JAMES 516

A LONDON CARTER NOVEL
(BOOK 1)

BY

BJ BOURG

WWW.BJBOURG.COM

D1519903

TITLES BY BJ BOURG

LONDON CARTER MYSTERY SERIES

James 516

Proving Grounds

Silent Trigger

Bullet Drop

Elevation

Blood Rise

CLINT WOLF MYSTERY SERIES

But Not Forgotten

But Not Forgiven

But Not Forsaken

But Not Forever

But Not For Naught

But Not Forbidden

But Not Forlorn

But Not Formidable

JAMES 516
A London Carter Novel by BJ Bourg
Originally published by Amber Quill Press
December 7, 2014

This book is a work of fiction.
All names, characters, locations, and incidents are products of the
author's imagination, or have been used fictitiously.
Any resemblance to actual persons living or dead, locales, or events
is entirely coincidental.

PUBLISHED IN THE UNITED STATES OF AMERICA

Dedicated to Brandon and Grace: Thanks for standing by me through everything. Your loyalty and support will never be forgotten.

Love, Dad

CHAPTER 1

Tuesday, August 16, 2011

"London, where in the hell are you?" Jerry Allemand's voice was laced with excitement—unusual for him—and I heard sirens screaming in the background. "We've got a hostage situation with shots fired at the First Gold Bank off of Highway Three in Gracetown!"

"Anyone down?" I rushed inside to dress in my sniper uniform—drab green coveralls and black boots.

"Not that we know of," Jerry said. "The guy walked in to rob the place, and one of the tellers hit a silent alarm. Warren Lafont was in the Food-N-Stuff parking lot and got there just as the suspect was walking out the door. They surprised each other, and the prick took a shot at Warren. Thankfully, he missed."

Warren Lafont was a two-year patrol cop who worked day shifts. "Did Warren return fire?"

"No. By the time he got his gun out, the man was back in the bank. Warren backed off and waited for backup."

"Do we have a description of the suspect?"

"White male, thick blond hair, tattoos on both arms and the right side of his neck. He's wearing worn jeans, a red muscle shirt and has a bandanna over his face."

I stepped into my coveralls and pulled the zipper up. "The rest of the team...are they en route?"

"I heard Dean, Ray and Alvin go out on the radio."

"What about Kent?"

"Not yet."

"Okay, I'm walking out the door. If you get there before me, get the guys set up." I flipped my phone shut and grabbed my tactical gun-belt from the closet in my room. After snapping it around my waist, I pulled my pistol from the closet and shoved it into my low-riding holster, then rushed out the door.

My lights flashed bright and my siren screamed as I rushed toward the hostage scene in my marked cruiser. My radio scratched from time to time as members of the SWAT team announced their arrivals at the scene.

Within minutes of leaving my house, I pulled my cruiser to a stop in front of Bestman's Market—a busy convenience store south of First Gold Bank—and stepped out. Betty Jo's Fried Chicken restaurant was located between Bestman's Market and the bank, and the Magnolia Parish Sheriff's Office's mobile command center had been parked in the south side parking lot of Betty Jo's. SWAT operators scrambled about in their ninja garb, utilizing the restaurant building as cover. Captain Anthony Landry—his bald head red from the sun's brutal rays and his forehead speckled with sweat beads—was barking orders at them.

I donned my utility vest and retrieved my sniper rifle—a black, police tactical system, chambered in .308 caliber, equipped with top-of-the-line glass and bipod—from where it had been secured in the rifle case in my trunk. After slinging it over my shoulder, I hurried to the mobile command center. Captain Landry met me by the front door and ushered me inside. "We need to talk," he said in a serious tone.

We walked to a large dry-erase board that covered the entire far wall of the command center. Gina Pellegrin—a detective I'd recently recruited to be my sniper coordinator—had already sketched out the surrounding parking lots and buildings. I nodded my approval when I saw the colored printouts of aerial satellite maps taped to the edges of the board. Gina looked up when we approached and smiled at us.

"Give us a minute, Gina," Captain Landry said. Gina nodded and walked off. When she was out of earshot, Captain Landry turned to me and frowned. "You're gonna have to kill this guy, London…first chance you get."

"You think?" I asked, as casually as I could, trying to ignore the surge of adrenalin that coursed through my veins.

"No, I know it. He took a shot at Warren, he killed a teller inside and now he's demanding something we can't give him."

"What's that?"

"He wants a blacked-out SUV and two hostages."

I pursed my lips, nodded my understanding. We could never let a suspect go mobile with a hostage...ever. "What happens when he realizes we won't do it?"

Captain Landry indicated with his head toward an enclosed glass room at the front of the command center where a team of negotiators were talking into headsets. "He told the negotiators he's going to start killing hostages if we don't park the SUV in front of the bank within the hour."

"What'll we do?"

"I'm trying to talk the sheriff into letting us set him up. I want to deliver the vehicle like he wants, but then I want you to drop him when he steps out of the bank."

"Will the sheriff go for it?"

"He's worried about something going wrong, but I assured him you're up to the task. He wants to give the negotiators some time to work their magic, but I don't see this guy giving up."

I stared up at the map Gina had drawn. The roof of Betty Jo's was much too close to the bank to be an effective sniper hide. A Food-N-Stuff was located west of the bank and, judging by the scale on the maps Gina had printed off the Internet, it was about a hundred and fifty yards away. I'd have an excellent visual of the entire front side of the bank from that rooftop, and the air conditioner units and the storefront would provide excellent concealment. I pointed to the center of Food-N-Stuff's roof on the map. "I'll grab Jerry and we'll set up here. We'll provide intel and when you're ready to rock and roll, just say the word—it'll be done."

Captain Landry slapped my back. "Get to it then, so we can wrap up this shit before another innocent person dies."

I nodded, then walked out into the blistering heat. Jerry was geared up and waiting for me, his thick brown hair already dripping sweat. He pointed to Block's Truck Stop and Casino two hundred yards northwest of the bank. "I sent Dean and Ray to the truck stop. They're gonna set up where they can cover the back of the bank."

"What about Alvin?"

"He's in the trees along the bayou, covering the eastern side."

We hurried to my cruiser, set our rifles on the back seat and then headed south on Highway Three for a quarter mile before turning down Green Oaks Street. The street led to a large subdivision that had sprung up years ago around the Food-N-Stuff shopping center, and it allowed us to get to the back of the building without being detected from the bank. We banged on the back door of the store. After several minutes, a manager inched it open and peered outside.

His eyes and mouth widened when he saw the rifles, but he quickly relaxed when I pointed to the badge sewn into my sniper vest.

"I'm London Carter," I began, "and this is Jerry Allemand. We're snipers with the Magnolia Parish Sheriff's Office."

The manager opened the door wider, nodding excitedly. "This is about the bank robbery, isn't it?"

"Yes, sir," I said. "We need access to your roof."

The man turned immediately and called over his shoulder, "Follow me!"

We walked through the stockroom—navigating a maze of pallets and buggies—until we arrived at a metal ladder bolted to the back wall of the store. It led to a square opening in the ceiling. The manager tugged a ring of keys from his belt and shuffled through them. He selected a small brass key from the dozens attached to the ring and held it out to me. "This is the key to the padlock."

"Thanks." I slung my rifle over my shoulder and scurried up the ladder. Hooking my left arm under the top rung, I turned the key in the padlock. I could feel the heat emanating from the metal door. When I removed the lock, I turned the handle and eased the access door open. I peeked through the slit in the opening and surveyed the rooftop, trying to get a bearing on our location. Air conditioners were scattered along the roof just like in the pictures Gina had printed, and the storefront made it impossible for me to see any of the buildings along the highway, including First Gold Bank.

I turned and tossed the keys into Jerry's waiting hands and then pushed my way into the bright daylight and onto the rooftop. Within seconds, Jerry's head and shoulders appeared in the opening and he sprung from the last step and landed lightly on his feet. At five-nine, he was the smallest of the snipers and arguably the most nimble.

Crouching low and keeping the storefront between the bank and us, we made our way toward the front of the store. We stopped about twenty feet from the edge of the roof and dropped to our knees. After grounding my rifle, I crawled until I could see around the storefront and had a good visual of the bank. A few squad cars were positioned at various angles in front of the bank. Deputies and SWAT officers were hunched behind them. Other than that, there was no activity down there.

I moved back to where Jerry waited. "I have a good shot of the bank from there," I said, nodding to where I had crawled. "Once I'm in position and have eyes on the bank, I'll motion for you to join me."

Jerry nodded.

Still hidden behind the storefront, I dropped prone on the boiling roof and cradled my rifle in the crook of my forearms. Inch by inch, I moved—the searing heat penetrating my uniform and tearing at my flesh—and little by little, the bank parking lot came into view. When I was far enough that Jerry could fit beside me, I carefully moved my rifle out in front of me, slowly extended the legs of the bipod and pulled the butt into my shoulder, all the while moving in exaggerated slow motion so as not to attract any attention from below.

Once my sniper rifle was snugly in the pocket of my right shoulder, my cheek naturally found the familiar stock weld—the result of hundreds of hours behind this very rifle—attaining perfect eye relief. I began breathing slowly and steadily. Within seconds, my muscles began to relax. My heart rate dropped to almost nothing. The pain from the scorching rooftop began to diminish. My right index finger stroked the trigger guard.

CHAPTER 2

Blinking sweat from my right eye, I peered through the scope and surveyed the front of the bank. It was a little over a hundred and fifty yards away, but my ten-power scope made it look like fifteen. I couldn't detect any movement from the shadows inside the bank. The suspect had obviously shut off all the lights and drawn several of the curtains. To an unsuspecting viewer, this could be any normal Tuesday in August, except the insane traffic was absent and there were no customers bustling about the usually congested area.

I felt Jerry's presence beside me. Without taking my eye from the scope, I asked him to turn up the police radio. Jerry set the radio on the hot roof in front of him and adjusted the volume so we could both hear the radio traffic. He then pulled out his spotting scope, extended the tripod legs and pointed it toward the parking lot below.

"I bet you wish you had a sniper mat now, eh?" he asked, referring to my unrelenting rebuke of snipers who relied on shooting mats, pinch bags and other shooting accessories to make them more comfortable.

"Not at all," I said softly, never taking my right eye off the bank. "Innocent people could die in the time it takes to set up all that shit. All a real sniper needs is his rifle, data book, lots of ammo and a radio."

"When you get old and retire," Jerry said, "I'm gonna take over the team, and we'll have blow-up mattresses, battery-operated fans and camouflage umbrellas."

I didn't reply, just maintained my visual on the bank. Nothing moved in the windows. I watched for what seemed like forty-five minutes...still nothing. The radio was silent, except for an occasional report from Gina saying the negotiators were trying to get the deadline extended. Sweat dripped from my pores. Jerry lay still beside me, and I could hear his steady breathing.

"You didn't fall asleep on me, did you?" I finally asked.

"Snipers don't sleep, they—"

Suddenly, the radio screeched and Gina came on. "Sierra One…standby. The suspect just stated he was going to kill a hostage and then he cut off communications."

I trained my crosshairs on the front of the bank, moving smoothly from the glass door to the windows that lined the front of the bank. "Can you see anything with the spotting scope?"

The spotting scope was four times more powerful than my rifle scope, but Jerry said he couldn't see any movement from inside. "The deadline's already past," he said. "I don't think he'll—"

A distant popping sound interrupted him. It sounded like a muffled *pop*. I frantically scanned the front of the bank. "Was that a gunshot?" I asked.

Jerry smashed the button on the police radio. "Sierra One to Command, was that a gunshot?"

"Ten-four, Sierra One, shots fired!" Gina answered.

I strained to penetrate the darkness inside the bank. Still nothing. "Damn it! I can't see shit. What about you?"

"I've got nothing. Wait a minute… I see something. Check window one. It looks like someone's moving toward the door."

I saw it. Two men were struggling with something…it looked like the limp body of a woman. They were dragging it toward the door. I focused my crosshairs on one of the men and then moved it to the other. "Neither one of them is the suspect." I moved my attention to the limp body. It was a young girl…couldn't be more than twenty. My blood began to boil. There was a bullet hole in her right temple. A trickle of blood had drained from the hole and spread down her cheek. Her eyes and mouth were open, frozen in terror. She wore a nice business suit with a nametag pinned to the front left lapel.

"She's a teller," Jerry said.

The two men pushed the door open and deposited the lifeless body on the sidewalk. One of the men, a paunchy fellow with a bald head and thick glasses, hesitated by the door and said something to his comrade. The other man glanced over his shoulder into the bank and reached for Paunchy's arm. Paunchy pulled away and made a halfhearted attempt to bolt across the parking lot.

I instinctively swung the crosshairs to the doorway, searching for the gunman and hoping I was wrong…I wasn't. Two more *pops* sounded from the interior of the bank and Paunchy stumbled and fell to his knees. He tried to get to his feet, but a third shot dropped him. He fell hard to his face. Blood began to spread across the back of his white shirt. I searched desperately inside the bank, trying to see past the other man. "Where the hell is the shooter?"

"I can't see shit inside!" Jerry yelled.

The other man rushed back into bank and the door swung shut. Before it closed, I saw him disappear to the left, between the counters. "They're behind the counter. Call Alvin; ask him if he can see the counter."

"Sierra One, Sierra Three, you have a visual on the counter?"

There was a slight pause and then Alvin's voice came on the radio. "Negative. A female subject pulled the curtains shut about an hour ago. I have nothing."

"London, standby," Captain Landry called over the radio. "Things are gonna move fast. We're bringing the SUV to the front of the bank as demanded. Hold on for more."

"Ten-four," Jerry replied for me.

Six SWAT members rushed toward the back of the bank. One of them carried a battering ram and another held a ballistic shield. When they reached the corner of the brick building, they crouched low, poised for an assault. Making entry into a building occupied by innocent hostages and a crazed gunman was too risky. This was shaping up to be a sniper-initiated assault, where I would take out the primary gunman and the entry team would move in to secure the hostages and take out any other threats.

"London," Captain Landry called a minute later, "we're live in fifteen. As soon as the SUV gets here and the suspect shows himself, engage him. When he goes down, the entry team will move in and secure the hostages."

"Ten-four," Jerry called.

I kept my crosshairs focused on the front door to the bank. The minutes ticked by like hours. The sun had slid low to the west and long shadows stretched across the southeastern side of the parking lot, but it did little to stifle the heat.

"It's here," Jerry finally said.

I moved my rifle slightly to the right and saw a white SUV with dark tinted windows pull into the parking lot behind Betty Jo's. Captain Landry walked over and spoke with the driver, a young patrol officer. After a brief moment, Captain Landry walked toward the eastern side of Betty Jo's and stood behind a patrol car where he could watch the exchange. The patrol deputy drove the SUV around

Betty Jo's and parked it directly in front of the bank, about twenty feet from the front door, with the passenger's side positioned toward the door. He then rolled out of the driver's seat and made a run for one of the patrol cars parked nearby. When he reached it, he squatted beside a SWAT officer who had been there all afternoon.

I saw Captain Landry lift his radio to his mouth and his voice boomed beside me. "All units...pull your vehicles out of the parking lot, ASAP."

The area suddenly came to life as officers scrambled into the cruisers stationed around the bank. They sped away, some pulling back as far as Food-N-Stuff and some driving around to Bestman's Market. Just as the bank parking lot cleared out, I detected movement from inside the bank. "Jerry, you catching this?"

"Yeah, is that..."

"It sure is!" From the number of legs moving, it looked like three people were walking toward the door. A large curtain was draped over their bodies. My heart began to thump in my chest. If they made it to the SUV and sped off, the hostages were as good as dead. I quickly surveyed their feet. The last person in line wore faded jeans and boots. The others wore slacks and dress shoes.

"The suspect's at the back of the line," Jerry said.

"Unless they changed clothes," I warned. "I can't take the shot unless I know for sure." They continued to walk, bumping into each other as they moved.

"They're almost to the car...you've got to do something!" Jerry called, his voice tense.

I didn't answer. As the curtain jostled with their movements, I strained to see beneath it. Nothing.

"Sierra One, they're almost out of runway. Take the shot," said a nervous Captain Landry.

I centered the crosshairs over the head at the back of the line, then hesitated. I couldn't shoot what I couldn't identify...period. I glanced back to their legs, hoping for some hint of verification. Still nothing.

Just as they reached the SUV, the person in the front jerked the curtain up and bolted from the group. In that split second, I saw that the person in the middle was a white male with blond hair and a tattoo on his neck, and his gun hand was starting to rise. The very instant my crosshairs touched the center of the suspect's right ear canal, my rifle bucked against my shoulder. The explosion made my ears ring.

By habit born of a million repetitions, I automatically bolted another round and prepared for a follow-up shot. Almost immediately I heard the *boom* from a flash-bang and a faint *pop* from somewhere near the bank. The two bank employees, one a woman and the other a man, were screaming as the entry team forced them to the ground and secured them. The suspect lay in a bloody heap where he had fallen, unaware that he had even died.

The police radio suddenly erupted in confusion. Amidst a dozen voices trying to talk over each other, one frantic voice dominated. "Shots fired! Officer down! Officer down!"

"Who in the hell fired that shot?" someone else bellowed over the radio. "Damn it, who fired that shot?"

I jerked my scope to the bank. *Are there two gunmen? Who is down?*

I searched frantically, but saw no other movement from inside. Several of the SWAT officers tore from the group in front of the bank and ran south toward Betty Jo's. They were yelling something I couldn't hear. I swerved my rifle in that direction, but before I could see what was going on, I heard Jerry gasp beside me.

"Oh, shit! They…they got him! They got Captain Landry!"

My heart began beating a thunderous rhythm in my chest. I moved my scope to the area where I'd last seen the captain. My stomach immediately turned sour. I gritted my teeth and swallowed hard.

CHAPTER 3

"Sierra One, where'd that shot come from?" a voice demanded over the radio.

Quickly regaining my composure, I twisted around and swung my rifle from left to right in a large arc, scanning the entire parking lot and surrounding area. "Did you see anything, Jerry?"

"I… I'm not sure what happened." Jerry's voice was strained. "I think the suspect got a shot off."

"No way. I dropped him before he could pull the trigger. He died instantly. Besides, he wasn't even aiming in Captain Landry's direction." I scanned the trees along the bayou side and spotted Alvin Reed, my newest sniper. His jungle hat was pushed high on his forehead and sweat had streaked a number of lines through his face paint. His rifle was rotating from side to side as he also searched for a possible shooter. His scope momentarily rested on our position.

Jerry saw him, too, and called him over the radio. "Sierra One, Sierra Six, you've locked on our position."

"Ten-four," Alvin returned. "I thought that was y'all. Tell Carter I've got nothing on my end."

"Call Dean and Ray," I told Jerry.

Jerry smashed the button on the radio. "Sierra One, Sierra Three, anything?"

"Negative," called Dean Pierce.

"Sierra Four, anything?" Jerry asked.

"I didn't see anything," Ray Sevin said over the radio. "But I thought I heard a report at my nine o'clock."

I rose to a seated position and pulled my left knee up, resting my left elbow on it. Supporting the fore-end of my rifle with the palm of my left hand, I peered through my scope and located Ray's position. I then searched directly to his left—his nine o'clock position—and came upon the highway. It was empty. Traffic had been diverted for miles to the north and south. Other than cops, there was no sign of life within a couple hundred yards of the bank in every direction.

"Sierra One," the voice bellowed again, "where'd that shot come from?"

I suddenly recognized the voice—Sheriff Calvin Burke. I grounded my rifle and took the radio from Jerry. "I don't know, Sheriff. There's no sign of hostiles anywhere."

There was a long moment of radio silence. Finally, Sheriff Burke came back on the radio. "Ten-four. Meet me at the command center."

I glanced down and found my spent casing on the tar roof. I snatched it up, dropped it in the chest pocket of my coverall and zipped it shut. I engaged the safety on my rifle and pulled the sling over my shoulder. Jerry gathered up his gear and followed as I hurried to the access door and pulled it open. We scurried down the ladder and ran to my cruiser. I screeched around the parking lot and raced up Green Oaks, swerved onto Highway Three and was in Bestman's parking lot within seconds.

A team of detectives had arrived, and they were carrying notebooks and toolboxes and preparing to process the scene. At around the same time, a second wave of SWAT officers arrived in one of the department's tactical vans and piled out of it. Michael Theriot, the captain of detectives, was barking orders to the SWAT officers, sending them out in teams to search the surrounding area in an attempt to locate the shooter.

Jerry and I found Sheriff Burke standing alone beside the mobile command center, staring down at Captain Landry's lifeless body. There were tears in his eyes. He quickly brushed them away when we walked up.

I looked down at what was left of Anthony Landry's head. There was a dark hole in his left eye. Although he was on his back, I could see that a large portion of the back of his head was missing. I pursed my lips and shook my head. Captain Landry had been more than just a supervisor to me. He had been a mentor, a friend, a father figure. Whoever did this to him was going to pay…and pay dearly.

I heard sniffling beside me and stole a glance at Jerry. His eyes were fire engine red and tears flowed freely down his face. I slapped his shoulder. "Let it out and then pull yourself together. We've got work to do."

"Wait," Sheriff Burke said. "I want y'all to hang around to brief the detectives."

I nodded, then pointed to Captain Landry's body. "Sir, what happened down here?"

The sheriff shook his head, face pale and blank. "I don't know. I was standing over there"—he pointed to the door of the mobile command center—"and I heard a loud gunshot. I assumed that was your shot. It was followed by a flash-bang and then another gunshot, but that one wasn't as loud. I figured it was a handgun. I heard Warren yell like something terrible had happened and when I looked…" Sheriff Burke shook his head and squeezed his eyes shut.

I glanced around until I found Deputy Warren Lafont. He was sitting slumped over on the curb in front of Bestman's Market. His face was buried in his hands. I made my way to him and dropped down beside him. "Hey, you okay?"

Warren was trembling. His thick, frizzy hair was wet and plastered to his scalp. When he looked up, his eyes were swollen and red. "Sarge," he said in a weak voice, "I was standing right beside him. One second he was saying that you got the bastard, and the very next second he was on the ground. He just collapsed."

"Did you hear anything right before he went down?"

Warren stared down at his hands, thinking. "I remembered hearing a flash-bang go off on the other side of Betty Jo's after the suspect went down. And then I heard the entry team yelling at the hostages to get down. I heard somebody scream. I thought I heard another popping sound. A second later, Captain Landry collapsed. At first, I thought he had a heart attack or something, but then I saw…I saw all the blood." Warren shook his head. "I've seen mangled bodies before, but his face looked hollow and empty, like everything inside of it just…just blew out the back of his head."

I looked back toward the Betty Jo's parking lot. The detectives had moved everyone back and roped off the area with crime scene tape. Sheriff Burke ambled over to where I stood talking to Warren Lafont.

"How are you, Warren?" the sheriff asked.

"I'm okay."

"If you need something, let me know."

"Sheriff, who's heading up the investigation?" I asked.

"I've got Bethany Riggs heading down here. The detectives will work the scene and assist her with anything she needs, but she's going to be lead. They'll answer to her."

"Why her? She doesn't have much homicide experience, if any at all."

Bethany Riggs had originally been hired to work undercover within the department. She'd made quite a name for herself—to most, that name was *rat*—by busting a steroid drug ring inside the department. When her undercover days were done, she became the assistant deputy in Internal Affairs. When Justin Wainwright retired after giving thirty-three years of service to the Magnolia Parish Sheriff's Office, she was promoted to lieutenant. From undercover officer, to assistant IA deputy, to lieutenant in IA—none of those things qualified her to be a homicide detective, especially lead on the most high-profile murder in the parish's history.

"Since it's an officer-involved shooting," Sheriff Burke explained, "I want her to spearhead the investigation. I'll assign a team of detectives to work side-by-side with her."

"I want to work with her on the case." I said it before I even realized I was thinking it.

"You're not a detective."

"Make me one."

"I can't make you a temporary detective for one case. I need you—"

"Then make it permanent."

Sheriff Burke stared sideways at me. "Are you saying you want to be transferred to detectives? Permanently?"

"If that's what it takes to get me on the case."

"You'd be willing to leave patrol? I thought you said you'd die a patrol dog."

"I want on this case—no matter what. I need to find out who did this to Captain Landry."

Sheriff Burke was silent for a long moment. "I don't have an opening for sergeant in the detectives division."

"I'll take a demotion."

"You're serious about this, aren't you?"

"Yes, sir."

"But how do I justify putting you on the case without having investigative experience?"

"I'm not exactly green, Sheriff. Shit, I've got twelve years on the job—that's more than some of your detectives. And that's more than Bethany Riggs."

"Let me think about it," Sheriff Burke finally said. "I'll get back to you in a day or two."

I nodded and walked to where the rest of the sniper team had gathered around my cruiser.

"Are we still having sniper training tomorrow?" Dean wanted to know.

"Absolutely," I said. "I need to meet with y'all so we can straighten some shit out." I looked at Gina. "Did Kenneth ever call in?"

Gina pursed her lips, shaking her head slowly. "I called him about eight times, left voice messages and sent four or five texts, but I never heard back from him."

That got my blood boiling. One of our department's great leaders had been gunned down that afternoon, and Kenneth hadn't even bothered to call in to say he couldn't be there. He had some explaining to do.

"Who the hell's that?" Ray asked, removing his hand from his slick, bald head to point at the entrance to Betty Jo's parking lot.

We all turned and saw a black unmarked car pull into the parking lot. It stopped at the edge of the crime scene tape, and the driver killed the engine. After a few seconds, the door opened and a tall female stepped out. She wore dark jeans and a navy blue polo shirt. The sheriff's office logo was embroidered over her left shirt pocket. A shiny shield was clipped to her belt, along with a pancake holster holding her pistol.

"That's Bethany Riggs," Gina said. "I spent a week with her at a homicide conference a few months ago. Definitely not the best week of my life."

Bethany Riggs paused in the doorway and gathered her shoulder-length, dirty-blonde hair and pushed it into a ponytail. She slipped a rubber band over it. She then snatched a metal clipboard from the front seat and pushed the door shut with her knee. Her eyes caught mine for a brief moment, and I nodded. She turned her head without acknowledging my existence and walked to the mobile command center. After talking to the sheriff for a moment, she strode briskly to where we waited. She stuck her hand out to me. "Sergeant Carter?"

I nodded, took her soft hand in mine and squeezed. She squeezed back, and I was surprised at her grip strength. I was also surprised at how blue her eyes were. "You can call me London," I said.

"London, I'm Lieutenant Bethany Riggs, Internal Affairs. You can call me Lieutenant Riggs." She glanced at the others, nodding. "The sheriff just informed me that I'll be lead on this case. I understand Captain Anthony Landry was a dear friend of yours."

I simply nodded.

"I know how it feels to lose someone close to you, and I'm really sorry for your loss."

I'm sorry for your loss usually sounded hollow rolling off the tongues of most people, but Bethany Riggs sounded sincere. "I appreciate that," I said. "I'm going to really miss that old bastard. He was a great man and a solid leader."

"That's what I hear." Bethany looked from one of us to the other, studying each of our faces. "In lieu of statements, can I get a report from each of you as soon as possible? That way I'll be able to better recreate what took place here just prior to the random shot being fired."

"We'll get on them right away," I promised. "But this was no random shot. Someone deliberately took out Captain Landry."

Bethany's eyebrows furrowed. "What makes you say that?"

"We had the place sewn up for a couple hundred yards in all directions," I explained. "So whoever took him out had to take the shot from outside that perimeter, and they shot him directly in the left eye. From that distance, to make that shot, they knew what they were doing."

Bethany Riggs began jotting some things down in her notebook. "And no one saw anything at all?"

"All eyes were on the hostage taker. No one saw a damn thing." I pursed my lips as realization slowly set in and whistled. "No shit. That's the perfect plan. The shooter knew we'd all be concentrating on the hostage taker and he took full advantage of it."

Bethany nodded her agreement and shut her notebook. "I'd appreciate those reports as soon as possible." She then walked away and met with a group of detectives who were examining Captain Landry's body.

"Let's go knock out those reports so we can get back to work." I led the way to the mobile command center, and we each found a vacant computer station and started typing. I finished my report first and printed it on one of the nearby printers. I snatched a pen from the counter and signed it. I then made my way out into the sultry evening air. Captain Landry's body was still on the ground, but it had been covered with a white sheet. A helicopter zipped by overhead. I'd heard on the police radio that the helicopter was a loaner from a neighboring department and two of our SWAT guys were onboard searching for the shooter.

I made my way around Betty Jo's until the front parking lot of the bank came into view, and it was only then that I remembered killing a guy. Two detectives were hunched over the hostage taker's body, taking measurements. "Any idea who he is?" I asked.

One of the detectives looked up. It was Lieutenant Corey Chiasson, second-in-command of the detective bureau. "According to the driver's license in his back pocket, this piece of shit's name is Pete Billiot."

"What happened in the bank?" I asked.

Lieutenant Chiasson paused, rocking back on his heels. "The prick walked in there with a gun and demanded all the money. When the bank manager hesitated, he shot one of the tellers. That lit a fire under the manager's ass and he gathered up as much money as he could and handed it over. One of the tellers hit the silent alarm during the ruckus.

"As Billiot exited the bank, Deputy Lafont drove up. Billiot fired a shot at him and then ran back into the bank. He ushered all the people behind the counter and bedded down there." Chiasson pointed at Pete Billiot's clothes. "He swapped clothes with one of the bank managers. Lucky you realized it."

"We're lucky the hostage made his move." I squatted beside Chiasson and studied the right side of Billiot's face, as though I were studying a paper target. My bullet had shaved the hairs off his ear canal—without hitting the rim—on its way to penetrating his skull and exploding out the other side, taking his brain with it. I was secretly pleased by the placement of the shot and oddly unmoved by the fact I had just taken a life for the first time. During my years of law enforcement and sniper training, a number of instructors had warned that taking a life could have severe emotional effects on a sniper. They'd told of officers turning to alcohol and drugs to cope with what they'd done and, for those who couldn't cope, how some had taken their own lives. I shook my head before I straightened. "Weak bastards."

Lieutenant Chiasson glanced up, a curious look on his face.

"Just thinking out loud." I walked around the outer edges of the scene until I found Sheriff Burke. "Anything new, Sheriff?"

He shook his head. "We've searched a mile in every direction, had the helicopter comb the entire area—nothing."

"What's next?"

"It's too dark now to do much good. Besides, whoever shot him is long gone. We'll have to rely on the investigation to solve this one, unless…"

I waited. When he didn't explain, I asked, "Unless what?"

"Some of the detectives are saying this is an accidental discharge."

"I don't think so, Sheriff. That shot was too precise and it was fired from a high-powered rifle."

Sheriff Burke nodded. "That's what they're saying. They think either a sniper or an entry team member touched off a round— accidentally, of course—because y'all were the only ones with rifles at the scene."

I bristled. "That's bullshit."

"I know, I know, but they have to attack this at every angle. You know that."

"I guess so."

"Look, don't worry about it. They'll get to the bottom of this." Sheriff Burke started to walk away, then stopped and turned. "By the way, you did real good today. Go home and get some rest. I have to put a press release together. I have a feeling we'll need the public's help on this one."

"What about putting me on the case?"

"I'll need to name a replacement for Captain Landry." Sheriff Burke rubbed his face. "Would you consider taking the job?"

I blushed. "Sheriff, I'm flattered, but I'm not captain material. Too administrative for my blood. I'd get bored and probably kill myself."

The sheriff sighed. "Well, get out of here and let me get back to trying to figure out what the hell I'm going to do."

I glanced down at my report. "This is for Lieutenant Riggs."

"Leave it in the command center. I'll let her know it's there."

I walked off and met up with the rest of the sniper team. They had finished their reports and stood talking in hushed tones by the doorway to the command center. They shut up when I approached.

"What're y'all whispering about?" I wanted to know.

Jerry looked down and studied his shoes, as though he had to take a test and wanted to make an A on it.

"Well?" I asked again.

"We were just talking about Kenneth and how it's messed up that he didn't show."

I nodded. "I'll take care of that tomorrow."

CHAPTER 4

Wednesday, August 17, 2011

I was the first to arrive at the rifle range the next morning. I set up six cardboards at the two-hundred-yard mark and stapled a face target on each. The other snipers began arriving a few minutes later and, as usual, Kenneth Lewis was the last to drive up. A narcotics agent, he drove a four-wheel drive the department had seized from some drug dealer. He jumped out the truck and rushed over to where we stood waiting near the shooting benches.

"Daddy, what the hell happened yesterday?" he asked. Kenneth had been calling me *Daddy* ever since I recruited him onto the team.

"Get your shit and let's do some shooting. We'll talk about yesterday in a minute."

Sensing he was in trouble, Kenneth only nodded and retrieved his rifle from the truck. When he had gathered his gear and was ready, I signaled Gina Pellegrin. In addition to recording our activities at the scene of our call-outs, Gina also issued the commands for the shooting drills I prepared for training. This enabled me to participate in the training and was a huge help to me.

After explaining what the first drill would entail, Gina cleared her throat. After a brief pause, she called out in a slow cadence, "Ready, ready, ready...fire!"

We burst off the shooting line with our rifles in hand, sprinted the two hundred yards to the targets, turned and sprinted back to the shooting position. We then dropped to the ground and each fired five rounds at our respective face targets. My rifle bucked repeatedly against my shoulder as I worked the bolt without thought. When I was done, I jumped to my feet and called time. Jerry was a few seconds behind me. I smiled. "You're getting faster."

"But I still can't catch your machine-gun ass." He shook his head. "I can't wait 'til you get old and slow."

When the others were done, we walked down to check the targets, and I nodded my approval. In order to be considered ready for duty, the first five rounds of every training session had to fall within the one-inch circle that covered the bridge of the target's nose…and every sniper had once again passed the bi-monthly test.

We tore down the targets, and I walked to my rifle to pick up my brass. I made a notation in my sniper log and then summoned the snipers to one of the tables. "Make sure everyone signs the training log." I waved to Kenneth. "Walk with me."

I took Kenneth to the far side of the overhang, away from the other snipers. Trying to keep my cool, I asked, "Where the hell were you yesterday?"

Kenneth dropped his head. "Daddy, I'm so sorry. I know I screwed up."

"Answer the question."

"Yvette's mom's not doing too good and she went stay with her for the week. She left Saturday." Kenneth shifted his weight from one foot to the other. "I…I was…"

"Was what?"

"Daddy, you gotta promise me this stays between us."

"Just tell me."

"I…I had a little sweetie come to the house. I can't sleep by myself."

My eyes narrowed. "You chose a piece of ass over your job?"

Kenneth quickly shook his head. "No, Daddy! I didn't hear my phone. Yvette usually calls every couple of hours, and I didn't want to have to sit there and talk to her while my girl was there, so I took the battery out of my phone. I put it back in this morning and got Gina's messages." He hung his head, and I saw tears form at the corners of his eyes. He brushed them away. "I feel like a piece of shit for not being there. I'll understand if you want to kick me off the team."

I sighed. "No, I don't want you off the team. I spent too much time training your ignorant ass."

He smiled. "Thank you, Daddy. I promise I won't let you down again."

"Yeah, well you might think about not letting your wife down."

Kenneth frowned, hung his head again.

I slapped his shoulder hard. "Let's go do some shooting."

When we rejoined the rest of the team—Alvin and Ray were holding targets against the cardboard while Jerry worked the staple gun—Kenneth cleared his throat. "I'd like to say something to y'all."

Jerry paused with the staple gun in midair; they all turned their eyes to Kenneth.

"I let y'all down yesterday," Kenneth began in a shaky voice, "and I feel really bad about that. Daddy and I talked, and I apologized to him. I want to apologize to all of y'all, too. I promise it won't happen again."

"If it does, I get to punch you in the balls," Dean mumbled around a clump of chewing tobacco. He turned and spat in the grass at the edge of the cement.

Gina pretended to gag. "You really need to stop that shit."

Dean just smiled, a sliver of brown saliva clinging to his swollen lip.

"When you two are done French kissing," I said, "we can get on with training."

One by one, the snipers walked over to Kenneth and either punched him in the shoulder or shoved him to show their forgiveness. We then each grabbed a cardboard target and began the long walk to put them up. As we walked, I moved beside Gina.

"I didn't expect you to be here," I said. "I figured you'd be working the case."

She shook her head. "They only have half the detective division working on it. Since I was there with the sniper team and Lieutenant Chiasson didn't want to interfere with anything you had me doing, he assigned someone else in my place."

We walked in silence until we reached the target stands. As we put up the cardboard that held multi-colored shapes with numbers in the middle, the sound of an approaching vehicle stopped us in our tracks. We all looked toward the shell parking lot, expecting to see Captain Landry's unmarked black cruiser. My heart sank as I quickly remembered he would never again be dropping by the range to see how our training was going.

"Who the hell is that?" Kenneth asked, as Bethany Riggs walked to where our rifles rested on the ground two hundred yards away. She stood with arms crossed, watching us. Kenneth shielded his eyes, squinted. "Damn, she looks hot."

"Watch your mouth. She's Internal Affairs."

Kenneth's face turned two shades whiter. "What is she doing here?"

"Your wife sent her," I joked. "Something about 'conduct unbecoming an officer' or some shit like that."

Kenneth's head jerked around to face me. "You serious?"

I laughed. "No, fool. She's heading up the investigation on Captain Landry."

Kenneth let out a lungful of air. "Damn, Daddy, don't scare me like that."

We finished setting up our targets and then walked back toward the firing line. Bethany moved past our rifles and met me at the five-yard line. She wore a low-cut, sleeveless shirt that exposed a bit of cleavage. I wasn't intentionally looking, but it was hard to miss. She handed me a sheet of paper. "The sheriff wanted me to deliver this to you immediately."

I glanced down at the memorandum that was printed on official sheriff's office letterhead and quickly read the message: *Effective immediately, Sergeant London Carter will be transferred from the Patrol Division to the Detective Division, under the command of Captain Michael Theriot. His new radio number will be 210. He will retain his sergeant rank and command of the sniper team.*

It was more than I'd asked for, but I was suddenly unsure if it was what I really wanted. I had worked patrol for so long that it was a part of my life. It was in my blood.

"You'll be working with me," Bethany said. "Because of your sniper expertise, Sheriff Burke wants you onboard as a consultant. That's it."

"When do I start?"

"As soon as you're done here. I'll wait for you, and you can follow me to CID."

The criminal investigations division was in Payneville, ten minutes from the rifle range. "Do you want me to just meet you there?"

"No, I'll wait." She nodded toward the row of rifles on the ground. "I'll need your rifle for evidence."

"Evidence?"

"Standard protocol." She fixed me with a stern look. "I'll also need the shell casing you took from the scene."

"*My* shell casing? Why?"

"In case you've forgotten, you shot a man last night. Although you've been cleared through our investigation, there'll most likely be a grand jury hearing to formally clear you. We'll need to present the rifle and casing as evidence to close out the case. Do you have another rifle to use while this one's being processed?"

I nodded, started to gather my gear. "I'll follow you to CID now. They can finish training without me."

We walked back to the firing line where I collected my spent casings and rifle and loaded them in the trunk of my squad car. Bethany stood waiting for me at her car. She was talking on her phone, but was too far away for me to make out what she was saying. I joined Jerry Allemand at one of the shooting tables.

"You got this?" I asked him.

"I guess I have to, since you're going play footsies with your new girlfriend."

I shook my head, thanked him and got in my squad car.

CHAPTER 5

I followed Bethany the nearly ten miles to CID, and we parked at the outermost edge of the overfilled lot.

"Why's it so crowded?" I asked when we stepped out of our cars.

"Everyone who responded has to meet today with a detailed report of what they did." She tapped a manila folder tucked under her left arm and walked briskly toward the front door to CID. "I have all of the sniper reports here. You guys did a good job. Your reports help paint a clear picture of what you all saw and it helped dispel the assumption this was an accidental discharge."

"Who came up with that bullshit theory?"

"I did," she said without slowing down.

I smiled sheepishly and pulled the door open for her. We made our way through a maze of hallways and finally arrived at the crowded conference room. Detectives bustled about the room gathering files and documents and taking seats around the large table at the center of the room. A giant poster board was plastered on one of the walls, and it contained a detailed sketch of the Food-N-Stuff parking lot and the surrounding roads and buildings. There were two human figures drawn on the sketch—on opposite sides of Betty Jo's—to indicate the bodies of Pete Billiot and Captain Anthony Landry.

"Sergeant Carter…" It was Bethany. She summoned me to a chair beside her at the crowded table. She then called out to the cops in the room, "Okay, let's get started."

The loud chattering dropped to a low buzz and everyone took seats. One by one, Bethany called on the detectives to provide a briefing of their activities. Photographs had been taken, neighborhoods canvassed, video surveillance from the surrounding stores confiscated.

Bethany shoved her pen toward Detective Melvin Ford. "Melvin, I need you to run background checks on every name on those canvass sheets. I want to know if any of them have criminal records, if they've had military or police training and if they're avid hunters." She turned to Detective Rachael Bowler. "Rachael, review the surveillance videos and see if anything suspicious turns up. The shootings had to have been caught on tape."

Melvin and Rachael abruptly jumped to their feet and hurried out of the room.

Bethany looked down at her notes and then scanned the table. "Show of hands...who was part of the search team trying to locate Captain Landry's shooter?"

Eight SWAT members—three from the detective division, four from patrol and one from the detention center—raised their hands.

"Did you locate any evidence or witnesses that can help us identify who this cop killer is?"

They all shook their heads. "Nothing at all," one of them said. "He vanished like a ghost."

Bethany drummed her pen on the tabletop. "How many casings were recovered from the scene?"

"We found six," Lieutenant Corey Chiasson said. "All of them nine-millimeter."

"What type of gun did the robber have?"

Chiasson flipped through his notes. "A black semi-automatic pistol, nine millimeter."

"Do we know why Pete Billiot tried to rob the bank?" Bethany asked.

"Yeah," Chiasson said. "When we located his wife, she said they were recently separated because Pete lost his job. He started drinking heavily and refused to go out and look for work. They lost both of their cars and were about to lose their house, so she took the kids and moved in with her parents. Her best guess is that he just snapped."

"What'd he do for a living?" I wanted to know. "Because he didn't act like no regular Joe. This guy had some tactical training, and he pulled the trigger like he'd done it before."

"Right you are," Chiasson said. "He worked security for a nuclear plant on the river. They're some kind of paramilitary organization."

Bethany looked sideways at me, impressed. "Good call."

"Just a lucky guess."

"Right," she said suspiciously. She turned back to Lieutenant Chiasson. "Who do you have attending the autopsies for the bank victims?"

"I'll handle them myself," he said.

"Good. Sergeant Carter and I will attend Captain Landry's autopsy. When are they?"

"I spoke with the coroner an hour ago. He'll do Captain Landry this afternoon, and he'll do the others tomorrow."

Bethany gathered up her notes and nodded to the group. "Okay, if there's nothing else, let's get back to work. You all know what to do."

I followed Bethany out to the bureau, and she led me to Captain Theriot's private office. "You've been promoted?" I asked.

"At least while Theriot's in Chateau"—the northern-most city in the parish that also served as the parish seat—"talking to the news reporters. I'll probably have to find another place to set up shop."

Bethany logged into Captain Theriot's computer, and I sat across the desk from her. Rachael suddenly burst into the office, her tanned face ashen. "I saw it!"

"What?" Bethany asked.

"The…the shooting. I saw Captain Landry get killed!"

Bethany and I traded glances and rushed out of the office, following Rachael down a long row of cubicles to her desk. Rachael dropped to her chair, moved the cursor over the *play* button on the video program and clicked it. She then stood and moved back so we could gather around the computer.

"I don't want to see it again," Rachael said. "Ever."

Bethany took the seat and I knelt beside her, and we both watched wide-eyed as the scene unfolded on the screen in front of us. The view was from across Highway Three and it displayed the eastern side of Betty Jo's parking lot. Captain Landry was standing in the parking lot beside Warren Lafont, holding his police radio and staring toward the bank. A cone of red mist exploded out of the back of his head and he collapsed. His knees buckled without warning and he crumbled straight down. Warren jerked his head around and his mouth spread open. Although the video had no audio, I thought I heard him scream.

Lieutenant Bethany Riggs' face had lost its color. I touched her shoulder. "You okay, LT?"

She nodded. "It's surreal, seeing a cop getting killed. When I see civilians dead or dying, it's easy to get my work done and depersonalize it, but when I see that"—she pointed to Captain

Landry's lifeless body on the cement—"I realize it could be me there on the ground. I mean, we wear the same uniform, the same badge…"

Counseling wasn't my forte, so I didn't know what to tell her to make her feel better. Myself, I was motivated by an intense desire to murder the person who did this to Captain Landry. Instead of saying anything, I leaned over Bethany and grabbed the computer mouse. I reversed the video and played it in slow motion. I clicked the *pause* button at the moment Captain Landry's head exploded.

Bethany winced. "Do you have to?"

"Yeah." With my index finger, I traced the edges of the cone of red mist. "You see this cone?"

Bethany nodded, forcing herself to look.

"It points toward the shooter's location."

This seemed to get Bethany's attention. She leaned forward and studied the frame. "So, the shooter was off to the north?"

"Yeah. Come with me." I stood and walked to the conference room, stopped in front of the large sketch and tapped on Captain Landry's body. I slid my index finger to the north and circled an area that encompassed the Pizza Hut and the truck stop. "The shot originated from here somewhere." I turned to Bethany. "Did y'all find the projectile?"

"No. We went over every inch of that place and didn't find anything. We figured the bullet broke up on impact, turned to specks."

I stared at the sketch, thoughtful. "I want to go out to the scene."

"Why?"

"I want to look for the remnants of that bullet."

The corners of Bethany's mouth hardened ever slightly. "I already told you—we've been over every inch of the scene and didn't find anything."

"I'm not suggesting y'all missed something."

"Then what exactly are you suggesting?"

I pointed to Bestman's Market on the map. "Did y'all check the northern wall of this building?"

"No. Why would we?"

"It's the backstop for the shooter's line of fire."

Bethany scowled. "There's no way the bullet made it that far. If there was anything left to it, it would've lost energy and fallen to the ground several feet from the body."

I shook my head. "The shot was fired from a high-powered rifle. It'll absolutely lose energy when it rips through the human skull, but it can travel for quite a distance afterward. Depending on the makeup of the bullet, it might not have enough energy to punch through the wall, but it could scar the paint and that would help me pinpoint the shooter's exact location."

Bethany pursed her lips and thought about what I'd said for a moment. Finally, she spoke. "What good would that do? We already know the general location from which the bullet was fired and we combed every inch of the area, but found nothing. I think it'd be better if we began looking into Captain Landry's background to find out who had a motive to kill him."

"He was certainly the target in this killing, but there's a chance it wasn't personal."

"Explain."

"He could've been a high-value target of opportunity. Snipers are trained to take out high-ranking officials, and if this shooter's had prior sniper training, he would've recognized Captain Landry's rank. But…"

"But what?"

"But snipers are trained to take out enemy snipers first, and high-ranking officers are the second group on the list of priorities." I studied the map. "I was probably out of his line of fire because of that air conditioning unit and the storefront, and Alvin was hidden in the trees, but Dean and Ray were clearly exposed out here by Block's Truck Stop. So why not take them out first?" Scratching my head, I mused aloud, "And why just kill Landry? The sheriff was out there and he's the chief law enforcement officer in the parish…it doesn't get any higher than him."

Bethany nodded. "If your *high value target* theory is correct, the sheriff would've certainly been taken out."

"I guess."

"What makes the most sense is that someone was pissed at Captain Landry and took him out, so our best course of action is to pursue that avenue of reasoning."

"You're the boss, but I'd still like to get out to the scene."

Bethany's blue eyes studied my face. After what seemed like a long moment of tense silence, she finally asked, "What exactly do you hope to accomplish again?"

"It's important that I figure out where he was when he fired the shot because his location alone will tell me some things about him."

She sighed. "Okay, but after we secure your rifle and spent shell casing in evidence."

CHAPTER 6

Twenty minutes later, Lieutenant Bethany Riggs parked her car in front of Bestman's Market. I jumped out and walked to the side of the building that faced the north. I began on one side and carefully searched every inch of the wall's surface. It was constructed of cinderblocks and painted white, which made the search much easier. It didn't take me long to locate a tiny crater in the wall that was about a quarter inch deep. It was about two feet above the ground and there was a tiny pile of powdered cinderblock on the cement beneath the hole.

Bethany was standing above where I squatted. She grunted. "I can't believe we missed that. I feel like such an idiot."

As I scoured the ground, I shook my head. "If you'd studied high-powered ballistics and test fired thousands of rifle bullets you would've found it just as easily as I did." Off the edge of the sidewalk, about six feet from where the round had impacted the wall, I found the remnants of a rifle bullet. The only thing left was the base of the brass jacket with a small bit of lead attached to it. "It's definitely a thirty-caliber bullet, quite possibly a three-o-eight round."

Donning a pair of latex gloves, Bethany recovered the projectile. "I guess it's a good thing the sheriff put you on the case." She said it more to herself than to me.

I moved back to the bullet hole and turned away from it, facing Betty Jo's. "LT, how tall are you?"

"Five-seven. Why?"

"Captain Landry was about five-nine. Can you go stand exactly where he was shot? Like we saw in the video?"

Bethany hesitated. "That's like asking me to climb into someone's coffin."

"I'll just need you there for a second or two, so I can use his location as a second point of reference. It'll help me line up the trajectory."

She sighed, walked across the parking lot and stopped at the very spot where Captain Landry had spent his last moments. I dropped to my right shoulder and put my head at a level even with the bullet hole. When I stared from there through the area two inches above Bethany's head, the trajectory led into the clouds. I began rising slowly along the wall to compensate for the drop in the bullet, keeping my eyes focused on the area directly above her head. The first thing that rose up from the earth and came into view was the Highway Twelve high-rise bridge that crossed over Highway Eighty, Highway Three and Bayou Magnolia. Highway Twelve extended east to west, cutting through the center of Magnolia Parish. "No shit!"

"What? What do you see?" Bethany called.

"Come on. We have to get up on the high-rise!" I jogged to her car, and she followed. It only took a couple of minutes to reach the eastbound shoulder of the Highway Twelve high-rise bridge. I exited the vehicle in a hurry, like a poor bastard heading to cash in his lottery ticket, and walked to the edge of the cement guardrail and looked over the side. Directly under us, cars zipped by along Highway Three. Bethany hurried beside me. From our vantage point, we could clearly see the parking lot where Captain Landry had been standing. I moved sideways to the east until I had lined up the approximate locations of the two reference points—the bullet hole in the wall of Bestman's Market and the spot where Captain Landry had been murdered. "This is it!"

Bethany shook her head. "It's impossible to hit someone from here. This has to be a quarter of a mile."

"Good eye." I straightened my arm, held my thumb up, gauged the distance. "Right at four hundred yards—about four-eleven. Very doable."

"Maybe for deer hunting," Bethany said, "but there's no way someone could hit a person's head from here."

"Not the head, the eyeball," I corrected. "And I'd bet a steak dinner I can prove you wrong."

"I don't eat dead cows." Bethany studied my face. "Seriously, you really think you can make that shot?"

"Not only can I make the shot, but I can do it with one eye

closed."

As Bethany pondered the meaning of my last comment, I began walking along the edge of the cement guardrail, searching for clues—black scuff marks on the rail to indicate a bipod, shell casings on the ground, shoe impressions in the gravel—but found nothing. Well, nothing but some graffiti painted onto the side of the guardrail.

"If this is the spot," Bethany began, "why haven't we found a shell casing?"

"Either the shooter didn't cycle another round, which isn't likely, considering he's obviously received sniper training of some sort, or he picked up his casing."

"Why would he pick up his casing?"

"Snipers are trained to be ghosts. When they leave an area, they erase all signs that indicate they were there." I scowled. "This is just one more indication we're dealing with a highly-trained individual."

"Is that why you took your shell casing from the scene?"

I nodded.

Cars zipped by at seventy-plus miles per hour, sending gushes of wind in our direction. This got Bethany's attention. "With all of this traffic, someone would've surely seen something."

I shook my head. "We sealed this area off. Traffic was diverted to the east at Highway Eighty-One and to the west at Exit Thirty-Eight."

"So this area was cleared of traffic?"

"Yep, completely. There were only cop cars and a few locals who had to travel this way to get home." I scanned the buildings between the murder scene and the bridge. "This is the highest point out here…the perfect spot. I can see over everything." I stepped back and looked up and down the four-lane highway. "And there're a number of quick getaways along this road."

"This guy knew what he was doing," Bethany said.

I nodded my agreement. "This is definitely a worst-case scenario."

"What do you mean?"

"We're dealing with a highly-trained sniper who can reach *far* out and touch anyone…anytime…anywhere, and we have no idea who he is and why he did this. This has the potential to turn into a cold case and go unsolved real quick."

"But once we find out who had a vendetta against Captain Landry, we should be able to figure out who the shooter is."

"I have a feeling it won't be that simple. If this were personal, the shooter could've killed him a hundred different ways. He could've shot him in his driveway, a dark parking lot, or at the boat dock on a lazy Sunday morning…any number of less conspicuous locations and at a closer and more manageable distance." I shook my head. "But not this guy. No, he waits until Captain Landry is in the middle of a high profile situation, surrounded by a small army of cops. There are a couple of things at play here."

I held up a finger. "First, this bastard's arrogant. He wants to show off his skills. At four hundred yards, a lot can go wrong with a head shot. Landry could've turned his head at the last second— sneezed, anything—and that bullet would've just whizzed by."

I held up another finger. "Second, by taking out a cop, especially a high-ranking officer, he's telling us he's not afraid of going to war with the entire department. That means he's either stupid or very good at what he does. Judging by the shot he made and his clean getaway, I'm thinking the latter."

"I agree," Bethany said, nodding. "But if it's not personal, then why do it? Why murder a cop in broad daylight in front of half the department? He's got to know the chances are high he'll be killed when he's captured, and, if he survives to make it all the way to trial, he'll get the death penalty. I can't imagine anything being worth *that*."

She did have a point, and as I considered possible motives, Bethany retrieved her camera. She began taking pictures of the surrounding area, while I stood where the shooter had been just hours earlier and tried to see what he saw…think what he thought. When Bethany was through taking her pictures, she walked up beside me. "What're you thinking?"

"Just wondering why he did this," I said, "and wondering what's next."

"What do you mean by that?"

"I have a strange feeling this is only the beginning of something really ugly." I turned to face Bethany, then sank back against the guardrail. "People are most afraid of what they can't see or hear and what they don't understand. There's a certain mystique surrounding snipers. Those who don't understand them fear them. Those who do understand them also fear them. In battle, there's nothing more fearsome than a sniper and his rifle."

"But this is not a battle or a war."

"Like I said, people fear the unseen and the unheard. Once word gets out that there's a mystery sniper on the loose, Lord knows what'll happen. It could cripple this place."

"But he killed a cop, so why would civilians be worried?"

"If someone's brazen enough to kill a cop, they'll kill almost anyone."

Bethany pushed a lock of dirty-blonde hair behind an ear and crossed her arms. "You really believe this person will kill again?"

"I'm almost certain of it. Hell"—I waved my hand around in a semi-circle—"he might be out there right now, with glass on us as we speak."

Bethany glanced around nervously, unfolded her arms and walked toward her unmarked car. "Well, let's get out of here and find out who wanted Captain Landry dead. The quicker we do that, the quicker we can put this case to bed."

"Have you eaten yet?"

She slid into the driver's seat and started the engine. When I got in and shut my door, she paused with her hand on the gearshift. "No…you?"

I shook my head.

"Okay," she said. "Let's grab something quick and then we'll go meet with Captain Landry's widow."

CHAPTER 7

Starla Landry was Captain Anthony Landry's second wife. They had been married for a little over a year. I'd met her once—during an awards banquet—and I didn't like her. There was something about her that rubbed me wrong, and it had nothing to do with her being half his age.

Now, Captain Landry's first wife, Olivia, was a good woman. She had taken the news of her husband's adulterous affair hard, the divorce harder and the marriage to Starla... Well, that had nearly killed her.

"We should be talking to Ms. Olivia," I said quietly to Bethany as we waited for someone to answer the door. "She was with Captain Landry for nearly thirty years."

"I know what you're getting at," Bethany said, "but the last days and weeks of his life are the most important. If anyone knows who Anthony Landry's enemies are, it's Starla." She knocked on the door again, waited. "Oh, by the way," she said, changing the subject. "When you report to work tomorrow, try wearing something that makes you look a little more like a cop and a lot less like a mercenary."

I glanced down at my sniper coveralls. "Sorry. You didn't exactly give me time to go home and change."

"Yeah, it was kind of sudden the way it—"

The door to the double-wide trailer burst open and a twenty-seven-or-so-year-old woman stood in the doorway. She wore thin shorts and a tank top with no bra. Her eyes were swollen, mascara smeared on her cheeks. "What do y'all want?" Starla Landry's voice was gruff. "I already talked to the other detectives. I don't know who did this to Anthony."

Bethany reached out and put a hand on Starla's arm. "I want to begin by offering our deepest condolences. As I'm sure you're aware, your husband was a legend to the men and women of Magnolia Parish and everyone loved him. It's impossible to think that anyone would want to do him harm, but we'd like to sit down with you and see if we can maybe recreate his activities for the past week or so and maybe come up with something—a lead, perhaps."

Starla threw the door open and stepped back. "Come in, I guess, but I don't know what good it'll do. I already told them other detectives that Anthony never got into it with nobody."

I nodded when I walked by Starla. She nodded back and said, "Your name is…let me see if I remember…London Carter, right?"

"Yes, ma'am, that's right. Anthony was like a father to me." I thought I saw Starla's face lose a few shades of color. I followed Bethany Riggs into the double-wide and we took seats around a small dining room table.

"Want something to drink?" Starla asked. "All I have is milk and beer."

We both declined the offer, and Bethany opened her notebook and set it on the table. "Can you begin with the night before Anthony was killed and tell us what he did leading up to the last time you saw him or spoke with him?"

Starla propped both elbows on the table and rested her chin in her palms. "He got home from work at about seven o'clock. We ate supper and then he watched TV while I ran to the store. When I got back, he was sleeping on the couch. I left him there and went to bed. When I woke up yesterday morning, he'd already left for work. I ran some errands during the day and then I went to my sister's in the afternoon. I'd planned to spend the night there because we were going shopping today.

"So…I guess the last time I saw him was when I got home from the store the night before he died." Tears welled up in Starla Landry's eyes and rolled down her face. "Had I known what was going to happen, I would've stayed home and spent time with him."

Starla was bawling now, chin trembling, hands covering her face.

Bethany waited patiently until Starla Landry regained her composure and then asked, "What store did you go to?"

Starla wiped her eyes. "Excuse me?"

Bethany glanced down at her notes. "You said you went to the store after you and Captain Landry ate supper. What store did you go to?"

Starla stared blankly from Bethany to me and back to Bethany before she spoke. "I...I went to the store up the road. Um, Food and Stuff Supermarket."

"What time did you go?" Bethany asked.

"It was after we ate, so it had to be about eight-thirty or nine o'clock."

"What did you buy?"

"Buy?"

"Yes, ma'am. What did you buy at the store?"

Starla Landry began wringing her hands. "I don't really remember."

Bethany raised a single eyebrow, fixing Starla with a cold stare. "I understand you've been through a lot, but we're only talking about the night before last. Surely you remember what you bought."

Starla nodded nervously. "Sure, I remember, it's just... I've been through a lot. Um, I bought some eggs and milk."

"How did you pay for it?"

"What does that have to do with Anthony's death?"

"Please, Mrs. Landry, these are important questions. Even though it might not seem like it right now, they all have a purpose and they'll help us determine what happened to your husband."

Starla Landry nodded her understanding. "I usually always pay with my debit card."

"Did you do so that night?"

Starla nodded, then hung her head.

"Okay," Bethany said. "Do you have a receipt?" Before Starla could answer, Bethany waved her hand. "Never mind. I'll get that from the bank. It'll help us establish a hard timeline."

As Bethany questioned Starla Landry, I studied Starla's face carefully. I was no detective—well, technically I was, but hadn't been for long—but I could tell she was hiding something. I was certain Bethany was on to her as well because of the questions she was asking.

"What time did you get home from the store?" Bethany asked.

Starla shook her head. "I don't remember."

"What car did you drive?"

"My car. Why?"

"The yellow one?"

Starla nodded.

"Okay, that's cool if you don't remember exactly what time you got back home. I can ask your neighbors. They might remember, and that'll help with our timeline." Bethany glanced over her notes.

"Okay, what about yesterday…what time did you wake up?"

"It was about nine o'clock."

"What did you do when you woke up?"

"I got dressed and went to the store."

I thought I saw Starla wince ever slightly.

"What store?" Bethany wanted to know.

"Back to the grocery store."

"What did you get?"

"Um, I was going to buy something for supper, but they didn't have what I wanted."

"What time did you leave and get back?"

"I left at about nine-thirty and I got back at about…" Starla's voice trailed off.

Bethany waited a few seconds and then pressed her. "What time did you get back? I could get it from your neighbors if you don't remember, but I'd rather hear it from you."

Starla sighed. "I think it was around three."

"Three?" Bethany asked. "PM?"

Starla nodded.

Bethany brushed her hair out of her eyes. "Where else did you go beside Food-N-Stuff?"

"I stopped by the Chinese restaurant in Payneville and got something to eat."

"What did you get?"

Starla's eyes narrowed, and I thought she was about to tell Bethany to go screw herself. "If you must know," she retorted, "I got some rice, sweet and sour chicken and an egg roll."

Unfazed, Bethany continued. "Did you eat at the restaurant or did you take it to go?"

"I took it to go."

"Where'd you eat it?"

"At my house," Starla said forcefully.

"Did you stop anywhere else?"

Starla shook her head.

Bethany frowned. "I'm confused. You left your house at nine-thirty and returned at three, yet the only places you went were Food-N-Stuff, where you didn't get anything, and the Chinese restaurant. Why'd it take you five-and-a-half hours for that?"

Starla stood abruptly. "My husband was just killed! Murdered! Do you know what it's like to have the sheriff come find you to tell you your husband has been killed? Do you?" Before waiting for an answer, Starla stormed to the door and jerked it open. "Get the hell out of here! I'm a victim and I will not be treated this way!"

That went great, I thought.

Bethany slowly closed her notebook and stood to leave. I followed her to the door and almost bumped into her backside when she stopped directly in front of Starla.

"You *are* a victim," Bethany said, "but you're acting like a suspect. If I find out you're lying to me, I'll bring the full force of the sheriff's office down on top of your ass for impeding a murder investigation. You might care more about your secret life than you do about your husband's murder, but my number one priority is finding Anthony Landry's killer, and I'll smash anyone who gets in my way."

Starla's eyes widened; her lower lip trembled. She asked what I was thinking. "How…how did you know?"

Bethany's face softened. She reached out and touched Starla's forearm. "Look, I know it's not easy to admit to something like this, especially in light of what's happened, but I need to know everything. It's the only way I can conduct a thorough investigation and locate your husband's killer. If I have to go around you to get the information I need, I'm wasting valuable time."

Starla Landry buried her face in her hands and wept. Bethany wrapped an arm around her and guided her back to the table. "It's okay," Bethany said. "Take your time."

When Starla had settled down somewhat, she began to talk in a low voice. "It started last year. I met someone at an awards banquet for the sheriff's office. We danced for a couple of songs, and he started flirting with me. I thought it was all innocent and fun. That night he came over to the house, and we all played cards—"

"Where was your husband?" Bethany asked.

"Oh, Anthony was there. It was the three of us playing cards." Starla wiped her face free of a stream of tears, but it only served to make room for more. "Anthony drank a lot that night and got up at some point to use the bathroom. When he didn't come back, I went check on him and found him in the bed. He was fully clothed, passed out on top of the bedspread."

"What was your new friend doing at this point?" Bethany asked.

"He…he had followed me to the bedroom and when he saw Anthony, he walked up behind me and started rubbing my back and my neck. It was kind of awkward—with Anthony lying there—so we went back to the living room. He kept rubbing on me and touching me and he tried to kiss me a few times. I told him no at first, but I was a bit drunk, too, and I eventually gave in." Starla was sobbing again.

"We…had sex in the living room that night," Starla said between sobs. "And I saw… We began seeing each other on a regular basis."

Bethany put a hand on her shoulder to comfort her. "The day your husband was killed, were you with this guy?"

Starla nodded.

I felt my blood boiling. I didn't know if it showed in my face, but I wanted Bethany to slap the shit out of this adulterous whore. On the very day her husband's brains were sprayed across Betty Jo's parking lot, she was out screwing some dude she'd met at a sheriff's office function.

"This mystery man," Lieutenant Riggs said softly. "Does he have a name?"

Starla nodded slowly, not looking up. In a muffled voice, she said a name.

"Wait," Bethany said. "I couldn't hear what you said. Can you speak up?"

"Ken…Kenneth Lewis. He's a sniper with the sheriff's office."

CHAPTER 8

I suddenly felt dizzy…sick even.

Lieutenant Bethany Riggs continued to question Starla Landry, but I was hearing none of it. Everything was a blur—one that was lasting longer than I could stand. I wanted to immediately rush out of the house and go find Kenneth. I wanted to beat his ass for having an affair with Captain Landry's wife. If he would betray his own captain, a friend, a fellow officer—who *wouldn't* he betray?

Bethany's voice suddenly cut through my evil thoughts and her question turned my blood to icicles.

"Ms. Landry," she said, "it's very important that you think really hard about my next question before answering. Okay?"

Starla nodded.

"Has Kenneth Lewis ever said anything about wanting your husband dead? Anything at all?"

Starla immediately shook her head. "No, never."

"Did he ever ask you to leave Anthony?"

Starla hesitated, then slowly nodded. "He did say he'd leave his wife if I left Anthony."

Bethany looked at me briefly, then turned her attention back to Starla Landry. "When did he tell you this?"

Starla shrugged. "I don't remember the first time, but he started saying it a lot during the past few weeks. He even told me he loved me."

"How did you respond?"

"I told him he couldn't leave his wife and I couldn't leave my husband. I told him I wanted things to stay as they were. He seemed cool with it." Starla nodded her head slowly. "Yes, he was definitely cool with it. He knew I loved Anthony despite our problems and he would never have done anything to hurt me."

"What about Anthony? Would he ever do anything to hurt Anthony?"

"No, he knew hurting Anthony would hurt me, so he would never—"

"Well, somebody did," I interrupted. "Other than Kenneth, is there anyone else who'd want to see Anthony out of the way…for any reason?"

Starla shook her head. Bethany glared at me. I guess she was pissed about me cutting into her interview, but I was beyond caring about anything except getting my hands around Kenneth's throat. I leaned across the table and stared Starla Landry directly in the eyes. "So, if what you're saying is true, Kenneth is the only person who would possibly have a reason to kill Anthony?"

Starla's eyes slowly widened as realization started to set in. "You…you really think he did this?"

Bethany cut in. "So, instead of being at Food-N-Stuff's or the Chinese restaurant…"

Starla frowned, nodded. "I was with Kenneth. We'd either meet at my sister's house in Doveport or at his brother's apartment in Chateau. I usually just told Anthony I was at the store or at my sister's. He'd never question me. I guess he trusted me."

"What time did you last see Kenneth yesterday?"

Starla rubbed her face with both hands, as though her cheeks had fallen asleep and she was trying to rub them awake. "Um, I'd picked up lunch for us, and he met me in the Food-N-Stuff parking lot. I left my car there and jumped in with him and we went to the Payneville Park. We spent most of the day there and then he dropped me off at my car about two-thirty. That was the last time I saw him. He was supposed to meet me at my sister's house last night, but…"

"But what?" Bethany asked.

"He never arrived."

"That bastard lied to me!" I blurted. I turned to Starla. "He said you went to his house last night because his wife went out of town."

"I've never been to his house." Starla's face suddenly twisted into a scowl. "His wife was out of town? He didn't tell me that."

Bethany stood and fished a business card from her back pocket. She handed it to Starla. "Call me if you think of anything else."

I followed Bethany to her car and we got in without saying a word. She pulled out of the driveway and headed south on Highway Three until we reached Highway Twelve. She took the onramp and headed west. I finally broke the silence to ask where we were headed, but I already knew the answer.

"The rifle range." She didn't take her eyes off the road as she rapidly picked up speed. "Kenneth Lewis has some explaining to do."

I only nodded.

I felt Bethany steal a quick glance at me. "You okay with this? Or do I need to get a new partner?"

"I'm okay with what we have to do, but I'm not okay with having been a fool for all this time."

"So, you didn't know about the affair?"

I jerked around in my seat to stare at Bethany. "Hell no, I didn't know about it! I would've kicked Kenneth's backstabbing ass had I known and I would've thrown him off the team. In our line of work, you have to be able to trust the man next to you one hundred percent, and that's a bit hard to do when you're sleeping with your partner's wife. Shit, that's the ultimate betrayal." I shook my head, still trying to wrap my mind around what I'd just learned. "Captain Landry was like a father to us. As a team, he gave us everything we asked for and always covered our asses. I can't believe Kenneth would betray him like that."

"Look, you're too close to the situation—on both sides—so it'll probably be best if you stay out of the interview."

"I'm fine."

"Right...like you were back there with Starla Landry?" Bethany shook her head. "Nope, I want you outside the room on this one. You can hang out in the observation room and watch the interview, but I can't afford any outbursts from you."

I started to argue, but something told me I wouldn't get very far with Lieutenant Bethany Riggs. "Okay," was all I said. And then, "How're we going to handle this?"

"We'll ask him to voluntarily come with us to CID."

"If he refuses?"

"I'll make a phone call to the sheriff, and he'll be fired immediately. At that point, we'll put a tail on him and apply for an arrest warrant. Once the judge signs it, we'll take him into custody and interrogate him."

"Wait a minute...an arrest warrant? We don't have a shred of proof he did it. All we have is speculation, and I'm still not positive Kenneth's capable of murder."

"You don't need to be positive. All we need is probable cause, and I think we can easily pass that test."

"How? With what?"

"He's got motive to want Landry dead, he's got the unique ability to pull off the shot and we just stomped a giant mud hole in his alibi. If you ask me, we've got more than enough for a warrant."

"There is one thing that doesn't fit."

"What's that?"

"I train our snipers to aim for the bridge of the nose when making a frontal shot to the head. Captain Landry was shot in his left eye."

"So? What's the difference?"

"Aiming at the left eyeball—or the right one—is okay if you're in the military and you're only shooting at targets of opportunity. If you pull your shot a little to the left you might graze the outer edge of his head and a follow-up shot would be necessary, but the consequences are nil. The worst thing that could happen is you don't get credit for a kill." I shook my head. "Law enforcement snipers don't have the luxury of missing. If they pull their shot and inflict anything less than an instantaneous kill shot, hostages could die...and that's not acceptable. By aiming at the bridge of the nose, you allow yourself some wiggle room. Pulling slightly to the left or right will still impact within the cranial vault and you'll drop your bad guy instantly."

"So, based on just that, you think Kenneth Lewis didn't kill Captain Landry?"

"I'm just saying it goes against his training."

Bethany was thoughtful for a while and then said, "He could've changed his aiming point just to throw us off. Think about it. If you were known for shooting people between the eyes, would you go out and shoot someone between the eyes? No...you'd shoot them through the mouth—or something different—just to throw off the investigators. You wouldn't want to leave a note saying it was *you* who did it."

"I guess you're right." I stared at the trees that blurred by, but didn't see them. "I can't believe I never picked up on it. He never seemed like the murdering type. Sure, he could take a shot to save a life, but he doesn't have a mean bone in his body."

"If priests can rape little boys," Bethany explained, "no one's safe."

She was right, of course. Every time there was a news story about some unsuspecting person committing a heinous crime—especially child molestation or rape—family members and friends would jump in front of the camera to express sincere shock that their loved one could do something so egregious. If there was one thing I learned after doing police work for twelve-plus years, it was that no one truly knew their neighbors or their friends—or their families. After working cases where fathers raped their daughters and mothers killed their children, nothing was sacred, and nothing surprised me anymore. I just couldn't believe I'd been so blind.

Bethany jerked the steering wheel and swerved into the shell driveway to the rifle range. She came to an abrupt stop near Jerry's cruiser and flung her door open. Her quickness surprised me. I hurried after her as she walked directly up to Kenneth Lewis. He started to open his mouth, but Bethany cut him off. "Gather up your shit and come with us."

Kenneth looked from her to me and then back to her. I felt Jerry and the others slowly gather around. All eyes were on me. If I said the word, Kenneth wouldn't be going anywhere and Bethany would find herself in grave danger. Snipers are a close-knit group and—with the exception of the imposter who stood before me—loyal to the death.

"What the hell's going on, Daddy?" Kenneth asked.

I bit my tongue until I tasted blood. It was clear from the way Bethany handled Starla Landry that there was some method to her madness and I didn't want to screw anything up. It was also clear that she could handle Kenneth on her own.

"I said, get your shit and come with us." Bethany's voice was stern, threatening.

Kenneth didn't seem impressed. He sneered and turned to walk away. Bethany quickly moved forward and grabbed his arm. Kenneth turned suddenly and shot a back-fist strike toward Bethany's face. With catlike reflexes, she slipped under it and pivoted around to his back side and wrapped her left arm around his neck, under his chin. Caught off guard, Kenneth clutched at her forearm, but she locked in a rear-naked choke and dropped to her knees, bringing Kenneth down with her.

The other snipers looked to me, and I shook my head. They relaxed and settled back to see what would happen next.

Kenneth's face turned to crimson and his clutching hands began to slide slowly down the front of his chest. Bethany released her grip on his neck and quickly pulled his arms behind his back. She produced a set of handcuffs from her back pocket and applied them to Kenneth's wrists. He was panting now, gasping for breath. Bethany slapped his back and pulled him to his feet. "You'll be fine," she said.

When he could speak again, Kenneth said, in a hoarse whisper,

"What the hell did you do that for?"

"You're under arrest for battery on a police officer," Bethany said. "And you're a suspect in the murder of Captain Anthony Landry."

There was a collective gasp from the other snipers. Kenneth shook his head in desperation. "No way," he yelled. "I didn't kill no one!"

"We'll talk about that at CID," Bethany said, escorting him toward her car. She called over her shoulder to me, "Get some gloves out of my crime scene kit and recover his rifle."

I did as she asked and secured the rifle in a large evidence box I found in the trunk of her car. I then locked up Kenneth's squad car and took the keys with me.

"We'll have a team come back to process his car," Bethany said as she strapped Kenneth into the back seat.

I walked over to the other snipers, looking from one wide-eyed person to the next. Jerry was the first to break the silence. "Is this shit for real?"

"As real as it gets."

"Sergeant Carter," Bethany called, "let's get him back to CID ASAP."

I nodded to my team of snipers and turned away. I'd barely closed the door when Bethany sped off.

"Daddy, this is bullshit," Kenneth was saying from the backseat. "I don't know what the hell's going on, but I didn't have nothing to do with Captain Landry's murder. He was like a father to me—to all of us. This bitch has it all wrong. I'd never do anything to hurt the captain."

"Right," I blurted, before I could stop myself, "and I guess screwing his wife was okay because that surely wouldn't have hurt him had he found out. Is that how you roll?" My eyes pierced his with a ferociousness that scared even me. Right at that moment, as I sat twisted in my seat looking into the eyes of the man who had possibly gunned down one of his own, I was sure I could murder him with a good heart.

In my peripheral vision, I saw Bethany wince. I kept staring at Kenneth until he looked away and then I turned back around. I mumbled an apology to Bethany, who only shook her head.

CHAPTER 9

"You think he did it?" asked Sheriff Calvin Burke. He stood beside me in the darkness as we stared through the one-way glass that separated us from the interrogation taking place in the adjacent room.

I watched as Lieutenant Bethany Riggs tried to work her magic on Kenneth Lewis. They had been in there for three hours and the only thing Kenneth would admit to doing was having the affair with Starla Landry.

"To be honest," I finally said, "I don't know what to think. If you'd asked me a week ago if I thought Kenneth would screw his friend's wife, I would've said you were crazy. I now know different, and I have no idea who he is anymore."

I turned my attention back to the interview. Bethany was leaning close to Kenneth and she was speaking in a low tone. I had to strain to hear what she was saying.

"You do understand you're going to get the death penalty if you're convicted, don't you?" she asked. "So you might as well explain why you did it. That might be the only chance you have to save your life."

"But I didn't—"

"I know, I know. You didn't do it," she interrupted. "Look, personally, I don't give a shit what happens to you. I'd rather you kept your mouth shut and we could just present our evidence and have you put to death as soon as possible. But I think you owe it to the friends and family of Captain Landry to at least say you're sorry for what you did."

"I am sorry for what I did, but I didn't kill him."

"Then why are you sorry?"

Kenneth threw his hands up. "For screwing his wife! I've told you that a thousand times. I'm sorry I slept with her. Look, I know that makes me a piece of shit and an asshole, but it doesn't make me a killer. I would never murder anyone."

"Not even for a woman?"

"Especially not for a woman."

Bethany studied her notes. "Well, I think that covers everything. I just have one final question for you. You told me earlier that you were home alone during the shooting. Why, then, did you tell Sergeant Carter that you were at home with a sweetie?"

Kenneth fidgeted in his chair, saying nothing.

Bethany's eyebrows rose. "Well? Which is it? Did you have a *sweetie* over or not?"

"No...I was home alone."

I shook my head, clenched my fists. *Lying bastard!*

Bethany smiled. "Perfect. This will be an easy case to present to the Grand Jury. You began having an adulterous affair with Captain Landry's wife. Things got serious and you wanted her all to yourself. You begged her to leave the good captain, but she refused to do so. This infuriated you. So, you did what any love-struck and desperate psycho would do—you took out the competition." Bethany stood and paced around the room, her arms folded. Finally, she stopped and glanced down at Kenneth Lewis. "When you woke up yesterday, did you know that would be the day?"

"I already told you I didn't do it!" The words spat from his mouth.

Bethany waved her hand dismissively. "I'm beyond that point. I'm at the part where you acknowledge you did it and want to offer an explanation so you don't get the death penalty." She sat at the corner of the desk and crossed her arms again. "You get the message that there's a SWAT roll. You know Captain Landry is in charge of SWAT and he responds to every callout. You're fully aware of the chaos that surrounds an event such as this, and you know how easy it would be for a police sniper to take advantage of this situation. You see it as the perfect time and place to execute your plan—"

"That's bullshit!" Kenneth's face was red, the veins in his temple protruding.

"What's not bullshit is that you had motive, opportunity and the means to carry out this crime," Bethany countered. "And what's most unfortunate for you is that there are only six people in this parish capable of making the shot that killed Captain Landry…and the other five were accounted for."

"I was at home!"

"Right, you were home alone when it happened, but you have no witnesses to verify that story, and you already lied once about it to Sergeant Carter." Bethany stood and gathered up her paperwork. She started to walk out, but stopped by the door. "Why didn't you just shoot him in the chest with a handgun like a normal person would do? At least then it would've been a little more challenging to figure out who did it."

Sheriff Burke and I were waiting in the hallway when Bethany stepped out of the interview room. "I think he did it," she said.

I frowned and nodded my agreement.

"As much as I hate to admit it, I think you're right," Sheriff Burke said.

I looked from Bethany to Sheriff Burke. "What's next?"

Sheriff Burke took in a deep breath and slowly exhaled. "Apply for an arrest warrant. If the judge signs it, arrest him."

Bethany nodded, turned to me. "Let's go."

I followed her down the hallway and to one of the empty cubicles. She took the driver's seat and fired up the computer. I pulled a chair from a neighboring cubicle and slid it beside her. I'd written my fair share of arrest warrants during my years as a cop, but I'd never drafted one for murder. "How do we apply for a warrant without evidence?"

"We have evidence. It's just circumstantial."

I suddenly remembered the autopsy that was to be performed on Captain Landry and glanced at the time on my cell phone. It was almost six o'clock. "LT, what about Captain Landry's autopsy?"

Bethany didn't turn away from the computer, where words were hopping onto the screen at a record pace. "I sent Corey a text message from the interview room. He and Sally will handle it for us."

Lieutenant Corey Chiasson and Detective Sally Piatkowski. I'd met Sally through Gina at a party once, about six months earlier. Gina later told me Sally wanted to go out on a date. Sally was a beautiful natural blonde with sky blue eyes and a nice body, and I was extremely tempted, but, as I'd told Gina, I had a strict rule against dating cops.

"What's the matter…you don't like strong women?" Sally had asked the next time she saw me.

"No, I love strong women. I just don't like strong women with guns," had been my response. Truth be told, I was a bit intimidated by how beautiful she was and I didn't—

"Hey, you daydreaming?"

I jerked my head up to find Bethany staring at me. "Wait...what?"

"I asked if you have some sort of documentation showing that Kenneth Lewis can make that shot from four hundred yards."

"Oh, yeah. I keep detailed records showing all of our training, which includes regular shots out to a thousand yards. I even have copies of the targets he—"

"Riggs! Carter! Shut it down," Sheriff Burke hollered from the hallway. "Get in here right away."

We exchanged worried looks, jumped to our feet and hurried to the conference room, where we found Sheriff Burke, Captain Michael Theriot and Chief Deputy Matt Garcia huddled around the boomerang conference-call phone.

"Yes, sir, I'm positive," a female's voice was saying. It sounded like Gina Pellegrin.

"Okay, hang tight until Bethany and London get there." Sheriff Burke smashed the hang-up button and turned to us, a somber look on his face. "Justin Wainwright"—the retired internal affairs captain Bethany had replaced—"was just found dead in his backyard. He was shot through the left eye."

CHAPTER 10

"We were wrong," I told Bethany as we drove to the scene. "It wasn't Kenneth."

"We won't know for sure until we get to the scene."

"Two cops get shot through the left eye in two days? It doesn't take a seasoned detective to figure out they're connected. And since Kenneth was in our custody during the second shooting, we can prove he didn't do it."

Bethany shook her head. "It's not always that simple, Sergeant. We have to go into every case with an open mind. Once we get there, we follow the evidence and let it dictate to us what happened, not the other way around."

Sure, I knew that, but I was certain this would be an exception. Kenneth had been with me since early this morning and he'd been in custody for hours. I said as much to Bethany, but she only said, "We'll have to wait and see what the evidence tells us."

We rode the rest of the way in silence, with the only sounds being the rhythmic clicking of the strobe lights and the whistling of the police antennas as they sliced through the evening air at eighty miles per hour.

It was almost eight o'clock when we arrived at Justin Wainwright's house. He lived off of Highway Three in Broadmoore, his house set back off the highway about three hundred yards. There were no neighbors for a couple of miles in either direction. Acres upon acres of sugarcane fields bordered his property to the north and south.

Six squad cars and two detective cars were parked in the front yard, their strobes flashing bright in the rapidly dimming evening light. Bethany and I found Detective Gina Pellegrin, Detective Sally Piatkowski and a crowd of patrolmen in the backyard. They stood around a red riding lawn mower. It was a crashed up against a young oak tree. The lifeless body of Justin Wainwright was positioned on his back several feet from the lawnmower. His head was turned sideways and the back of his skull was a mushy mass of broken bone and brain matter. There was a crimson hole where his left eye had once been.

Gina looked up when we approached. "The bullet went right through his left eye, just like Captain Landry."

I walked closer and leaned over to see his face. He looked bloated and his skin was blistered. The warm breeze peeled a healthy dose of rancid rot from his body and rubbed it into my nostrils, singeing my nose hairs. "Jesus, he's ripe!"

Gina nodded. "He's been dead at least two days."

"No shit." I turned slowly to Bethany. "You were right."

"Only because I've been wrong too many times. I learned to reserve my opinion until after I see the evidence...all of it." She turned to Gina. "Let's get this scene processed. I want photos and detailed measurements of the position his body's in now. We need to figure out his exact location when he was shot, so Sergeant Carter can determine the sniper's position when he fired the shot."

Bethany turned to me. "After we're done here tonight, we'll station a deputy to guard the house until daybreak. We'll come back then and you can get a fix on the sniper's shooting position. Maybe we'll get lucky this time and find a shell casing we can match to Kenneth's rifle."

I nodded. There were no streetlights out here in the country, and it would be next to impossible to conduct a thorough search at nighttime, even with ambient light.

Bethany handed me a pair of latex gloves and turned toward the house. She waved at me to follow. "While they process the scene, we'll search the house to see if we can figure out what he's been doing since he retired. It might shed some light on why Kenneth wanted him dead."

We walked up the steps to the back door and Bethany tried the knob. It opened. "I guess it would be unlocked," she mused. "He was in the backyard cutting grass. It would've been daytime."

I thought back to what Gina had said. "If he's been dead two days, then that would put him cutting his grass on Monday. Kenneth's wife left on Saturday to go to her mom's house, so, unless he has some other alibi, he's got opportunity and the means to kill

Wainwright, too."

"We just have to figure out what his motive would be for killing a retired captain." When Bethany walked through the door, I followed. We found ourselves in a dated, but clean, kitchen. "How well did you know Captain Wainwright?"

"He was on SWAT when I first started with the department. He was pretty squared away. I got called into his office once for an excessive force complaint, and he was cool about it."

"Was it a valid complaint?" Bethany had stopped walking and pierced me with her blue eyes.

"No, it was a complete lie. This punk said I broke his nose for no reason, but I never even hit him."

"Did you have physical contact with him?"

"Oh, yeah, I arrested him for pulling an armed robbery. I had to chase him down and tackle him to the ground, but that was the end of it. He complained to a jailer that his nose hurt, so they brought him to the hospital. Several x-rays and hundreds of taxpayer dollars later, they concluded there was nothing wrong with his nose."

"But he filed an IA complaint anyway?"

"Yeah...he claimed I punched him in the face, but Wainwright knew immediately that he was lying."

"How'd he know that?"

"I break what I hit...and there was nothing broken on him. Wainwright was cool about everything and didn't even put it in my jacket."

Bethany studied me, nodding slightly. "Okay," she said, "let's finish tossing this place." She began digging through drawers and cabinets in the kitchen. "Tell me more about Wainwright."

"You worked with him. You should know more than I do."

Bethany shook her head. "He never talked about his past or his personal life. Hell, the only time he talked to me at all was to tell me what to do. So, if you don't mind enlightening me..."

"I don't know a whole lot about him. His wife died a few years before he retired and he went into business for himself after leaving law enforcement. PI work or something. I think he handled divorce cases and accidents more than anything else." I dug idly through some of the drawers as I followed Bethany around the room. She went to the living room, searched it and then made her way down a carpeted hallway. We turned left into the first room, and she flipped on a light.

"This must be his office," she said.

A desk and bookshelves—all of them a cluttered mess—were

built into a closet and a row of filing cabinets lined one wall. She moved to the desk area, and I approached the filing cabinets. I stopped short when I saw pry marks on one of the filing cabinet drawers. I tested it and it screeched open. The locking mechanism dangled. "I've got something here," I called out.

Bethany hurried up behind me. "What is it?"

I looked over my shoulder and was surprised at how close she was to me.

"There must be something in there that's worth killing for, and we need to find it." When she spoke, the smell of Big Red gum clung to the words that floated from her mouth. As I watched her mouth move, I felt an intense desire to shut her up with a kiss—to press my mouth against her moist lips.

Blinking the thought from my mind and wondering where it had come from, I turned back to the filing cabinet. "What if the killer already found it?"

Bethany surveyed the room, then nodded slowly. "I thought it odd that a person who keeps such a neat kitchen would have a messy desk, but it's obvious the killer came in here and rummaged through the place. Whatever he was after, it must've had something to do with Wainwright's business."

"How can you be so sure?" I wanted to know.

Bethany smiled, pointing to the filing cabinet in front of me. I looked down and blushed. A small label on the damaged drawer read *Wainwright's Private Investigative Services.* Bethany walked around the room, examining the ceiling, pushing on the walls, testing the floor with her boot. "London, where did you hide your porn?"

I jerked my head up from where I was searching through the files in the cabinet. "Excuse me?"

"When you were a kid—where'd you hide your porn?"

"What makes you think I had porn?" I felt my face redden.

She smiled. "Every boy has porn at one time or another...and they all hide it."

She was right, of course. I sighed. "I'd take some of my dad's older magazines—the ones I figured he wouldn't miss—fold them in half and put them in the inside pocket of my winter jacket."

Bethany immediately walked out of the office and continued down the hall until she found the master bedroom. I followed her and watched as she searched all of the pockets in every piece of clothing hanging in his closet. Nothing. "Either Wainwright had better hiding spots than you or he didn't have porn." She stood by his closet door and surveyed the bedroom. Her eyes fixed on a wall socket and she pointed to it. "What's odd about that socket?"

I looked where she pointed, then checked the other walls. Every wall had one electrical socket, while the wall she was pointing at had two…and they were close together. She moved closer and whistled. "This screw has been worked quite a bit. The paint's been chipped off it."

I fished a knife from my pocket, flipped the blade open, and handed it to her. She used it to turn the screw until it fell to the floor. Passing the knife back to me, she used her fingernails to pry the wall plate off and put it to the side. She tugged on the socket and it fell free. The area behind it was empty and dark. "I think we're onto something."

I dropped to my knees beside Lieutenant Riggs to watch as she slipped her gloved hand through the opening in the sheetrock and began feeling around in the wall. She bit her lower lip and leaned in, trying to fit more of her arm into the hole.

"Is there anything in there?" I asked.

"No, nothing. I can only feel the floor, the studs and the opposite wall." She started to pull out, but stopped. "Wait a minute."

"What is it?"

"It feels like some sort of a latch in here."

There was a sharp metallic click from inside. Bethany removed her arm and light emanated from the rectangular hole in the wall. "The wall on the other side opened up," she said. She peered through the hole. "It's his office."

We hurried to our feet and walked out the bedroom down the hall. When we reached Justin Wainwright's office, we stopped and looked around. Bethany pointed to the desk. "It's under there."

We both dropped to our knees to get a better view of the trap door. The wall under the desk was constructed of a dark wooden panel. The trap door—two feet high by two feet wide—had been cut from this wall and now stood open, suspended by a narrow hinge attached to the inside of the door. Squeezing my way under the desk, I pushed the trap door shut to inspect it. The top edge of the door coincided with the trim under the desk and the bottom edge of the door coincided with the top of the baseboards.

"This is ingenious," I said. "By attaching the latch and hinge to the inside and making it accessible from the adjacent room, he totally disguises this as a trap door. The splices are seamless at the top, bottom and both sides. Fine craftsmanship."

Bethany squeezed beside me, her left shoulder pressed firmly against my right shoulder. "But I didn't feel anything inside, so why go through all that trouble for nothing?"

I pulled the door open wide and it exposed two separate compartments, separated by a treated stud. The compartment to the right of the center stud was empty, and it was where the electrical socket was located. The other compartment to the left of the stud appeared empty as well, but the space extended beyond the cutout of the trap door and disappeared into the darkness between the walls. I twisted my body, extremely conscious of Bethany's body pressed beside my own, and carefully reached into the opening with my gloved hand. I felt something.

CHAPTER 11

"What is it?" Bethany Riggs asked, the whisper of her breath tickling the side of my neck.

I pulled out a large manila envelope. We scurried out from under the desk and stared at each other, then at the envelope.

"What do you think is inside?" I asked.

"We're about to find out." Bethany took the envelope and turned it over. There was a white label with a name and address typed into it. She gasped. "It's labeled *Anthony Landry.*"

"What the hell?" I was beyond curious. "Hurry…get it open."

She rolled to a seated position and scooted to the center of the floor of Wainwright's office. She eased the clasps on the envelope open and separated the edges so she could look inside. She gasped. "There're pictures in here—lots of them—and they're large prints." She turned the envelope over and allowed the prints to slide out and onto the floor.

"Holy shit!" I blurted when I saw the picture on top.

"Are those what I think they are?" she asked.

"Yes, they are."

She rifled through the pictures. "What is Wainwright doing with surveillance pictures of Kenneth Lewis and Starla Landry?"

"I guess Captain Landry hired him to spy on Starla. He must've suspected she was cheating on him."

We went through all of the pictures—about two dozen of them—and found there were about eight pictures each from three different locations. The first location was in front of Captain Landry's house. Starla was hanging onto the side of Kenneth's squad car and, in most of the pictures, they were only talking, but the last two shots showed them kissing. I shook my head before I flipped to the next location.

The Gator Inn in Chateau. That series of pictures showed Kenneth getting out of his truck, Starla getting out of her yellow car, both of them entering room 118 together, then leaving the room together. It wouldn't take a genius to figure out what took place inside that room.

The third set of pictures had clearly been taken from across the practice field at Central Magnolia High School. Because of the distance between camera and subjects, these pictures were not as clear as the others, but there was no mistaking Kenneth's truck and Starla's car parked beside the Baptist church located at the end of Journey Drive. In that series of photos, Starla got out of her car and climbed onto Kenneth's lap as he sat in the driver's seat of his truck. They both disappeared beneath the level of the dashboard for a number of the shots, and when they reappeared, Starla was topless. Another shot showed her pulling on her shirt, and the last one had her stepping out of Kenneth's truck.

"This ain't good." I tossed the last of the pictures into the pile on the floor. "At least Captain Landry died before he had to see this shit."

Bethany nodded. "If these pictures would've made it to him, we'd be working Kenneth's murder."

Having known Captain Landry for a dozen years, I knew she was correct. I watched as she collected the photos and returned them to the envelope. "Kenneth must've found out Wainwright was investigating him," I mused aloud. "He couldn't take the chance this gets to his wife, so he kills Wainwright, searches for *this*"—I pointed to the envelope—"but doesn't find it, so he kills Captain Landry in case Wainwright told him what he'd found. "

"How'd he find out Wainwright was investigating him?" Bethany wanted to know.

"Because—like all of us snipers—he's an expert in counter-surveillance techniques. It'd be next to impossible for someone to follow him and take these pictures of him without him noticing."

Bethany chewed her lower lip, a thoughtful expression on her face. She finally stood and walked back to Justin Wainwright's desk. She dug around for several seconds and then turned toward me holding an expensive-looking camera and four memory card cases. "There's no memory card in the camera and these cases are empty," she said. "I noticed it earlier, but didn't realize what it meant. And look"—she pointed beneath the desk—"under there. The computer hard drive is missing."

I stared blankly at her, wondering what she was getting at.

"Kenneth took all of the memory cards and the hard drive. He had no idea Wainwright had that envelope stashed away—how would he?—so he just did what anyone in his situation would do. He snatched up all of the potential evidence and killed the only two men who might know about him and Starla." Bethany leaned against the desk and bit her lip again. "But why use his sniper rifle to carry out the murders? That's like leaving a calling card with his name and number on it."

"It's what he knows." I picked up the envelope of pictures and held onto them while Bethany finished searching Justin Wainwright's house. When nothing else of interest was found, we made our way out back and rejoined Gina and the other officers. Sheriff Burke, Captain Theriot and Chief Garcia had arrived at some point and were standing around Wainwright's body.

"Sheriff, take a look at these," Bethany said, handing Sheriff Burke a pair of latex gloves and then the envelope.

After donning the gloves, Burke shuffled through the photos. "Jesus Christ, what on Earth was Kenneth thinking?" Burke handed the pictures back to Riggs. "How'd Wainwright get his hands on these?"

"It appears Captain Landry hired him to follow his wife," she said.

"So, it's pretty clear Kenneth had motive to kill them both?" Chief Garcia asked.

I glanced at Bethany; we both nodded.

"When can we expect both cases to be wrapped up and your reports done?" Garcia asked.

"Carter and I are going to interview Lewis again," Bethany explained, "and then we'll return here in the morning to finish working up the trajectory. After that, we're pretty much done."

Sheriff Burke nodded. "Good, I want this case put to bed as soon as possible. The media is going haywire over this, speculating there's a terrorist out there killing cops. I want to be able to make a press release as soon as y'all are done."

Bethany inclined her head toward Captain Theriot. "Have you heard from Lieutenant Chiasson? He was supposed to attend Captain Landry's autopsy, but I haven't heard back from him."

Captain Theriot nodded. "He got to the office just as we were leaving."

"Any surprises?" I asked.

Theriot shook his head. "Cause of death was a gunshot wound to the head, and the coroner ruled it a homicide."

"Did the coroner say if he suffered?" Bethany asked, a look of concern on her face.

"No, he didn't mention it."

"I hate to break up this party," Sheriff Burke said, "but we have to get going."

Captain Theriot and Chief Garcia nodded and both followed Sheriff Burke through the backyard and around the house to where their car was parked.

"Captain Landry didn't feel a thing," I assured Bethany as we watched the trio walk away.

"How can you be so sure?"

"A high-powered rifle round to the cranial vault instantly destroys the brain stem—kills you deader and quicker than lightning strikes. He never knew what hit him. Shit"—I spat on the ground—"poor bastard probably still thinks he's standing out there watching that hostage situation go down."

"How do you know all that?" Bethany wanted to know.

"It's my job to know what a bullet does when it leaves my rifle barrel."

She considered this. "So, everything you know, Kenneth knows?"

I nodded somberly. "I didn't just teach him how to kill people, I taught him how to kill instantly, how to make no-reflex kill shots, and then how to deal with it emotionally."

Bethany placed her hand on my shoulder and squeezed. "It's not your fault. You had no way of knowing—"

I pulled my arm away. "Look, it's nice of you to say that, and I certainly appreciate the gesture, but don't waste your sympathy on me. I don't need it."

Bethany scowled. "Jesus, I was just trying to be nice. You don't have to be such a prick."

"I'm not being a prick. I just don't want you to feel sorry for me because I don't feel sorry for myself."

"I don't understand," she said slowly.

I sighed, not knowing how to put it into words. How do you tell someone you haven't felt a thing since you were a kid? That no matter how hard you try, you can't muster up a single tear? "Just please understand that I sincerely appreciate the gesture. I've learned a lot about you today, and I know you're a great person. I just don't like good people feeling bad for me when I can't even feel bad for myself."

I could tell by the look on her face that Bethany was slipping deeper into a state of confusion. I smiled. "Why don't we just forget about it and go finish interrogating Kenneth?"

She nodded. Before we walked off, she turned to Gina Pellegrin. "Can you line someone up to secure the scene overnight?"

Gina was still crouched over Justin Wainwright's body. She was recording measurements on her diagram as another detective called them out to her. Without looking up from her notepad, she called over her shoulder, "I ain't your secretary."

I thought I saw Bethany's eyes flash. She opened her mouth to say something I was certain would only start a catfight, so I interrupted her. "Damon," I called to one of the patrol deputies who used to work on my shift, "you working nights?"

Damon nodded. "I got it, Sarge."

As we walked to Bethany's car, she grumbled, "What's that bitch's problem?"

"She's cool," I said. "You just have to get to know her. She's definitely someone you want on your side in a pinch."

Bethany grunted, climbed in and slammed her door shut. Neither of us spoke on the ride back to CID. I stole an occasional glance at her profile.

"What the hell?" Bethany slammed on the brakes and jerked the steering wheel to the right.

I turned to see flashing lights in my face and knew instantly that something was drastically wrong. An ambulance had cut us off and was racing into the parking lot at CID. Before we could park, two medics jumped out of the ambulance and ran toward the front entrance. Chief Garcia shoved the door open for them and they all disappeared into the office, with us hot on their heels. We followed them to the interview room, but we got stuck in the crowded hallway.

"What's going on?" Bethany demanded, as Chief Garcia pushed his way through the sea of officers, making a hole for the medics. No one answered Bethany, and she grabbed the collar of the nearest deputy and jerked him back, nearly took him off his feet. "I said, *What the hell is going on?*"

The deputy turned, his face ashen. "It's...it's Deputy Kenneth Lewis. He...he killed himself!"

CHAPTER 12

Bethany Riggs stood with her back against the one-way glass in the interview room, lips pursed. I stood beside her and looked down at Deputy Lester LeBouef. His face was a waterfall of sweat and his feet twitched under his chair.

"Start talking," Bethany said forcefully.

"He asked to use my cell phone," Lester explained in a feeble voice. "I didn't know he would do that. He just said he needed to—"

"Why in the hell didn't you stay in the room with him?" she asked.

Lester hung his head, then shook it from side to side. "I don't know. He asked for some privacy…said he needed to talk to his wife. I was just outside the room. I could hear his entire conversation."

"What did he say? All of it," she demanded.

"He told her he didn't do the things they said he did, but it sounded like she didn't believe him. It sounded like she was accusing him of doing something with someone named Laura, because he kept saying that Laura was a liar."

Bethany looked at me, then back at Lester. "You sure he wasn't saying Starla?"

"Oh no, because he mentioned Starla, too. He said that was also a lie." Lester wiped the sweat from his face, but more beads sprouted from his pores. "He kept telling her he couldn't go to prison. Said he wouldn't survive it."

"Did he say anything else?" I asked.

Lester shook his head. "He was quiet for a while, so I thought his wife was talking and he was listening. But then…then I heard some strange sounds, like gurgling. I tried to open the door, but something was blocking it. I had to fight for a few seconds to break through and that was when I found him."

"How'd he do it?" Bethany asked.

"He got up on the chair and removed the hanging ceiling tile. I guess he took off his coveralls next, tied one leg over the metal beam, and made a noose with the other end because when I found him that's how he was hanging. He used the desk to block the door." Deputy LeBouef wiped his face with both hands, sighing. "Will I lose my job?"

Bethany pushed off the wall and walked to the door. "That'll be up to Sheriff Burke. But if I had my way, you'd be fired and arrested for malfeasance in office."

"Kind of harsh on the kid, don't you think?" I said as we made our way to the conference room.

Bethany stopped walking and turned to face me, her hands on her hips. Her cheeks were flushed, eyes narrow. She opened her mouth to speak, but her eyes turned suddenly curious. "Why are you looking at me like that?"

The one thing that had been going through my mind was how beautiful she looked when she was angry, but I hadn't realized it showed in my expression. I tried to recover quickly. "Um, what do you mean?"

"You were staring at me all funny-like."

"No, I wasn't." I waved my hand to dismiss the issue. "I was just thinking about something else."

"About what?"

"Stop trying to divert attention away from the real issue."

"Which is?"

"How mean you were to poor Lester."

"Well, he really screwed up."

"Look, he was just trying to be cool with a fellow officer. You know how it goes." I tilted my head sideways, reconsidering. "Wait a minute…no, you don't know how it goes."

Bethany Riggs' eyebrows furrowed. "What's that mean?"

"You're IA, so you don't know what it's like to be cool to another cop." When I saw her fists ball up, I immediately told her I was joking.

"You'd better be joking," she warned. She turned and started walking again. "Lester shouldn't have left Kenneth alone. It's his fault Kenneth's dead."

"No, it's *Kenneth's* fault that Kenneth's dead. He made a selfish and cowardly decision to take his own life. That's nobody's fault but his own."

"Yes, but it's Lester's fault Kenneth killed himself while he was in our custody. If Kenneth had killed himself at home or in some cane field, no big deal, but he did it *here*. Now we're responsible, you and me, because he was our prisoner."

"Well, since you put it that way, I'm pissed at him, too."

When we walked into the conference room, Sheriff Burke was on the phone and the entire senior staff was seated around the table, talking in hushed whispers.

"No," Sheriff Burke was saying, "I'm not prepared to make a statement... Right... Maybe then... Yeah, call me in the morning... Okay, goodbye." He slammed the phone down. "How in God's name did they find out about this shit so fast?"

"Was that the news media?" asked Captain Trevor Abbott, commander of the support division.

"No," sneered a red-faced Burke, "it was the Russian consulate."

A bewildered look fell over Captain Abbott's face. I tried hard to stifle a grin, but it was no use. His level of ignorance was legendary and many often wondered—out loud—what he was doing leading an entire division. Burke looked from Abbott to Bethany. "What did Lester say?"

Bethany filled him in, and he only nodded as she spoke, staring a hole into the wall opposite where he sat. When Bethany was done, he sighed. "Yesterday and today are the worst days in our department's history. This is a black eye that's not going to heal very soon."

"It needs to heal before October," Chief Garcia said. "You're up for re-election."

"I don't think this'll hurt you," I offered.

Sheriff Burke broke his gaze on the wall and turned to look at me. "Explain."

"A rogue cop cheated on his own wife with a captain's wife. He learns that a former cop was investigating him, so he kills that former cop. He then kills the captain just in case the captain knew anything about it. And it—"

"Wait a minute." Sheriff Burke raised his hand. "None of this is sounding good for me."

"Except," I continued, "that we caught this rogue cop mere hours after he killed Captain Landry. He was in custody before the body of Justin Wainwright was even discovered. Sure, our department and our community were hit hard yesterday and today, but we rose to the challenge. Although he was one of our own, we took Kenneth into custody immediately—without hesitation—and we got this case wrapped up within twenty-four hours."

"And don't forget all the lives we saved yesterday at the bank," Chief Garcia reminded the sheriff.

Burke frowned. "All that's nice and great, but we still had a cop kill himself while he was in our custody."

My cell phone suddenly vibrated in the chest pocket of my coveralls. I fished it out and looked at the number. It was Kenneth Lewis' house number. "Shit! It's Kenneth's wife!"

The room turned graveyard quiet. I flipped open my phone. "Hello, this is London."

"London, please tell me it's not true!" Yvette Lewis wailed. "Please!"

"Yvette, calm down. Where are you?"

"Is it true? Is he dead?" Yvette was crying uncontrollably.

"Where'd you hear that?" I asked, stalling.

"God damn it, London," Yvette screamed into the phone. "Just tell me! Is Ken dead?"

"Okay. Yes. Yes, he's dead. The medics did everything they could for him, but it was no use. It was too late. I'm so sorry, Yvette—"

I heard a thump and a chorus of pitiful wails in the background. "Yvette...are you still there?"

"What's going on?" Sheriff Burke asked.

I shook my head. "Yvette, can you hear me?"

Bethany Riggs slapped my arm and headed for the door. "Let's go."

Keeping the phone pressed to my ear, I rushed after her.

"Keep me informed," Sheriff Burke hollered from the conference room.

CHAPTER 13

There were three cars in the driveway at Kenneth Lewis' house, so we had to park on the street. I jumped out, rushed to the door, banged on it loudly.

A tearful lady answered. I recognized her as being one of Yvette's aunts.

"Is Yvette still here?" I asked softly.

The woman nodded and stood back for us to pass. I led the way into the kitchen and through to the living room, where Yvette sat in a ball on the sofa, clutching a box of napkins in her hands. When she saw me, she lurched to her feet and ran to me, threw her arms around my neck, sobbed.

I held her for a long and awkward moment. Her cries slowly subsided and she finally pulled away from me. "I'm sorry," she whispered and turned back toward the sofa.

"Don't apologize," I said.

When Yvette was seated beside her aunt, she motioned for Bethany and me to join them. "I'm sure y'all have some questions," she said.

Bethany nodded. "We understand he called you tonight…from a patrolman's cell phone?"

"Yeah, he called me from a number I didn't recognize." Yvette sniffed, then blew her nose. "He said he was calling to say he didn't do the things y'all said he did, but I told him I didn't want to hear his shit. I told him it was over and that I was filing for divorce."

I scratched my head. "You were filing for divorce because we arrested him?"

"I'm filing for divorce because he's been sleeping with my sister for the past three weeks! While I'm away taking care of our sick mother, she's back here at my house screwing my husband. If I could, I'd divorce that deceitful witch, too."

"How do you know Kenneth had an affair with your sister?" Bethany asked.

"I suspected something was going on," Yvette explained. "The last two times I got back home from being at my mom's for a few days, I found empty wine cooler bottles in the outside garbage can. Ken never drank wine coolers and he never took out the trash, so I knew something was going on. I was back at my mom's a couple of days ago and I tried calling him, but he wouldn't answer. I couldn't leave my mom alone, but I couldn't take it anymore, so I called one of my friends last night and asked her to drive by my house. She called me later to tell me that Laura's car was here. She drove by again at midnight, and Laura's car was still here."

"Laura…is that your sister's name?" Bethany asked.

Yvette nodded.

"What time did your friend drive by and see Laura's car here the first time?"

"It was about eight o'clock."

"And when did you get back home?" Bethany asked.

"I wasn't supposed to get back here until late this afternoon, but I got my other aunt to go sit with my mom so I could come home early. I wanted to try and catch them in the act." She shook her head. "I was too late. They were already gone. I remembered Ken saying he had sniper training today and I was going to wait until he got back home to confront him, but he got arrested before that could happen."

"How'd you know about that?" I asked.

"I found out from Ray's wife, but it was already out because Laura came over here to see if I'd heard." Yvette shook her head. "It was all too much for me, and I confronted her right there in my driveway, out in the open." Yvette fought to choke back the tears. When she had regained her composure somewhat, she continued talking. "Laura admitted coming over here three different times and sleeping with my husband. She said it happened at her house a couple of times, too, while her husband was offshore. The worst thing about it…when she'd come here to be with Ken, she'd tell her husband she was going stay with Mom, and she's never lifted a finger to help Mom."

"Did she say how it all started between her and Ken?" Bethany asked.

Yvette nodded her head slowly. "She said Ken started patrolling by her house when her husband was offshore and he'd stop if she was outside. She said he started flirting with her and would joke about staying overnight and keeping her safe." Yvette rolled her eyes. "I can't believe she fell for his crap. She did say his advances made her feel pretty. I know her husband was away a lot and I guess it can get kind of lonely, but why do that to me? I'm her sister. Why *my* husband?" Yvette's already swollen eyes welled up again and she buried her face in her hands. "I feel so stupid!"

Bethany moved beside Yvette and put an arm around her shoulder. "You're not stupid, honey. You did what we all did—we trusted him, and he betrayed that trust."

After a few minutes of muffled sobbing, Yvette looked up. "I…I know I might get in trouble for telling y'all this, but I knocked the shit out of Laura."

The corners of Bethany's mouth curled up into a smile. "No, you won't get into trouble for that. If I had my way, you'd get a reward."

"But I made her nose bleed!"

"She had it coming," I said.

When we finished questioning Yvette Lewis, we stood to leave, and Yvette followed us to the door. Bethany walked to her car, while I stopped to give Yvette a hug. She wrapped her arms tightly around my torso, pressing her face against my chest for a long moment. When she released me, she looked up into my eyes and in a mournful voice asked, "What am I supposed to do now?"

I just shook my head and walked away. I joined Bethany at the car, and we stopped at Laura LeCompte's house next.

Laura's eyes widened when she answered the knock and saw Bethany and me standing there. "Laura LeCompte?" Bethany asked.

Laura nodded, her eyes shifting from Bethany to me.

"Can we ask you some questions about Kenneth Lewis?" Bethany asked.

Laura stole a nervous glance over her shoulder, stepped outside and closed the door. "Um, sure, what can I do for you?"

"We understand you were having an intimate relationship with Kenneth Lewis," Bethany began.

Laura's chin trembled, as she wrung her hands in front of her chest. "Does my husband have to know about this? He'll kill me."

"You mean, you haven't told him yet?" Bethany asked.

Laura shook her head. "I can't."

Bethany pursed her lips. "While I don't agree with what you've done, it's certainly none of my business outside of this case. So, you have my word he won't hear about it from us."

Appearing a little more relaxed, Laura took a deep breath. "Okay, what do you need from me?"

"It's simple, really. What time did you go to Kenneth Lewis' house yesterday?" Bethany asked.

"I think it was about six o'clock," she said.

"What do you mean by you *think?*"

"I was waiting for my husband to call me from offshore—he usually calls the house phone first—and I wanted him to know I was home. I left right after his call, and I'm pretty sure he called right at six."

"How long did it take you to get to Kenneth's house? Did you go straight there?" Bethany asked.

"Yes, ma'am. It only took me about five minutes to get there."

"So," I interjected, "you got to Kenneth's house at about six-o-five PM?"

Laura nodded. "Thereabouts."

I gave Bethany an *Oh shit, Kenneth might not have done it* look, but she calmly turned to Laura and asked, "Is it possible you're mistaken about the time? Could it have been later than six?"

"It's possible," Laura acknowledged. "I wasn't really looking at the clock."

"Once you got to his house, did you leave at some point?" Bethany asked.

"Yeah, I left early this morning, about three."

"Did Kenneth act strange at all when you were with him?" I asked.

Laura shook her head. "He was his normal self. I was sure shocked when I heard he killed that cop—and a little scared. He could've killed me, too."

Bethany thanked Laura LeCompte for her time, and we walked away.

"Shit, Beth—"

"Lieutenant Riggs," Bethany corrected.

"Shit, LT," I said. "How could Kenneth have killed Captain Landry if he was with Laura?"

"There are two problems with her story," Bethany explained. "First, she was sleeping with him, so she could absolutely lie for him, and second, she's not sure about the time."

CHAPTER 14

Thursday, August 18, 2011

It was eight-thirty when I pulled into the CID parking lot. Lieutenant Bethany Riggs was already there. I hadn't been given my pass code for the super-secret CID entrance, so I was forced to walk around to the patrol division side of the building. As I walked through the squad room, I heard a television blaring from Captain Landry's old office. It sounded like news from the shooting, so I hurried to catch it. Jerry Allemand was sitting on Captain Landry's desk. He nodded toward the forty-two-inch flat screen.

I sat beside him on the desk, watching intently as the blonde anchor talked.

"A sex scandal has turned deadly for three Magnolia Parish deputies—two of them high-ranking officials—and has shocked the sheriff's office to its core. It couldn't have come at a worse time for Sheriff Calvin Burke, who faces a tough opponent in the upcoming October election for sheriff.

"Sources say Deputy Kenneth Lewis, who is a member of the department's elite sniper team, was involved in a sex triangle with an undisclosed female. On Tuesday night, Deputy Lewis drove to the top of this bridge"—the cameraman faded away to show that the anchor was standing on the Highway Twelve high-rise—"and fired a fatal shot that killed Captain Anthony Landry, a decorated officer with nearly thirty years of dedicated service to the department, while he supervised the successful release of a dozen hostages during a mid-afternoon bank robbery. In that incident, an unidentified sniper shot and killed the hostage taker seconds before Lewis fired his fatal bullet.

"While it is unclear if Captain Landry's widow was involved in a sexual relationship with Kenneth Lewis, Channel Seven News has learned that detectives named Lewis a suspect in the murder shortly after interviewing Mrs. Landry, and he was taken into custody without incident early yesterday afternoon.

"Late last night, the body of former Internal Affairs Captain Justin Wainwright was discovered in his backyard, the victim of an apparent sniper attack, and Deputy Lewis was named a suspect in that shooting as well. Before detectives could question Lewis about that shooting, he reportedly used his sniper coveralls to hang himself in the interview room at the Sheriff's Office CID building in Payneville."

When I looked over at Jerry his eyes were wide. "If Kenneth could turn bad, any of us could."

I slipped off the desk and punched his shoulder hard. He winced and rubbed away the pain. "Kenneth didn't *turn* bad," I said. "He always was bad. We might not have known it, but he certainly did."

Jerry shook his head, unconvinced. "I don't know…"

"Well, I do know, but if you don't believe me, there's nothing I can do for you." I left him to his troubled thoughts and walked down the long corridor that separated the patrol division from CID and stopped by the locked door. I banged on it and waited. After what seemed like too damn long, it swung open.

It was Gina Pellegrin. A smile played across her face as she stood in my way, looking me up and down. "Damn, you look yummy," she said. "I never thought I'd ever see you wearing dress slacks and a button-up. You look like church material."

I scowled and tried to walk by her. She put a hand on my chest, stopping me. "Here, let me fix your collar." She reached up and began fussing with the collar, her face inches from mine. My neck tickled as her cool fingers brushed against it. When she was done, she stepped back and cocked her head from one side to the other, admiring her handiwork. "There, now you look like a real detective."

I mumbled my thanks and made my way to the cubicle where, just the night before, Lieutenant Bethany Riggs had started typing the arrest warrant for Kenneth Lewis. Bethany was sitting there typing. She looked up casually when I approached, started to turn back toward the monitor, but then jerked her head back toward me. "Damn, you clean up good!"

I blushed, pretending not to hear her. "Ready to check out the trajectory on the shot that killed Justin Wainwright?"

"Yeah, I'm getting cross-eyed here. It's time for a break." She shut down the computer, and we walked outside. I caught a glimpse of Gina Pellegrin watching us from across the room near the secretary's desk. When our eyes met, she quickly turned away. Strange, I thought, but then dismissed it.

When we arrived at Wainwright's house, a patrolman I'd never met was sitting in the driveway. We flashed him our badges, and he nodded. As they often do, things looked much different in daylight. We walked to the tree where Justin Wainwright had sucked his last bit of air, and I stood where they had marked his position. The lawnmower was still where we'd found it, crashed up against the tree.

"Look at the cut pattern," Bethany said. "He was cutting a circle around the tree and it looks like the wheel jerked to the left when he fell off the mower, driving the lawnmower into the tree."

I moved to the spot just before the abrupt turn to the left and surveyed the entire area. I dropped to my hands and knees and studied the grass carefully. It didn't take me long to locate minute specks of blood and brain matter. "LT," I called, "this is where he was shot."

Bethany walked over and crouched beside me. "No shit. You're really getting the hang of this detective stuff."

"I know guns and ammo, but detective work is something that'll take me a while to master," I admitted. I stood and looked in the direction opposite the blood evidence. I was staring directly at the tree branches. An oddity on one of the leaves caught my attention and I moved closer. "Here we go!"

Bethany Riggs sidled beside me and looked where I pointed. "The bullet went through that leaf before it hit him?"

"Yep," I said triumphantly, closing one eye and looking through the trees to the land beyond. Off in the distance across a desolate cow pasture and nestling against a row of trees sat an old wooden shed. "That's the spot."

We set off across the barren field, and it wasn't long before my shirt started sticking to my back. I lifted my arms and checked the armpits of my shirt. Wet...and growing. A bead of sweat had gathered above Bethany's upper lip.

"I can't wait until winter," she complained.

"No matter how hot it gets, I'll always prefer summer to the cold."

"Not me! I love cuddling up in front of a fireplace with a good book while the world outside turns to ice."

We reached the shed and I calculated my paces. "Four hundred yards," I said, looking back toward Justin Wainwright's backyard. The lawnmower was visible from where we stood. "I think this is the location."

Bethany Riggs was walking around the area, scouring the ground for clues. I heard her gasp. "This is it!"

I walked to where she stood staring down at the dusty ground. There, cut deep into the dry earth, was a simple message…James 516. I stared at it for a long moment and realization struck me. The graffiti on the guardrail of the Highway Twelve high-rise bridge! "This message…it was on the guardrail!"

Bethany's mouth dropped open. "That's right!"

I studied it carefully, trying to figure out what it could mean. I asked Bethany what she thought.

"I have no clue," she said. "Do you know any cops named James?"

I searched the folders of my mind, but could think of none. "No."

She swung her camera off her shoulder and took a picture of the message. "Could five-sixteen be the distance from here to the target?"

I shook my head. "It's four hundred and nine yards."

Bethany bit her lower lip and mumbled, "James five-sixteen."

CHAPTER 15

An hour later, Bethany and I were standing at the front of the dark conference room with the photograph of the James 516 message plastered on the seventy-inch flat screen. All members of the detective division, absent Captain Theriot, were seated around the table.

Bethany pointed to Detective Melvin Ford. "Did you get anything on the hotels?"

Melvin stood, shook his head. "I checked every hotel in the tri-parish area. There are none with a fifth floor. But"—he pulled out his notebook—"I reversed the number and name and did an internet map search for five-sixteen James Street. There're a couple of them within a hundred and fifty miles of here, so I contacted the agencies in those jurisdictions and asked them to make contact with the homeowners, just to see what they're all about."

"Rachael, did you get anything?" Bethany asked Detective Rachael Bowler.

"We don't have a single James—first or last name—in our system that was born on May sixteenth of any year. I checked jail records, our complaint database and I called the DA's office to have them check their records...nothing."

Lieutenant Bethany Riggs bit her lower lip—I found it to be very distracting—and drummed her fingers on the lectern.

"No shit," Gina Pellegrin said, breaking the silence. "We're looking at this all wrong."

I thought I saw Bethany bristle. "How's that?"

Without saying a word, Gina stood and left the room. She returned moments later carrying a small book.

Using the light from her phone, she flipped through the pages. She looked up at the picture, looked back down and stabbed the book with an index finger. "James five-sixteen is a Bible verse that talks about confessing your sins and praying for each other. He was sending a message for—"

Bethany scoffed. "I hardly think Kenneth Lewis was a religious person."

"No, he wasn't," I said. "The only time I heard him say God's name was when he was cursing."

"Maybe someone else left the message," Rachael said. "It's quite possible—"

"What the hell are y'all doing with the light off...having an orgy?" boomed Captain Theriot's voice from the doorway. He flicked the light switch on, and everyone squinted.

"We were trying to figure out what that message meant," Bethany explained.

Captain Theriot frowned, apparently confused.

"The one I told you about that we found at Justin Wainwright's house," Bethany said. "The same message painted on the guardrail of the Highway Twelve high-rise."

"Oh that," Theriot said, remembering. "Forget about that message. This case is closed. Wrap up your report and label it 'Closed, Offender Killed.'"

"But, sir," Rachael interjected, "we think it was a biblical message, like a warning. There might be—"

"I don't give a shit if it was a message from God Himself...shut it down. We know who did it and we know why he did it. Enough said. Case closed." Captain Theriot waved his big paw. "Now get out of here and stop hogging up the room. The sheriff's on his way here to plan the funerals."

We all stood, gathered up our stuff and began filing through the door.

"Wait up a second," Captain Theriot barked. "While all of y'all are in one place, the funerals for Captain Landry and Captain Wainwright are scheduled for eight o'clock Saturday morning at St. Margaret's in Payneville. They'll both be buried with full honors and there's gonna be a pretty lengthy graveside ceremony. I need all of y'all in dress blues and I need y'all there early. There's gonna be about a hundred cops from other agencies there, so I need y'all to stand out. I want spit-shined boots, sparkling brass and pressed uniforms that'll stand up on their own if y'all step out of them. Got it?"

"We got it," we said in awful unison.

"What about Kenneth?" Lieutenant Chiasson asked.

This turned Captain Theriot's face a deep purple. "I don't give a shit if they burn his corpse and dump the ashes in a sewer. My only regret is that I didn't get to watch him die."

Everyone scattered, leaving Theriot there to seethe. I followed Bethany to the desk she had claimed as her own and we each dropped into a chair. "There's more to this story," she said.

"I agree, but what's the use in going forward? Kenneth's dead. No one's in danger anymore and there'll never be a trial, so why bother?"

"I just don't like loose ends."

CHAPTER 16

Saturday, August 20, 2011

Even though I was in an overly crowded church, I stood completely alone. Everywhere I looked there were men and women in full uniform sobbing. Not a dry eye in the house. Gina Pellegrin stood bawling on one side of me, her face buried in her hands. Jerry Allemand was on my other side, staring straight ahead, tears racing down his flushed face. I looked from Gina to Jerry, and then back to Gina. Jerry was on his own.

I wrapped my arm around Gina's shoulders and squeezed tight. She turned and collapsed against my chest, pressing her face against my neck. I felt the moisture as her tears leaked onto my flesh. "It's okay," I whispered, not knowing what else to say. After she had settled down and pulled away from me, I stepped out of the row I was in and made my way to the back of the church. Once I'd made it to the quiet security of the vestibule, I relaxed. I loosened my tie and released the top button on my shirt, then shifted my gun belt. I couldn't wait for this shit to be—

"Why'd you leave?"

The voice startled me, and I turned quickly. Lieutenant Bethany Riggs. Her eyes were red and moist.

"I…I don't do well at funerals," I admitted.

"You look like you're doing *quite* well. Yours are the only dry eyes in the building…shit, probably in the parish. I saw people crying in the store this morning when I stopped to get some coffee." Bethany studied my face. "If I didn't know better, I'd think you weren't bothered at all by the deaths of Captains Landry and

Wainwright."

"It just takes a lot to get me worked up."

I got to the graveyard early, so I decided to pay my family a visit. I was there an hour before the first sirens greeted my ears. Not wanting to fight the crowd for a sideline spot, I quickly made my way through the maze of tombstones until I found the two open graves positioned side by side. Both officers' families had agreed to bury the men beside each other.

I took up a spot where I could see and hear everything that would be taking place and waited while carloads of officers and family members began arriving. There were two columns of folding chairs, each positioned in front of one of the open graves, for the families of Captain Landry and retired Captain Justin Wainwright, and these filled up first and fast.

A wooden platform had been constructed on the side of the graves opposite the columns of chairs, and it was there that Sheriff Burke and Chief Garcia would make their speeches and presentations of the American flags. A row of chairs sat along the backside of the platform and the various speakers began taking their seats.

The dress rehearsal had taken place on Friday and, although everything had gone off according to plan, the practice ceremony took every bit of three hours. I glanced down at the time on my phone. There was no way we'd be done before noon.

Familiar officers from the Magnolia Parish Sheriff's Office and strangers from law enforcement agencies across the state began crowding in. Within an hour, the entire graveyard was saturated with blue uniforms. There was standing room only. A man I'd never seen got up on the platform and stood in front of the microphone. I'd heard someone say he was the master of ceremonies—whatever that meant—and it looked like he was going to be introducing the other speakers.

"Ladies and gentlemen of the badge, citizens of this great parish, and everyone who has traveled from afar to be here on this difficult day of mourning…greetings." The master of ceremonies' voice echoed authoritatively through the aisles of tombs and mausoleums. "We are here today to mourn the loss of our two law enforcement brothers, Captain Anthony Landry and retired Captain Justin Wainwright, to celebrate their short—but rewarding—lives and to honor their sacrifices to the people of the community they served."

I scanned the officers nearest me in the crowd and tried to locate a familiar face. Other than some of the commanders on stage— Captain Trevor Abbott was one of them, and I desperately hoped he wouldn't speak—I didn't recognize any of them. I thought I caught a fleeting glimpse of Gina Pellegrin walking through the crowd to the right of where I stood, but I couldn't be sure.

One by one, the speakers took their turns at the microphone, including Captain Abbott, and one by one, they broke down during their mostly self-absorbed speeches, many of which were too long. Sheriff Burke was the last to take to the microphone. Sniffles and sobs reverberated through the crowd as he spoke in a strained and shaky voice. I shuffled my feet often, trying to find a comfortable standing position. Sweat dripped from my pores. My polyester uniform felt like wet sandpaper as it rubbed against my clammy body. My gun belt tugged at my right hip, putting a strain on my lower back. I shifted my stance for the umpteenth time, praying for the ceremony to be over soon.

Finally, Sheriff Burke turned and handed the microphone to the master of ceremonies. The man walked to the edge of the platform and faced east, where seven well-dressed officers stood side-by-side in a grassy clearing about fifty yards away. They all held old wooden rifles at port arms, and they waited for the command to fire the three-volley salute. A bugler moved into position at the center of the platform and a deathly hush fell over the crowd.

The master of ceremonies suddenly belted out a command, and the seven members of the honor guard threw the rifles to their shoulders and aimed at an upward angle over the gravesite.

I sure hope they're firing blanks, I thought, as I calculated the distance to the neighborhood west of the cemetery.

On the next command, the rifles exploded into the air, resulting in gasps and startled outbursts from people throughout the crowd. Several people cried hysterically. The second volley brought about the same reaction from the crowd, but my attention was not on them. It was on the seven riflemen. I stood admiring their smooth handling of the rifles. They moved as one unit—firing, pulling the rifles down, working the bolt-action with fluid smoothness, shouldering the rifles again. As a sniper who understood the amount of dedicated time and effort that went into attaining that level of proficiency, I was impressed by the expert synchronization of their shots. All seven sounded like one shot, with not even a hint of a misstep. I suddenly became suspicious—what if only one of the riflemen had bullets?

When the master of ceremonies belted out the third command, the riflemen fired, and I thought I detected a slight glitch in the harmony of their last shot—

"Oh my God!" someone screamed from the crowd.

CHAPTER 17

Rapid movement caught my eye. I turned just in time to see a uniformed officer crash to the floor of the wooden platform. The head bounced once and lay still, staring at me through one lifeless, open eye. The other eye—the left one—had been reduced to a gaping hole of torn flesh and blood. In the split second before the area exploded in stampeding officers and civilians, I recognized the face of Captain Trevor Abbott. Abbott had been facing me several seconds before the shot, and I realized that the shot had come from my six o'clock position—behind me.

I did a fast survey of the area and spotted most of the command personnel running for their lives through the graveyard, along with hundreds of other officers and civilians. People jostled by me, and I had to shove a few of them away as I searched frantically for Sheriff Burke. Amidst the confusion of screaming and fleeing officers— many of them not knowing where to go—I located the sheriff. He was still on the platform. As people hurried by him, Sheriff Burke stood dumbfounded and motionless, staring down at the lifeless body of his longtime friend and employee, Captain Trevor Abbott.

I rushed to the platform, taking the wooden steps two at a time, and tackled Sheriff Burke to the ground. Scooting across the floor of the platform, I pushed him ahead of me and over the edge. He fell the five feet to the ground and I dropped down beside him.

"Stay down!" I yelled above the swarming chaos.

"What happened?" Sheriff Burke asked, his face ash gray.

Without answering, I dug my phone out of my pocket and flipped it open. I lifted my left hand above the level of the platform and took a quick picture of the area south of our location. I pulled my hand down and studied the picture I'd taken. It was blurry, but it would do. Off in the distance, the peak of a white building stood above the rows of mausoleums in the graveyard. There were two windows facing our position—and both looked to be open. I quickly glanced around. Dozens of officers were huddled behind tombs and mausoleums while others were still fleeing for the security of their cruisers. I shoved my phone in my shirt pocket, then jerked my pistol out of its holster.

"What are you going to do?" Sheriff Burke asked, a horrified expression on his face.

"The shots must've come from that building, and I need to get to it."

"You'll get killed before you get to the building."

"There's a lot of cover between here and there. I should be fine." I took a deep breath, exhaled. "Stay down," I called and bolted from behind the platform and raced to the nearest tomb. I dropped down behind it and fished my phone out again. I took another picture and checked it out. It was impossible to penetrate the darkness of the rooms. Ten snipers could be crouched at the back of the room with rifles trained on my position and I'd never know it.

I was about to move to the next tomb when a movement to the left of my position caught my eye. I craned my head to survey the area where I'd seen the movement, while trying not to expose my head to the sniper, and was surprised to see Jerry Allemand crouched between two tombs, holding a semi-automatic rifle.

"Jerry," I hissed.

He turned and nodded when he saw me. "You ready to get this bastard?"

I nodded. "Did you get a fix on his location?"

"The shot came from somewhere to the south, but—"

"It came from the old school." That was Gina's voice. "It's been abandoned for ten years. There's nothing around it, so it'd make the perfect spot."

I leaned back and looked to my right. Gina was standing beside a mausoleum, pistol in hand. "Y'all want to do this?" I asked.

"Hell, yeah!" Jerry said. "I'm tired of our cops being gunned down."

"No prisoners," Gina said.

"Okay, let's leap frog our way to the end of the graveyard," I said. "I'll go first. If I draw a shot, unload into those two windows."

When they both acknowledged they'd heard me, I jumped out in the open and rushed forward to the next row of tombs. I threw myself over a low grave and rolled up against a mausoleum. I scurried to my hands and knees and made my way to the right side of the wall so I could cover Jerry and Gina's advance.

"It's about time you got here!" called a female voice I'd come to know well.

I turned to my right. Lieutenant Bethany Riggs was lying prone behind a low grave, her pistol out and aiming in the direction we were heading. "We need to do something before another cop gets killed!"

I pointed toward the old school building. "The shot came from the upstairs windows. Help me provide cover for Gina and Jerry."

Bethany nodded and peeked out from behind her tomb with her pistol aimed at the building. I did the same. "Go! Go!" I called.

Moments later, Jerry and Gina bolted past our location and took cover twenty feet closer to the building. Bethany and I moved next, and we continued that pattern until we reached the last row of tombs.

"What now?" Gina asked. "It's at least seventy-five yards of open space between here and the building."

Jerry nodded. "That's too far to run without cover. It'll be suicide."

Of course, he was right. "If that bastard gets me, y'all better kill him." I rolled to my feet and shot off the ground, making a mad, zigzagging dash for the old schoolhouse. As I ran across the dry, crackling grass, my eyes and pistol were trained on the upstairs windows. Within seconds, I was diving toward the side of the building and rolled to a seated position. Before I could get my bearings, a body crashed into me and we both slammed against the wall of the building. Something had smashed into my chin and I tasted blood. I swept the body and reversed positions to be on top of... "Bethany? What the hell are you doing? Are you crazy?"

I scrambled off her and helped her up. She started to open her mouth, but I put a finger to my lips, listened. There hadn't been any movement from inside that I could tell. I looked to where Gina and Jerry crouched. Jerry was peeking around the side of the tomb, and I made a hand sign for him to stay put. I turned to Bethany and pressed my lips against her ear. "We're going in. Get in my back pocket and stay there. You hear?"

Eyes wide with anticipation, Bethany only nodded. I could almost hear her heart beating against her chest. I inched along the edge of the building, making my way to the doorway that loomed ahead. Bethany stayed right behind me, her hand resting on the small of my back. If I were to die today, I couldn't think of a better person to die alongside. When I reached the doorway, I found the wooden door already ajar. I placed a cautious foot on the wooden steps and eased it open farther. The ancient hinges screamed their protest, and I winced, my hand tightening around the grip of my pistol.

I waited several seconds. When the squeaking hinges brought no response from within, I slowly entered the room. It was a large room—looked like an old classroom—with a stairway at the far side of the building. The smell of mildew hung thick in the air, making my nose tickle. I had to stifle a sneeze before moving farther.

Bethany and I tiptoed across the open area and reached the stairway without incident. Training our pistols toward the top of the stairs, we began our cautious ascent. The door at the top of the landing was closed. When we reached it, I looked at Bethany and raised my eyebrows to inquire if she was ready. She nodded.

In one swift motion, I stepped in front of the door, kicked it open and rushed inside. Another large room and, like the one downstairs, it was empty. A table was positioned at the center of the room about twenty feet from one of the two open windows. I stood beside the table and leaned over it to where I thought the shooter might have been and looked out the window. I had a perfect view of the wooden platform where Captain Abbott had been standing twenty or so minutes earlier.

"This is the place," I said weakly. I sat on the edge of the table to ponder what this meant.

Bethany walked to the window and waved her hand to Jerry and Gina. "All clear," she called.

"Kenneth didn't kill Landry and Wainwright," I finally said. "The real killer sniper is still out there and he's still targeting cops. We've got to—"

"Stop second guessing ourselves. This is certainly not Kenneth, but it doesn't mean Kenneth is innocent of the other murders. We've got hard evidence against him that can't be ignored. This"—she waved her hand around the room—"could be the work of a copycat killer."

We heard boots clunking against wood as Gina and Jerry stomped up the stairway. They walked to the window and stared out.

"Damn," Jerry muttered, pointing. "I was standing right over there by that thick cross. He could've dropped me easy from here."

"Me, too," Bethany said, walking around the room, searching for evidence.

"We were like turtles on a log out there." Gina shuddered. "It could be any one of us lying dead out there right now. How'd he even pick his target out of all those cops? Was it just a random thing? Someone on the stage? If he wanted to make a point, why not kill the sheriff? He was right there next to Abbott." Gina stepped back and started to turn toward me, but suddenly stopped and gasped. "Hey! Look at this shit!" She was pointing to an area just below the windowsill.

The blood in my veins turned to ice when I saw it…there, carved into the weathered wooden planks, was the familiar message…James 516.

CHAPTER 18

Bethany rushed to Gina's side and dropped to her knees. "This is definitely not a copycat killing."

"How do you know for sure?" I asked.

"No one knew about James five-sixteen." Bethany turned to me. "You were right all along. Kenneth died for nothing. The real sniper's still out there...and he's picking us off one by one."

The four of us huddled together at the center of that abandoned room, the graveness of the situation beginning to sink in.

"Who's next?" Jerry asked.

"That's what we have to try and figure out." Bethany held up three fingers. "So far three cops have been assassinated by this sniper's bullets...and they're all captains."

"So," I mused aloud, "do you think he's only targeting captains?"

"It could be," she guessed.

"What happens when he runs out of captains? Does he start in on...on lieutenants?" Gina asked.

When she said it, I saw Bethany's eyes widen slightly. In my mind's eye, I caught a glimpse of her lying on the ground with her left eye blown out, and I didn't like it one bit. "Maybe he's moving upward," I said. "If he takes out the entire command staff all the way up to the sheriff, he can take down the department. If you cut off the head, the snake dies."

"But who would want to do something like this?" Jerry asked.

Bethany shook her head. "I don't know, but we need to get a crime scene team up here quick and cast as large a net as possible to try and catch him. He could still be out there, walking around in that crowd, hiding amongst the cops. We need to check out everybody before letting them drive off. At this point, everyone's a suspect."

"It'd be hard for him to blend into the crowd carrying a sniper rifle," Jerry countered.

I walked to the window and surveyed the area. Civilians and cops were starting to come out from behind tombstones and mausoleums—the cops with their guns drawn—and some were hurrying to their cars, which were parked everywhere. I leaned out the window and looked to the right and left of the building, along the road that connected the parking lot of the old school to Highway Three. Cars...everywhere.

"Shit," I said. "There're a hundred cars within twenty feet of all sides of this building. The sniper could've stashed his rifle in any of them and just melded into the crowd."

Bethany snatched up her phone, punched in some numbers. After a short pause, she began speaking. "Captain Theriot, we need a crime scene unit and some detectives to the old school south of the graveyard... Yes, the building's secure... No, the suspect was gone when we got here."

I moved out of earshot, flipped open my own phone and scrolled through my address book until I got to Sheriff Burke's number. He answered on the first ring.

"Talk to me, Carter," the sheriff said in a strained voice. "Tell me you got this asshole!"

"When we got here he was gone." I paused for a moment. "But he left behind a message."

"Message? What kind of message?"

"The same message that was left at Captain Wainwright's house and on the guardrail—James five-sixteen."

Sheriff Burke was silent for a long moment. "Does this mean Kenneth didn't kill Landry and Wainwright?"

"I think that's exactly what it means."

"God help us." I heard the life drain out of Sheriff Burke's voice.

After almost a minute, I glanced down at my phone to make sure we were still connected. We were. "Sheriff?"

"I'm here," came the voice of an exhausted man. "I'm just trying to think of what I'm going to tell Lewis' widow. Wainwright, Landry and Abbott...that crazy piece of shit out there killed them. But Lewis... Lewis' death is on us...on *me.*"

"Look, Sheriff, Lewis made a conscious decision to do what he did, and what's done is done. There's nothing we can do to change it. What we need to do now is focus on getting this sniper before he kills again."

"You're right." Another pause. Finally, he asked, "What do you think we should do next?"

"Lieutenant Riggs is getting with Captain Theriot. They're gonna get the crime scene unit up here to work the building and hopefully find some evidence that'll lead us to the suspect."

"Okay, that sounds good. What about the shooter?"

"We think he hid his rifle—probably in a car—and then melded into the crowd. There're a hundred or so private vehicles parked in the vicinity of this building, and I need some deputies to help us search them before they drive off."

"I'll have Carmella meet you with a squad of patrolmen," Sheriff Burke said, "and you can let her know what you want them to do."

"Carmella *Vizier?*" I asked. Last I'd checked, Carmella Vizier didn't command the patrol division. She was a former narcotics agent who had been promoted to captain of the personnel division when Calvin Burke first became sheriff of Magnolia Parish back in 2000. Word from some of the oldtimers was that she couldn't cut it in the narcotics division anymore, but she had been screwing the sheriff so he took care of her.

"I'm moving her to commander of the patrol division," Sheriff Burke explained. "The transfer was supposed to take effect Monday, but under the circumstances…"

I shook my head, but didn't comment on the wisdom of that decision. "While they search the vehicles, I'm gonna take Jerry and the other three snipers, possibly a couple of SWAT members, and start a search of the outlying areas. We might get lucky."

"Good idea. Keep me tight in the loop."

"What're you going to do?"

"I was thinking about hanging around here, doing what I can."

Although he couldn't see it, I shook my head. "No! You need to get with Chief Garcia and y'all need to get the hell out of here. I think this sniper is trying to take down the command structure of the department."

"But why?"

"I don't know. Once we figure out the *why* of it all, I think we'll find out the *who.*"

There was another long pause, then Sheriff Burke spoke in a somber voice. "You saved my life today and I'll never forget that. I've always taken care of those who've taken care of me, and I owe you my life. As long as I'm sheriff, you'll want for nothing…that I promise."

"That's not necessary, sir." I hung up and waved Jerry over. I told him the plan, and he started calling the guys to meet us outside of the old school. Bethany approached.

"I've got a crime scene team en route and they'll tear this place apart. We'll get something, I'm sure of it." She glanced at Jerry Allemand, who was talking hurriedly on the phone. "What's going on with you guys?"

"We're gonna check the surrounding area to see if we can't get lucky."

"I'm coming with you."

I looked into those blue eyes and knew I could never tell her no. "Sure thing, LT."

"Guys," Gina called thoughtfully from where she was still standing, staring out of the window. "We're dealing with an extremely dangerous and cunning person, but he's not as smart as he thinks."

Jerry, Bethany and I walked over and stood around her, trying to see what she saw. A team of patrol officers led by newly appointed Captain Vizier was making their way toward the old schoolhouse. Some of the cars were already leaving, and I tried to make a mental note of the descriptions of each of them as they drove off. A group of detectives were huddled over Captain Abbott's body. Other uniformed officers ambled about, seemingly unsure of what to do next or what to make of what had just happened.

"What're you thinking, Gina?" I asked.

"These are not random killings of some madman, and this is not some terrorist plot to take out the command structure of the department. I believe each victim was targeted for a specific reason and I think they're all connected."

"Um, I think we all already knew the killings were connected," Bethany said.

Gina ignored the sarcasm in her voice. "Not the killings...the victims. The victims are all connected to each other and to the killer. We need to find out who else shares a connection with Landry, Abbott and Wainwright and we need to find out soon, before we lose another cop."

"What kind of connection?" Jerry wanted to know.

"Anything," Gina said. "A case they've all worked...a married chick they've all banged...anything."

"I guess the most obvious common denominator between them is their rank," I said. "Of course, Wainwright was retired, so..."

"If this is involving a case they worked," Jerry mused, "it would have to be from their past because they've been commanders for years and haven't done any real work in a long time. We'll have to interview the other captains to see if they can think of anything. Once we find the connection, we'll find the bastard who did this."

"I don't think he cares if we make the connection." I pointed to the message under the window. "He's trying to give us the connection. James five-sixteen…it has to mean something to somebody."

"I think it's a Bible verse," Gina said. "I think the message is telling them to confess their sins, to admit to doing something wrong, and that makes me think it has to do with a case they worked. Maybe they put the killer in jail for something he thinks he didn't do and he just got out and is seeking revenge." She pulled a notebook from her shirt pocket and scribbled something in it. "We need to check to see if anybody they've ever arrested has been recently released from prison."

"But what did Kenneth have to do with it?" I wanted to know. "Why frame him for the murders? It seems senseless."

Gina squinted. "I've been trying to figure that one out myself. Maybe the killer was trying to buy some time. The longer we're out chasing ghosts—or an innocent cop—the longer he can operate undetected. If he set Kenneth up, that means he had to know about the affair. If we find out who knew about the affair, we find the killer! Bethany"—Gina turned to look at her—"don't you handle cases of officer misconduct? Conduct Unbecoming an Officer or whatever the hell y'all call it now?"

"Yeah, but no one's ever filed a complaint against Kenneth about anything. He was clean as a whistle."

"How about you follow-up on that angle when we're done here, Gina," I suggested. "Check the complaint database to see if there were any complaints filed against him that never made it to IA, and canvass his neighborhood to see if anyone saw anything suspicious. We do know that Justin Wainwright was following him, so maybe the killer was following Wainwright and found out that way."

Gina scribbled some more in her notebook.

Footsteps echoed on the hollow floor downstairs. "Y'all up there?" a voice called from the bottom of the stairway.

CHAPTER 19

We walked to the edge of the staircase and looked down to see a team of crime scene investigators, clad from head to toe in white crime scene suits and carrying crime scene cases, looking up at us.

"Yeah, but we'll be getting out of your way," Bethany said. She then led us downstairs and out into the smothering afternoon air.

A group of patrol officers under the command of Captain Carmella Vizier had teamed up with five detectives and they were searching all the civilian vehicles in the area. The civilians stood patiently beside their vehicles, none of them uttering a single complaint. It wasn't every day they saw a high-ranking cop get the back of his head blown out during the funerals of two other cops who'd died identical deaths, and even if they didn't like their stuff being searched, I guess they figured it would be better if they didn't add to the sour mood of all the officers involved.

Roadblocks had been set up along Highway Three to the north and south of the graveyard and other officers were stopping and searching everything and everyone that approached. Many of the officers were SWAT members, and they had quickly changed into their tactical gear. The black garb, ballistic helmets, low-riding holsters and semi-automatic rifles dangling across the front of their bodies made for an intimidating presence, and no one dared resist the polite requests to search their vehicles.

As I watched them wave cars to a stop, I caught several of them glancing anxiously up and around, as though expecting a sniper's bullet to whisper out of the sky and snatch the life right out of them. I scanned the surrounding graveyard and observed the same actions from officers and civilians alike. I shook my head. This killer had everyone on edge. What these officers didn't realize was that even if they were targeted, they would never know it...just like Wainwright, Landry and Abbott never knew it. One instant they were standing in this world doing their own thing and the very next instant they were standing before their Maker, trying to explain away the transgressions from their all-too-short lives. Their deaths were so sudden and unexpected they didn't know how it was that they'd come to be standing before God, nor did they know why they were there.

We met the other snipers in the backyard of the old school, and I turned to Bethany. "Come...walk me to my car. I have an extra rifle you can use." As we turned to leave, I caught Gina studying us. There was a strange expression on her face. When she saw me looking, she turned her head and busied herself checking the chamber of the semi-automatic rifle Ray Sevin had given her.

Bethany and I rushed through the empty graveyard to where my new unmarked cruiser was parked. It was a nice car, but the trunk was just big enough to fit all my sniper gear. I smashed the trunk button and removed my semi-automatic rifle from the rifle rack mounted to the trunk lid. "You know how to use this?" I asked Bethany.

Wide-eyed, she shook her head.

"It's not as mean as it looks." I gave her a quick lesson on how to operate it.

"Does it kick?" she asked when I handed it to her.

"I've shot it with the butt against my...um, you know, my jewels, and nothing broke."

"No, I'm serious. Does it kick?"

"I've done it a number of times to demonstrate how little it kicks. I'd do it for you here, but"—I waved my hand around—"these jumpy bastards would all drop dead from a heart attack."

Bethany cocked her head sideways. "Why aren't you jumpy?"

I shrugged into my sniper vest. "What do you mean?"

"I noticed how scared and panicky all these officers were when the shooting started, those who pretend to be so tough and who act like bad-asses. But you...you come across as just a normal guy, but you didn't panic at all."

"I *am* just a normal guy." I locked my tactical gun belt in place and slammed my trunk shut.

"No, you're normal until the shit hits the fan. At that point, while everyone else is freaking out, you're cold as ice, even when you're under fire. I mean, I saw how you saved the sheriff's life. It was almost as though…"

I started making my way back to the old schoolhouse. "As though what?"

Bethany hesitated. "Um…as though you wanted to die."

I stopped and turned to face her. "Are you saying I'm suicidal?"

"No…no, not at all," Bethany said. "I just… It just seems like you don't care about dying. You threw yourself between the sheriff and the sniper. Who does that?"

"Bethany—I mean, LT—I do care about dying. I have a strong will to survive and I'll always do everything I can to keep myself and everyone around me alive." I turned my eyes away, not wanting her to see into my soul. "It's just so much easier when you only have yourself to think about. Cops with families…they're distracted on the job. They might not think so or want to admit it, but every time they get into a life-and-death situation they're wondering what'll happen if they die—who'll raise their kids, how'll their families pay for the house, who'll be sleeping next to their spouses. All that shit rips through their minds and distracts them from the task at hand. That's why so many mistakes are made during stressful situations."

"I don't have a family"—her voice was sad—"but it's not easy for me. This scares the shit out of me. I'm always looking over my shoulder, wondering—"

I put a finger to her full lips. They were soft and moist. I'd thought she would pull back, but she didn't. "I won't let anything happen to you."

Lieutenant Bethany Riggs—Internal Affairs investigator, the cop of the cops—nodded and took my hand away from her face. "I know you won't," she said softly.

What the hell are you thinking, London? I asked myself as we continued on our walk toward the old schoolhouse. The other snipers were there and had their gear. Gina stepped forward and motioned with her head. "Can I talk to you for a minute?"

"Sure." I followed her to the side of the building out of earshot of the others. "What's up?"

"Why don't you tell me?" Her eyes were narrow, penetrating.

"I don't understand what's happening here."

"Something's going on between you and Bethany."

"No, there isn't." I glanced over my shoulder to where Bethany stood, her blonde hair blowing in the light summer breeze, her face a sculpture of perfection. I turned back to Gina and leaned closer. "Are we really having this conversation? In case you haven't noticed, I'm single, and most importantly, a cop just got killed. Whatever's going on with you, you'd better put it far behind you and get your head in the game. I need you sharp. I need everyone sharp. We ain't got time for petty bullshit."

"You know you can be such a prick sometimes." Without saying another word, Gina huffed and stormed away.

"Hey, Gina," I called out, "wait a minute."

Gina continued walking. She placed her closed hands against the small of her back and subtly extended both middle fingers my way. I shook my head, as I followed her to the group.

There were nine of us—six from the sniper team, two from SWAT and Lieutenant Bethany Riggs—and I split us up into three teams.

"Team two will cover the northern sector of the graveyard, and team three will cover the southern sector. The patrol guys are checking cars to the east." I nodded to Ray Sevin and Bethany. "We'll take the western sector."

"Let's do this shit." Ray's voice was somber.

"Keep your eyes peeled and your index fingers close to the trigger," I warned. "That bastard's still out there and until he's caught, no one's safe. *No one!*"

We spent the remainder of the day trudging through cane fields, dense woods and blackberry pickers, but there was no trace of the shooter or any evidence of his comings or goings. It was as though he'd appeared in that old schoolhouse, murdered Abbott, left his message behind and then disappeared into the humid air. He was a ghost…a sniper. The tattoo on my left shoulder bore the sniper's creed, and this evil bastard was adhering to it.

We met team two and team three back at the old school. They looked as tattered as we did. The sun had crept behind the distant trees and the temperature had cooled to about a hundred and two degrees. The crime scene detectives had left, and the graveyard was empty except for us.

I wiped grimy sweat from my forehead. "Anyone heard from the sheriff?"

"I spoke to Captain Theriot a few minutes ago," Gina offered, "and he said all the commanders are camping out at the main office tonight."

"All of them?" I asked.

Gina nodded. "Every last one of them."

I glanced at Bethany, whose blonde hair was plastered to the sides of her head. Her cheeks were flushed and her makeup had long since disappeared from her face. I found it hard to peel my eyes from her perfect complexion—

"Did you hear me, London?"

Sure, I'd seen her lips moving, but I hadn't heard a word Lieutenant Bethany Riggs had said. "I'm sorry. What'd you say?"

Bethany tried to act annoyed, but I thought I saw her face blush slightly and wondered if Gina was on to something. What if there was something happening between us? Would that even be possible?

"I *said*," Bethany repeated, "that this is the perfect opportunity to get all of the captains together in one room. We can meet with them to see if they have any idea what the hell James five-sixteen means."

"Good idea. One of them has to know something." I turned to the rest of the team. "Y'all get home and get some rest, but be careful. Even though we're not captains, we all need to be on high alert until we know who we're dealing with and what he wants. Change up your patterns of movement, don't stand in front of windows, get in and out of cars and buildings as quickly as possible...shit like that."

CHAPTER 20

Bethany turned her car into the large parking lot across the street from the main office, and I parked beside her. My eyes were on the building as I shut off my car. Something looked different. I opened the door and saw Bethany staring, too.

"Why's the building so dark?" she asked.

I scanned the roofs of nearby buildings, searching the dark skyline for any signs of a shooter. Nothing.

"Let's go find out." I started across the parking lot, and she followed. As we walked closer to the main office building, I saw slivers of light at the very top and bottom of the windows and realized what had happened. "They blacked out the windows. It looks like they used cardboard."

Bethany's nose scrunched up. "Cardboard? They don't really think cardboard will stop a bullet, do they?"

"No. Snipers can't shoot what they can't see, and this particular sniper is selecting specific targets, so the cardboard will suffice."

"But can't he just shoot at random and still hit someone inside?" she wanted to know. "He could just take an automatic weapon and shoot out all the windows, killing nearly everyone inside."

"We're not dealing with some crazy gunman who's trying to run up a number." I shook my head. "No, we're dealing with a highly trained killer on a very specific mission. He's only going to kill who he needs to kill to accomplish his mission—not a person more."

"If you say so. After all, you're the expert on this shit."

We used our key and entered through the back door, then strolled up the long hallway toward the front of the building. Military cots were strewn along the hallway and in some of the rooms. When we neared the end of the hall, I glanced into Sheriff Burke's plush office. It was empty. I found him around the corner and two doors down in Chief Garcia's office.

"I'm not about to sleep in an office with windows," Sheriff Burke explained.

"Good thinking," I said. One wall of Burke's office was solid glass and it faced a number of three- to five-story buildings across the city. Chief Garcia's office, on the other hand, was located at the center of the building, with no windows or doors leading to the outside.

Bethany didn't waste time with pleasantries. "Sheriff, we need all the commanders in the conference room as soon as possible so we can try and figure out if any of them have any connections to Wainwright, Landry and Abbott. We need to know if James five-sixteen means anything to them."

"It's getting late," Sheriff Burke said. "Why don't we wait until the morning?"

"Sheriff, I think Bethany's right. We need to get this done as soon as possible," I said. "That way we can start following up on any leads first thing in the morning. If we waste time and someone else dies, it'll be our bad."

"That piece of shit is killing captains and"—Sheriff Burke shot a thumb over his shoulder toward the back of the office—"they're all safe and secure in here. We've got half the SWAT team surrounding the building and up on the roof. No one's dying tonight…I guarantee that. You kids go on home and get some sleep." Burke glanced at his wristwatch. "Be back here at six in the morning. I'll have all the commanders waiting for y'all in the conference room."

Worry lines had etched deep grooves into Sheriff Burke's face and his eyelids drooped slightly. This had been a rough week for everyone. As much as I wanted to get right to work, I knew we had to sleep at some point, and now was probably the best time. Once we dived further into this case, there was no telling how long we'd be running around.

My eyes met Bethany's and I nodded. We both turned and made our way back into the night. The city streets were deserted. I walked Bethany to her car and paused there for a minute. "Will you be okay?" I asked. "I mean, I know you can take care of yourself, but we've already had three capable cops get killed and…and I'll worry about you."

She stood there quiet, staring down at the keys in her hand.

I swallowed the sand in my throat. "Would you like some

company tonight? Maybe I could cook you something to eat. You know, I'd feel more comfortable if everyone stayed paired up—"

"You cook?" Bethany's face bore an expression of skepticism.

"I cook a mean peanut butter and banana sandwich."

Bethany's eyes narrowed. "London Carter, are you trying to lure me to your place so you can seduce me?"

My cheeks caught fire. I stammered, the words tripping over themselves. I finally managed to say, "No! I just thought it'd be better if we stayed together. At least until we know what we're dealing with."

"You mean, for safety's sake?"

"That's it," I said. "For safety's sake."

Bethany smiled, her eyes glistening in the dark. "Okay, you're on. Let me go home and shower first and—"

"I've got a shower," I offered, before I realized what I was saying. "And hot water, clean towels, an old T-shirt…whatever you need." I braced myself for what would happen next.

Bethany studied me for a few moments before a tired smile slowly spread across her face. "It's been a rough week. I could sure use some company and pampering. Follow me to my house so I can get a toothbrush."

My heart began pounding in my ears. As soon as Bethany was in her car, I slipped into my unmarked and followed her across Chateau to her house. I waited as she retrieved her things and then she followed me to my house.

I showered quickly in the master bathroom, while she showered in the hallway bathroom. Her water was still running when I walked into the kitchen to put supper on. It was a little after midnight when she called from the bathroom.

"London, where's that T-shirt you promised?"

I'd just finished heating up a frozen pizza—the smell torturing my aching stomach—and was making drinks. I froze in mid-pour. "Say again," I called back, not believing my ears.

Bare feet padded behind me and I turned to see Bethany Riggs— *Lieutenant* Bethany Riggs—standing there wrapped in a bath towel, droplets of water hanging precariously from her hair and ears. "You promised me a shirt." Her nose wrinkled and her eyes darted to the oven. "Hey! You also promised peanut butter and bananas! Will I get *any*thing you promised?"

It felt as though my chin were dragging the ground as I stared. Tanned and toned legs shot out the bottom edge of the towel and smooth shoulders extended from the top. She lifted her hands and ran a towel through her wet hair. I caught my breath. I didn't remember her breasts being that pronounced. One wrong move and the bath towel would be on the floor around her ankles.

I blinked back to the issue at hand. "Yeah, I'll keep at least two of the promises. You'll get some company…and a T-shirt." I put down the bottle of soda. "After the day we've had, I figured you deserved a hot meal."

"Pizza certainly sounds good right about now." She smiled and tapped the front of the towel. "Can I get that T-shirt, or do you want me to wear this towel all night?"

My face flushed. "Coming right up." I hurried to my bedroom and had just snatched a large shirt from a drawer when her voice called from the bathroom.

"Do you have a pair of boxers I could borrow?"

"Boxers?" I asked myself quietly, my mouth dropping. And then, aloud, "Sure thing, LT."

I met her in the doorway to the bathroom and handed her the bundle of my clothes.

"Bethany," she said.

I must have looked confused.

"Call me by my name, Bethany…not LT."

"Sure thing, LT." I smiled.

I returned to the kitchen and finished making the drinks. It was then I noticed my hands shaking. I couldn't remember the last time I had a woman in my house. What with work and running the sniper team taking up every facet of my life—

"Can I help?" Bethany stood there in the doorway to the kitchen wearing my oversized T-shirt and loose boxers.

"I hope you don't mind me saying this," I said, "but that shirt and those boxers look better on you than they ever looked on me."

She walked up and took the glasses of soda from my hands. "Thank you. I knew there was a heart in there somewhere."

I slipped a couple slices of pizza on two plates and led the way to the living room. I put the plates on the coffee table, sat on the sofa, nodded toward the recliner. "You can have my chair."

Bethany shook her head and sat next to me on the sofa. "I hope you don't mind, but I'd like to be close to you. I feel like… I don't know… This case has been very difficult for me, and I just feel lonely for some reason. I don't really have any family and most of the cops steer clear of me. You're the first officer here who has been nice to me and treated me like an equal. The rest treat me like an outsider, like I have a contagious disease or something. I guess I asked for it, though. I mean, what cop would want to hang out with the person who helped put away a dozen of their brothers in blue?"

I was surprised by her sense of vulnerability. "Those cops you put away were criminals who should've never been cops. You did the right thing."

"So why don't I feel good about it?"

"The right thing is not always the easiest to do," I said around a mouthful of pizza. As hungry as I was, I would've sworn that pizza was the absolute best meal I'd ever eaten.

"God, this is so good," Bethany said, her eyes closing in ecstasy. "Who knew pizza would make me forget about my troubles?"

I nodded and wolfed down the rest of my food. After we were done, we settled back on the couch facing each other and began making small talk. Our conversation eventually turned to the case.

"Do you think we'll ever catch the person doing this?" she asked.

"I know we will. The only problem is catching him before he kills again."

"It's scary that someone's out there picking us off one at a time. Lately, I keep feeling the hair on the back of my neck stand up and I think he's watching me through his scope…that he's going to start targeting lieutenants and I'll be the first to go. I feel like I'm going crazy. It's so scary."

Bethany hugged her shoulders and shuddered. "And then there's the pressure from the sheriff and every other cop in the department to solve the case. Everywhere I go I feel like they're looking at me wondering why I haven't solved it yet and questioning whether I'm capable of working the case. Every time someone else dies, I feel like they think it's my fault."

A twinge of guilt tugged at me for being one of those who doubted her abilities. I quickly shrugged it off. "It's not your fault at all. You're doing the best you can—we all are—and we'll get this piece of shit eventually."

"Like earlier today when some of the mounted patrol officers who worked for Captain Abbott were huddled together staring at me and talking. I know they were blaming me for what happened."

"Who were they? I'll beat the shit out of them! How dare they give you even an ounce of attitude! You're working harder than anyone to solve this case."

Bethany was silent, and I thought I saw her eyes glistening.

"Are you okay?"

She pressed her lips together, then shook her head. "I don't know if I can keep doing this. The case is really starting to get to me.

Seeing all those dead cops wearing the same uniform I wear…" She shook her head. Tears were steaming down her face now. "I just don't know if I can handle it anymore."

CHAPTER 21

I leaned up and reached out for Bethany's arms. I pulled them open and drew her to me, wrapping my arms around her. I straightened my legs, and she stretched out on top of me and melted into my chest. I felt her body relax on top of mine, as she allowed the tears to fall freely. I rubbed her back with one hand and caressed her hair with the other.

"It's okay," I whispered into her ear. "Let it all out. You'll feel better afterwards."

I lost track of time. It could've been minutes we lay there wrapped in each other's arms, or it could've been hours. At some point, she lifted up on her elbows and looked down at me. Her eyes were glassy as she stared into my own. Her lips parted just a little and her tongue traced a line across them. Her face tilted and began to lean slowly into mine. I felt a stirring in my loins and my heart rate increased as her mouth moved closer. Just as I felt the sweet moistness of her full lips pressed to mine, I jerked back, shook my head, pushed to a seated position.

Bethany moved in deft unison with me, as though we'd done this countless times, and ended up in my lap with her arms wrapped around my neck. "What's the matter?" she asked, her bottom lip pouting.

I looked down to avoid her tantalizing eyes, but caught sight of her breasts and observed her excitement pushing through the thin T-shirt she wore—*my* thin T-shirt. With all the strength I could muster, I turned and looked to the side. "I don't want it to be like this."

"Like what?" Her arms were draped over my shoulders, her

hands rubbing my ears.

Weak with desire and frustrated, I sighed. "I want you *so* bad, believe me, but—"

"I know," she interrupted, a mischievous grin spreading across her face. "I can feel you."

"But I don't want to take advantage of you."

"How on earth would you be taking advantage of me?"

"You…you're an emotional wreck right now. I don't want you doing something in your current state of mind that you'll regret later."

"First off, I'm a big girl. Second, I would *never* regret it!" She cocked her head to the side. "I don't know how to read you."

"Try English," I mumbled. "It's the only language I know."

She gave my shoulder a playful punch. "No, silly…what I'm saying is that I don't get *you.* When you're working, you're so cold and calloused, but here you are, outside of work, and you're such a sweetheart."

I leaned back, frowning. "Why do you say I'm cold and calloused?"

"I'm not saying it in a bad way," she explained. "It's just that you're so good at what you do. I mean, you killed that hostage taker without batting an eye. You handled the murders of men you've worked with for years and didn't even shed a single tear at their funerals. I mean, there wasn't a dry eye in the house except yours. How can you watch all that heartbreak without breaking down yourself? You were the absolute *only* person not crying. That's just bizarre. Even the sheriff was bawling like a newborn. When I saw that I thought you were just a coldhearted ass, but then you're so sweet to me. I just don't get you."

I sighed. "What I'm about to tell you doesn't leave here. Okay?"

"Sure."

"No, I'm serious. I've never told anyone what I'm about to tell you, and I need your word you'll never repeat it."

Bethany cupped my face in both of her hands and looked me in the eyes. "I swear I will take your secret to my grave and beyond."

My brow furrowed. "Beyond?"

"I won't even talk about it in my afterlife," she said.

"Okay, that'll work." I smiled, cleared my throat. "I-I can't cry."

Bethany looked confused. "Like, you have a medical condition? You don't produce tears or something?"

I laughed. "No, nothing like that. Sometimes I wish I could cry. There have even been times when I've tried to make myself cry, but nothing comes out. I just can't do it. I can't get myself to that place where I feel so terrible that I start crying."

"How is that even possible?"

"It started when I was eight. That was the last time I ever cried."

Bethany crossed her arms and cocked her head. "You expect me to believe you haven't cried since you were eight years old? Not a single tear?"

"Well, tears leak out from time to time when I yawn, but no, I haven't cried since I was eight. That was when my entire family got wiped out in a car crash—my mom, dad, brother and sister."

Bethany grabbed her chest, gasped. "Oh God, that's horrible! What happened?"

"I was competing in an amateur boxing match in Texas and I drove up with my coach and some of the other fighters. My dad was following us, and my mom, sister and brother were with him. It was late on a Friday night and we were driving through this little town west of the Louisiana-Texas line when a car ran a red light. It just missed my coach's car, but it sideswiped them. The car was so messed up. There was blood everywhere.

"They were trapped inside. I tried as hard as I could to get to them, but people kept holding me back. I cried so hard there was a piercing pain in my head. I was punching and kicking at the people who were holding me back—I got one of them right in the jaw—but I couldn't get to the car. It burst into flames, and I could hear them screaming. It seemed like they screamed in agony for hours, but it was probably only minutes."

Bethany was bawling again. I pulled her forward, and she rested her head on my shoulder.

"I'm sorry," I said. "I'll stop."

"No, no, finish. I want to hear it."

"I cried all that night and into the next day. It was around five o'clock in the morning when I had an epiphany. I suddenly realized that I wasn't crying for them. I was crying for myself. I was feeling sorry for myself. I felt so selfish and ashamed at that moment. They had endured the most agonizing type of death and here I was feeling sorry for myself. My pity turned to hate…a deep, dark hatred that still burns inside my chest to this day." I sighed. "Anyway, that was the last time I cried."

After several long moments of silence, Bethany—her lips rubbing my neck as she spoke, causing a chill to reverberate up and down my spine—asked, "Who was your hatred directed at? The driver of the other car?"

I nodded. "Dan Stevens…he was drunk."

"Oh, no. Did they arrest him?"

"Yeah, but he didn't do any time for it. Because he had a clean record, the judge gave him home incarceration."

Bethany jerked her head up from my shoulder. "Are you shitting me?"

"Nope. Home incarceration. And he was allowed to leave his house to go to work and church. Of course, no one cared that my family would never get to do any of those things again."

"I can't believe you turned out as good as you did, considering. It would've been easy for you to just go crazy and rebel, turn into a criminal."

"You have no clue," I said. "I spent a lifetime of hours fantasizing about killing that asshole. When I finally got my driver's license, I'd drive by his house on a regular basis and just watch him, wondering what it would be like to beat him to death."

"Why didn't you go after him?"

"It would dishonor the memory of my family. My dad worked hard to make a good name for himself and for us, and I didn't want to ruin his name for one selfish act. It's not what he would've wanted. So…" I studied her face, wondering how much to tell her.

"What is it?" she asked.

"I'm just wondering how much I can trust you. You are IA, you know."

"It is *so* against policy for me to be sitting here in your lap wearing your T-shirt and boxers," Bethany said, rubbing my face with her hand. "I'm hoping I can trust you—otherwise I'll be looking for another job tomorrow."

"Your job's safe," I said. "I know how to keep a secret."

She winked. "So do I."

After a brief hesitation on my part, I sighed. "Okay…the only reason I became a cop was to find a way to get back at that piece of shit legally, without bringing disgrace on my dad's name. When I realized it would never work—that the case was over legally—I'd been doing this job for five years. I thought about leaving law enforcement work, but then it dawned on me…"

"What dawned on you?"

"I figured I could start training as a sniper, then I could take him out from far off without anyone ever knowing. That way I could do what I felt I had to do, as a man, and I wouldn't disgrace my family name. So, I trained religiously. I'd dry-fire my rifle several hundred times every night at my house, and I'd spend hours upon hours at the shooting range. When I felt I was ready, I began planning how I was going to take him out. About three days into my planning, I got a call from a friend of mine who works for the department where that piece of shit lives. Dan Stevens had been killed in another DWI-related crash. Suddenly, just like that, my whole reason for existing was gone. I felt like I had trained for nothing…had lived for nothing."

Bethany's eyes widened and her body stiffened.

"What's wrong?" I asked.

"Was…was the hatred you felt also directed at the criminal justice system?"

I frowned. "I don't follow you."

"Did you blame the justice system for him going free?"

"Somewhat, I guess."

More silence. I could see the wheels inside of her head turning. She was biting her lower lip and looking down at her hands.

"What is it?" I asked.

She shook her head.

Like a punch to the solar plexus, it dawned on me. I burst out laughing. Bethany looked up, confused.

"What's so funny?" she asked. "Why are you laughing?"

"You think I'm the killer! You think I'm the one killing cops because the system failed me and my family."

Bethany's face flushed. She looked embarrassed. "No! That's absurd. I know better than that. You're capable of killing if you have to—you've already proven that in a big way—but you're no murderer."

I squeezed her waist, tickling her. She squirmed, giggled.

"For a second there," I said, "you really thought I was the killer sniper. I saw it in your face."

Still giggling, Bethany held up a hand, holding her index finger and thumb about an inch apart. "Maybe this much, but then I dismissed it. I mean, when you said how you trained to do that and then he died and you had nothing left, I just thought…"

"You thought I was a murderer? That I'd kill someone who didn't deserve killing?"

"Just for a second my mind wandered, you know, because you're like one of the only people in this area who can make that shot and—"

"You know," I interrupted. "I've been accused of a lot of things, but murder has never been one of them…until now."

Bethany slugged my shoulder. "I didn't accuse you of anything." That mischievous grin returned. "I realized right away it couldn't be you because you were standing right next to Captain Abbott when he was shot. But even if you were the killer and I'd have to arrest you, I think I'd sleep with you before turning you in."

"Wait…what did you say?"

My heart began racing as Bethany wrapped the fingers of both hands behind my neck and pulled my mouth to hers. It was a rough kiss—animalistic—and it excited me. I pulled her body firmly to mine. Her full breasts pushed against my chest as our tongues and hands explored each other. Unable to contain myself any longer, I gripped her bottom and stood to my feet, holding her against me. She squeezed her legs around my waist and kissed me wildly. Moving one foot at a time, trying to feel my way as I went, I carried her toward my bedroom, drunk with passion. We continued to kiss and my chest began to ache with desire.

When I reached my bedroom door, I kicked it open and rushed through it. As I stumbled across the room, Bethany tugged at my shirt and ripped it toward my head. I tossed her onto the bed. As she fell backward onto the plush mattress, she took my shirt with her. She tossed it aside and squirmed out of the boxers I'd loaned her. I clutched at the button of my shorts and, as I kicked out of them, she pulled off the T-shirt she was wearing. I fell on top of her and our warm, hungry bodies melded into one.

CHAPTER 22

Sunday, August 21, 2011

The sun beamed through the crack in my bedroom curtains. I squeezed my eyes tighter and rolled over in bed, turning my back to the window. Bethany stirred beside me. I reached for her waist under the sheets, and she instinctively drew her body closer to mine. She snaked up through my arms and found my mouth with hers. I rolled onto my back and pulled her on top of me.

A thunderous boom suddenly sounded from the front door of my house. Bethany lurched in my arms, shooting a panicked look around. "Who's that?" she hissed.

"I don't know." I bolted upright, pulling on my shorts and shirt fast. I snatched my pistol from the nightstand and hurried to answer the knock. Before I opened the door, I glanced through the peephole. Gina Pellegrin. *What the—?*

I shoved the pistol in the back of my waistband and pulled the door open. Gina's hands were on her hips, her lips pursed.

"Do you know what time it is?" she asked. "The sheriff's been looking for you for an hour. You were supposed to be back at the main office for six. We thought you were dead." She paused, then shot a thumb toward Bethany Riggs' car. "And what the hell is *that* doing here?"

I scowled. "What are *you* doing here? Why didn't you just call?"

"I did call you—a dozen times! Do you even know where your phone is, or were you too busy—"

"Okay, that's enough. I appreciate your concern. I appreciate you coming here to check on me, but I'm fine. Let the sheriff know I'll be there in thirty minutes."

"Tell him yourself." Gina spun on her heel and stormed off.

I shook my head and swung the door shut. I turned and was surprised to see Bethany standing there. Her eyes were suspicious. "What's her problem?"

"I have no idea."

"I'm so sorry. I shouldn't have come. It was a bad—"

I put my finger to her moist lips and then moved in to kiss her. Afterward, I said, "I wouldn't have had it any other way."

She smiled. "You sure?"

"Positive." I grabbed her hand and pulled her toward the bedroom. "Now let's get ready for work before we both have to start looking for another job."

CHAPTER 23

The five remaining captains for the Magnolia Parish Sheriff's Office, Majors Doucet and Day, Chief Garcia, Sheriff Burke, Detective Lieutenant Corey Chiasson, Detective Gina Pellegrin and three other detectives were seated in the conference room when Bethany and I walked in—and they *all* looked up.

Sheriff Burke glanced at the wall clock, then back at us. "I'm glad y'all finally decided to join us."

I nodded my apologies. "I'm really sorry. It won't happen again."

"It had better not." Sheriff Burke frowned. "We started thinking one of y'all had been killed. We tried calling both of your phones, but…"

Bethany mumbled an apology—her face a bright shade of crimson—walked to the front of the room and flipped open her notebook. She stared out over the room of commanders. "We asked the sheriff to get you guys together so we could try and figure out why this killer is targeting captains. In order to figure out who the next target will be, we need to find some common denominators among Wainwright, Landry and Abbott, and we need to figure out if any of you share that connection." She grabbed a dry erase marker and wrote James 516 on the board. "Does this mean anything to any of you?"

I studied the faces of the captains who sat around the conference table. They passed glances amongst each other, shrugged, and shook their heads.

"Anything at all?" Bethany pressed. Still a host of blank stares. "What about cases? Have any of you worked any cases with Wainwright, Landry or Abbott?"

"None of us have worked cases in years," Captain Theriot said, "and I've never worked the same division as any of them. I was in narcotics when Landry and Abbott were in patrol. Wainwright was in IA back then. Shit, he was in IA for as long as I can remember. I think he was born there."

Bethany quickly wrote some notes on the board. "So, Landry and Abbott were in patrol at the same time?"

Captain Theriot nodded.

"Any of you were on patrol at the same time?" Bethany asked.

Captain Martin Thomas, commander of the narcotics division, raised his hand. "I worked patrol at the same time they did, but we were on opposite shifts."

"Do you remember them being involved in any major cases together? Where they might've put someone away for a bunch of years?" As Bethany spoke and moved about at the front of the room, my mind wandered to the perfect body that rippled under her clothes. I had to shake my head a few times to jog the image loose and I had to force myself to concentrate on the task at hand.

Thomas shook his head. "We never really handled major investigations on patrol. If we caught a major complaint, we'd call out the detectives and they'd handle it."

Bethany studied the board and bit her lower lip.

As her mind worked, I stepped up. "Have any of you ever arrested an ex-soldier or law enforcement officer who might've been trained as a sniper?"

More blank stares and shoulder shrugs.

"That's not something we would've known," Theriot said. "I did handle some cases in narcotics that involved some pretty unsavory characters, but those guys weren't precision shooters. They were the *spray-n-pray* type. They liked doing drive-bys with cheap semi-automatic rifles. Besides, they were too stupid to pull off this type of organized attack against us, and they wouldn't know the difference between a captain and a trustee."

Heads nodded and a low buzz of agreement sounded around the room. Chief Garcia spoke up. "Detective Pellegrin, you seem to think this was some sort of religious warning. They told me you said James five-sixteen is a Bible verse that says something about confessing your sins?"

Gina—very careful not to make eye contact with me—nodded her head. "That's the most likely meaning of the message. It says something about"—she glanced down at her notepad—"confessing your sins and praying for each other. I'm thinking the killer wants someone to confess to something."

"But we're the good guys," Captain Theriot said, "so we wouldn't be the ones needing to confess any sins. It seems like they'd leave that kind of message for criminals, or Kenneth Lewis— for committing adultery."

"You bring up a good point," Bethany interjected. "Whoever killed them knew about Kenneth Lewis' affair with Landry's wife and they knew Wainwright was investigating it. Did any of you know about the affair?"

There was a long moment of silence and then a low voice came from the back of the room. "I did." It was newly appointed patrol division commander, Captain Carmella Vizier.

Chairs rattled and tables creaked as people shifted in their chairs and every head turned to face her.

"How'd you know about it?" I blurted, remembering Gina had surmised if we found the person who knew about the affair we'd find the killer.

"Anthony told me he'd been suspecting it," she said quietly.

I studied Captain Vizier. She couldn't be the killer. I'd seen her at yearly firearms qualifications, and she couldn't hit water if she aimed out at the ocean, so she definitely didn't have the skills to pull off the kinds of shots that had been killing our captains.

"Did you tell anyone else about the affair?" I wanted to know.

"No. He asked me not to say anything, so I didn't."

"What else did he tell you?" Bethany asked.

"Nothing, really. He asked what he should do, so I told him he should file a complaint against Kenneth with IA, but he said he didn't know you"—she nodded toward Bethany—"very well and didn't know if he could trust you to keep it quiet. I told him he should hire a private investigator to follow them around." She shrugged. "I guess that's what he did."

"Why didn't you say anything about this earlier?" Sheriff Burke demanded.

"Because I didn't think that had anything to do with what's happening."

That got my attention. "Why not?"

"I think that was all a distraction to get us looking somewhere else while the killer was setting up his next victim."

"Where'd you dream up this theory?" Captain Theriot asked harshly.

"This is purely speculation on my part," Vizier said, her eyes focusing on the table in front of her, "but I don't think the affair had anything to do with the killings."

Major Lawrence Doucet leaned forward, resting his thick, hairy forearms on the table. His beady eyes focused on Captain Vizier. "If you know something about these murders, you'd better speak up."

The color drained from Vizier's face. "I-I don't know anything," she stammered. "I just don't think it's connected to the affair."

"You're a potential victim, not an investigator," Captain Theriot said. "So you might want to keep your hunches to yourself."

Bethany and I traded curious looks. I shrugged, while she continued addressing the group. She pointed to Detective Ford. "Melvin, did you run background checks on all the people listed on the canvass sheets from the neighborhood where Captain Landry was murdered?"

Melvin nodded. "They were all clean, except for a few kids with criminal records, but those were misdemeanors. Nothing that stood out."

Bethany bit her lower lip as she studied her notes. She glanced up and nodded toward Gina. "Did you ever get to complete the canvass of Captain Landry's neighborhood?"

I held my breath as I watched Gina's eyes narrow and her lips press together. She was silent for a long count of three, and then her face relaxed. She scanned her notes.

"Yes, *ma'am*," she said in a strained voice, "I did canvass Anthony's neighborhood—like I said I would—and I also checked our database to see if there'd been any suspicious person complaints filed. No one from Anthony's neighborhood saw anything suspicious and the only complaints we've had out of that neighborhood over the past six months have been for lock-jobs"—someone locking their keys in their car—"and animals roaming at large."

"London," Sheriff Burke cut in, "what type of skills would someone have to possess in order to make those shots?"

"His farthest shot was on Captain Landry at four hundred and eleven yards. An average sniper can shoot a four-inch group at that distance, so this guy is exceptional. He knows how to read wind and how to accurately compensate for it. He either has a range finder or he knows how to manually determine distance and compensate for the bullet drop at four hundred yards. If he's shooting the same type of bullet we use in our sniper rifles, that would be a thirty-five-inch drop—hardly a walk in the park, even for a skilled sniper."

"You mean this guy's better than an average sniper?" Captain Theriot asked.

"The average police sniper trains once or twice per month and can generally shoot one minute of angle—about one inch at one hundred yards—and they usually only shoot out to a hundred yards because the average shot for a police sniper is between seventy and seventy-five yards." I pointed to the board where Bethany had written the word Suspect in red. "This guy trains at least once a week, and he's had extensive experience shooting at longer distances, probably even out to a thousand yards."

"Who has a one thousand-yard range?" Theriot asked.

"There's one here in Chateau," I said. "But anyone with the right amount of property can make their own thousand-yard range. Shit, there's enough public land around that they could be practicing right under our noses and we'd never know it."

"What kind of artillery are we looking for?" Sheriff Burke asked.

"Depending on the brand name, your average sniper rifle typically shoots one minute of angle out the box," I said, "but that won't get the job done in these cases. This prick's not shooting the average sniper rifle. If it's not a custom made job, it's definitely been tuned to shoot sub minute of angle. It'll be topped with a high-quality scope."

Sheriff Burke turned to Captain Vizier. "Carmella, you still have that contact at the *Daily Magnolia Times*?"

Carmella nodded.

"Go call her and tell her to put out the word we're looking for anyone with information on people shooting rifles at shooting ranges or in backyards. If they were at a shooting range and the person next to them was shooting what looked like a sniper rifle, I want to know about it. If they hear regular gunshots in the woods behind their house, I want them to call. If a friend of a friend's step-uncle's wife has an older brother who likes to shoot, I want his name." Burke turned back to me as Carmella gathered her notes and hurried out of the conference room. "Where do people have to go to get sniper training? Wouldn't they have to be a cop or in the military to attend sniper school?"

"Normally, yes," I said, "but nowadays, with all the private security companies employing counter-snipers and conducting their own training, it's hard to keep track of who's receiving this type of training. Also, there's an ass load of literature available to the general public on the finer points of sniping, so anyone can train themselves to be a sniper."

"You expect me to believe someone could train themselves to be this good from reading books?" scoffed Captain Tyrone Gibbs, who was the commander of the juvenile division. "Bullshit."

"That's not bullshit," Gina hissed before I could open my mouth. "London trained himself to be a sniper, and he was the best sniper in the state long before he even attended his first sniper school. He took top shooter at every sniper school he attended."

Gibbs looked from me to Gina, then to the sheriff. "Is that true?"

Sheriff Burke nodded. "We sent him to a national sniper competition, and he took first place. I got to attend the awards ceremony and the instructors didn't believe us when we told them he hadn't been to a school yet."

"How'd you do it?" Gibbs asked. "I mean, what does it take to get that good? Maybe knowing that will give us an idea of what to look for."

"Well, I trained twice a week—four hours on Wednesday nights and eight hours on Sundays—and I shot about five hundred rounds per month." I rubbed my index and middle fingers against the thumb of my right hand. "It was expensive. Cost me more than a dollar every time I pulled the trigger. But I loved sniping more than anything else in the world and it was worth it to me. This person we're dealing with…he went through a lot of trouble and expense to become good at killing."

I looked from one captain to the other, staring each of them directly in the eye for a full second before moving to the next. "Somebody…somewhere…did something really bad to piss this bastard off, and now he's taking it out on y'all."

"Why do you think that?" Captain Theriot asked. "These could just be random killings by some lunatic."

"If they were drive-bys—that would be one thing. Anyone can do a drive-by." I shook my head. "This guy's on a mission. If any of y'all have any idea why someone would want to target y'all, speak up…or more of y'all will die."

"What if he's already killed who he wanted to kill?" Captain Thomas asked.

"Do you want to stand out there"—I pointed to the streets—"and find out?" When Thomas didn't respond, I continued. "Y'all need to think really hard. Is there anything any of you have ever been involved with—good or bad—that might make someone want to target y'all? Come on. Now's not the time to be bashful. Cough it up."

"Are you trying to blame us for these murders?" Captain Theriot asked. His face was red and his thick eyebrows were furrowed. "Are you saying we're somehow responsible for what this cowardly bastard is doing?"

"No," I said. "Nothing, no matter how horrific, justifies the murders. We're just trying to do our jobs. If we can figure out *why* this is happening, we can figure out *who* is doing it."

The entire room fell into a long silence. I scanned the faces, trying to read the expression on each of the captains, wondering which one of them held the keys to why this was happening. I wondered if one or more of them had been involved in something shady in their past—and if that something shady was now catching up with them. What if Gina was right? What if James five-sixteen was a Bible verse? What if the killer did want them to confess to some sin? Would they give in and confess, or would they allow more blood to flow just to protect their own selfish—

"Sheriff Burke!" Kimberly Weimer, Sheriff Burke's secretary, burst through the door of the conference room. "Quick! Turn on the TV!"

CHAPTER 24

Someone grabbed the remote and switched on the large flat-screen television. It was already set to the local news channel, and we immediately recognized that the news reporter was standing right outside our main office building. We all leaned forward to hear what he was saying.

"…outside of the sheriff's office in Magnolia Parish, where three captains have been gunned down in recent sniper attacks. Sources tell us that the remaining captains and other high ranking officials are barricaded in this building and they are expected to remain inside until investigators apprehend this highly skilled and elusive killer."

"Who the hell told them that?" Sheriff Burke wanted to know.

"When asked earlier if he planned to bring in the FBI, Sheriff Calvin Burke said that this is a local matter and that his deputies are more than qualified to bring this case to a successful resolution. Calls to Sheriff Burke have gone unanswered. Dawn, back to you."

The image switched to the studio and the woman named Dawn smiled into the camera.

"With us tonight in our New Orleans studio is nationally-renowned FBI criminal profiler Dexter Myers. Mr. Myers, can you tell what type of individual might be responsible for these heinous crimes?"

The suit flashed a fake smile and nodded. "Thank you, Dawn. In a nutshell, this killer is most likely a white male in his mid-thirties and he was probably recently fired from his job. He will be a weapons collector and will most likely have a library of military and police books. His personality traits will include—"

The television suddenly went black. Sheriff Burke tossed the remote on the conference table. "To hell with them idiots. That's nearly the same profile they released for the DC-area sniper and the Baton Rouge serial killer…and they were wrong both times."

"They play the numbers game," Captain Theriot said. "Sometimes they get lucky and sometimes they don't. When they don't, they waste precious time and get more people killed."

Most of the officers in the room nodded in agreement. Some of them grumbled their disdain for the FBI. Sheriff Burke leaned against the table, exhausted. He rubbed his face. "Where do we go from here?" He was met with silence. "Anyone got any ideas?"

More silence.

"I think the answer's in this room," I finally said. "We've got to sit here until somebody figures out what it is they have in common with Abbott, Landry and Wainwright—no matter how slight."

The men and women in the room stared at each other. Some whispered back and forth, presumably trying to figure out what was getting them killed off one at a time. Five minutes later, the phone at the center of the conference table buzzed and Kimberly Weimer's voice came through the loudspeaker, calling Sheriff Burke's name. Sheriff Burke acknowledged her. "What is it?"

"I've got a call for Sergeant Carter," she called through the loudspeaker. "It was patched in from dispatch. It's some man who says he knows something about the case. I told him Sergeant Carter was in a meeting and asked if he wanted to speak with someone else, but he said he would only speak with the sergeant."

Sheriff Burke shot me a look. I quickly moved to the corner of the table, near the phone.

"Put him through," Sheriff Burke ordered. He turned and shushed the rest of the room. "Not a word!"

The phone buzzed again, and Sheriff Burke looked up at me. "Ready?"

I nodded.

Sheriff Burke pressed the button that was blinking and stepped back.

"Hello, this is London Carter," I said, leaning forward. "I understand you have some information about the case we're working."

"Sergeant London Carter," a muffled voice said through the phone's speaker, "I know why these killings are taking place."

Bethany and I traded wide-eyed looks. "Really? Why's that?"

"I won't talk on the phone. We need to meet in person."

My brow furrowed suspiciously, and I tried to think of what I might have in common with Landry, Abbott and Wainwright. Was I the next target? This would certainly be a good way for the killer to draw out his next victim. "How do I know this isn't a trap?"

"You'll have to take my word for it."

I hesitated, glancing at Bethany. She shook her head and mouthed the words, *No way.*

"Look, you've got to give me something. How do I know you're for real?"

"Again, you'll have to take my word for it. You need me—I don't need you."

"Well, you obviously want something," I said, "otherwise, you wouldn't be calling us. So, what do you want? Why are you doing this?"

"I want the truth to come out—the *whole* truth."

"The truth about what?"

"I won't talk over the phone. Meet me at ten o'clock tonight…the Payneville Park in Payneville. Go to the gazebo on the eastern end of the park and wait for my signal. If you're late, I'm gone. If you bring company, I'm gone. If you tell anyone else, I'm gone."

"What about my partner?"

"Lieutenant Bethany Riggs?"

Bethany's eyes dropped to the phone, her brows furrowed.

"Yeah," I said slowly, "Lieutenant Bethany Riggs. Is it okay if I involve her? After all, it's her case."

"That's fine—she's cool. Bring anyone else and I'm gone. You'll never hear from me again and you'll be left to figure this shit out on your own. I'm already taking a big risk just calling you."

"Can you give me some sort of hint as to what type of information you have?" I pressed. "You know, something I can feed the sheriff so I can convince him to let me—"

"Not a word to anyone!" the man said in a forceful voice that drew an odd look from Captain Theriot. There was a brief pause and then the man continued in his muffled voice, "I have contacts within the department"—this drew curious glances from all in the room— "and I have a police scanner. If I find out you told a single soul or if I hear a peep on the scanner, I'm gone."

I became more suspicious. "If you're so scared, why go through all this trouble? Why not just tell me what you need to tell me and let me go do my job?"

"I have original documents that will prove why this is happening and it will name the sniper's next targets. These documents can *not* fall into the wrong hands. They're the only proof of what really happened that night."

"What night? And where'd you get these documents?" I asked, hoping the mystery caller would keep talking, but sensing that his reluctance was growing.

"Just meet me at the park and don't be late."

Click!

The line went dead, and the room was draped in silence. I checked the clock on the wall. Nine-fifteen AM. We had nearly thirteen hours to find out as much as we could about this caller.

"Listen up, gang," Sheriff Burke barked. "I don't give a shit who asks—*no* one outside of this room will know about this conversation. Got it?"

There were nods all around the table.

"Melvin," Bethany said, "can you get to communications ASAP and find out as much as you can about the number this guy called from?"

"Sure." Melvin gathered up his stuff and stood.

"I'll be on the road," Gina said. She was still avoiding eye contact with me. "Call me if y'all need anything."

"You know," Captain Theriot said, addressing me, "when he snapped at you, he lost his disguise and his true voice came through a bit. He sounded familiar."

"Familiar how?" I asked.

Theriot shook his head. "I'm not sure where I know the voice from, but it sounded vaguely familiar. I'll have to think about it. The call wasn't recorded, was it?"

"No," Sheriff Burke said. "None of the lines in here are recorded."

As we talked, Captain Carmella Vizier walked in. "Sheriff, the newspaper's going to put out an ad asking anyone with information about snipers to call our hotline."

As they continued talking, I moved to where Bethany stood. "You ready, LT? We have to hit the road, too. I want to get a few things done before tonight."

"Wait a minute," Sheriff Burke called. "Aren't we going to get a team together to provide over-watch protection?"

"You heard the man," Bethany said. "If we bring company, he's gone, and we might never find out what's going on."

Sheriff Burke traded glances with Chief Garcia and Captain Theriot and then sighed. "Okay, but I want to know when y'all are leaving and I want to know as soon as y'all have the document. Call me on my cell. Oh, and London…"

I looked up. "Yes, Sheriff?"

He pulled me to a corner of the room out of earshot of everyone else. "Bring the document straight to me. I don't want anyone looking at it."

I nodded, and Bethany and I left the office and headed for my place. She drove.

CHAPTER 25

After she parked in my driveway, Bethany followed me to the doorway. I stopped to unlock it.

"Why are we here?" she asked.

I pushed the door open and stepped back for her to enter. "I have to get some things together."

"What things?"

"You'll see."

We walked into my living room, and I selected a silver key from my key ring and went to my gun closet. The door was constructed of reinforced steel and it was always padlocked shut. I unlocked it and pulled open the door. Bethany whistled. "Damn, you've got a lot of guns!"

I pulled my backup sniper rifle from the wooden pegs on the wall and slung it over my shoulder. I grabbed a ballistic vest from another peg and tossed it to Bethany. "You'll be needing this."

"For what?"

"I want you wearing it tonight...just in case."

She hoisted it in her hand. "This is heavier than my vest."

"This one's made to withstand rifle rounds...three-o-eight rifle rounds."

She frowned. "It wouldn't do me any good since he makes headshots."

Bethany was right, of course, but it made me feel better knowing she had some sort of protection. "I can get you a ballistic helmet if you want."

"No, I don't do hats." She nodded to the rifle across my back.

"What's that for?"

"I'm going to set up on the top of the Payneville Bridge and you're going to meet our mystery man at the gazebo. That way I'll be able to keep an eye on your surroundings *and* keep an eye on our contact. If he even sneezes while he's in your presence, I'll drop him." I grabbed a three-ring binder from a shelf in my closet and thumbed through the book until I found what I was looking for.

"What's in that binder?"

"Over the past few months I've gone to a bunch of high points in the parish and ranged the surrounding area. I started in the southern part of the parish and began working my way north, visiting every bridge, hospital and building over three stories high, and—lucky for us—the last place I ranged was the Payneville Bridge. I hope to get the entire parish done before the end of the year." I flipped it shut and returned it to the shelf, shut the door and locked it. "It's five hundred twenty-eight yards from the bridge to the gazebo. We'll stop at the rifle range on the way out so I can zero my rifle. The last time I shot this rifle was last winter and it was about sixty degrees."

Bethany chewed her lower lip as she watched me gather up my gear. "I don't know about this. I think I'd feel more comfortable if you came with me."

"You'll be fine. I can do a better job of watching you from the bridge than I can from right beside you. In fact, you'll be safer in that gazebo than the sheriff will be in the main office."

"If you say so."

I turned to her and touched her face, kissed her gently on the lips. "I won't let anything happen to you, I promise."

Bethany moved in for another kiss, and I couldn't resist. When she pulled back, her eyes were half closed. "I could get used to this," she murmured.

"Me, too." I reluctantly pulled away and set my rifle down on the couch, along with some ammunition and two sets of ear mikes for our cell phones. "Let's get this into the car, then go grab something to eat while we have a minute and then we'll head to the range."

*   *   *

After we took our time devouring a couple of fried shrimp po-boys, French fries and drinks at Bill's Seafood, we strolled out into the bright sunlight and pulled ourselves into Bethany's car. We then proceeded to the shooting range. As we drove into the shell parking lot near the rifle range, I was surprised to see a car parked there and a figure standing directly above a rifle grounded on the firing line. The shooter was wearing drab green coveralls and a matching cap.

"Who's that?" Bethany asked.

"Not sure." I stepped out and strained to see downrange. There were five little white dots set out on a narrow platform at the three-hundred-yard line. Suddenly, the shooter dropped prone behind the rifle and snapped off five rounds in rapid succession. I was impressed by how smoothly the shooter manipulated the bolt. With each thunderous shot, a white dot exploded into the air, sending a yellow mist cascading toward the backstop. I nodded my understanding. The targets were chicken eggs.

When the last echo of the last shot had faded into the warm afternoon air, the shooter stood and turned. She stopped when she saw us approaching. "What are y'all doing here?" Gina Pellegrin demanded.

I pointed to the sniper rifle on the ground. "Where'd you get that? And where'd you learn how to shoot? You're pretty damn good!"

I saw the anger lines in Gina's face relax. She tried to stifle a grin. "My dad bought it for me last Christmas."

"Where'd you learn to shoot?" I pressed.

"I pay attention when you talk and I come out here during my lunch hour a few times a week."

"But…why?" I asked.

"I mentioned to the other snipers that I wanted to be the first female sniper ever in Magnolia Parish," she said a little bashfully, "and they all laughed at me. They said women can't be snipers."

"That's bullshit!" I said. "I've met three female snipers over the years who were every bit as good as their male counterparts. Keep shooting like that and you'll be blowing Jerry and them away at training."

"No kidding." Bethany nodded her agreement. "That was super impressive! Way to represent!"

"What do you mean by 'at training'?" Gina asked.

"There's no need for you to shoot in the dark anymore," I said. "It's time for you to come out of the closet and show off your stuff."

I walked to Bethany's car to retrieve my rifle, and Gina followed. She was beaming. "Hey, London, can I talk to you real quick?"

"Sure," I called over my shoulder as I pushed the button to open the trunk. I swung it open and reached for my rifle.

"I just want to say I'm sorry about this morning." Gina was staring down at her hands. "I guess I just got a little…um, a little jealous."

I froze, then turned slowly. "Jealous? Why on earth would *you* be jealous?"

Gina's freckled cheeks were red. "I don't know. I guess I…"

"What? You guess you what?"

"It's not easy to say."

"Just blurt it out."

Gina took a deep breath, blew it out. "Okay, I guess I have…"

"Have what?"

"I was just surprised to see Bethany at your house."

"I didn't know I had to check in with you," I joked.

"Well, now that you know, we shouldn't have this problem again." Gina smiled. "Seriously, I just wanted to apologize for the way I reacted and to make sure we're still cool."

"We're still cool." I gave her a half-hug and grabbed my rifle and a box of bullets to walk toward the firing line where Bethany was waiting for me.

CHAPTER 26

It was fifteen minutes to ten and we were approaching the Payneville Bridge along Highway Three.

"Slow down to about five miles per hour when you pass the service station," I told Bethany. My rifle was in my left hand and my right hand was on the door handle. "I'll jump out and make my way to the top of the bridge. Cross over it and take a left down Allard Street, go down—"

"To Main Court and take a left until I reach River Road. Park right alongside the gazebo...I got it." Bethany grabbed my knee and squeezed. "We've been over this a million times."

I sighed. "I'm sorry. I just want to make sure you're completely safe."

"I'll be fine."

Rick's Service Station was coming into view. I turned to Bethany to offer last minute instructions. "Remember to turn your headlights off before you step out and don't silhouette yourself against the night sky. If you hear even a bump, drop to the ground and take cover, and whatever you do, don't leave the gazebo."

"Damn, you've suddenly turned into quite a worrywart. What happened to the London Carter who didn't give a shit about anything?"

"I'm just being selfish," I said, poised to jump out.

"Selfish? What do you mean?" As she spoke, Bethany slowed to a roll.

I pushed open the door and leapt to the ground—running forward to keep my footing—and called out, "If something were to happen to you, I wouldn't get to spend more time under the sheets with your beautiful ass."

Before she could reply, I slammed the door shut and, crouching low, sprinted across the highway and up the slight ramp to the western side of the vertical lift bridge, holding my sniper rifle close to my chest. When I reached the rusted stairway that extended up toward the top of the bridge, I slung my rifle over my shoulder, palmed my pistol and began the long ascent. I quickly and silently scaled the three flights of steps. A few cars whizzed across the metal grating beneath me, causing the bridge to rattle and shake under the weight, and it helped to mask any sounds I might have made. As I neared the landing, I began to inch my way onward—my pistol muzzle leading the way—until I could see over the landing.

When I was certain the catwalk was clear in both directions and that the killer had not taken a position up there, I strode across it until I reached a point where I had a clear view of the gazebo and the surrounding area. I holstered my pistol and shrugged my rifle off my shoulder. I snapped out the legs of my bipod and dropped to the floor of the catwalk, settling in behind my rifle. I carefully scanned the entire area, searching first for other sniper positions that might conceal our killer, and then for any movement that might indicate the approach of our mystery caller.

There was no movement along River Road. The lights glowed from the windows of only a few houses that lined the southern side of the street. I rotated my scope to the left and scanned the length of the bayou—no boat traffic whatsoever. Everything was quiet. A flicker of light caught my eye at the right of my scope and I turned my attention to that area. Headlights bobbled from Main Court and grew brighter as they approached River Road. When the side of the vehicle came into full view, I recognized Bethany's car. It turned the corner, traveled in my direction, slowed to a stop beside the gazebo. The headlights were blinding, and I couldn't see beyond her car.

I reached for the redial button on my cell phone and pressed it. Bethany's phone rang loudly into my left ear and she picked up on the second ring. "Hey, do you see anything?" Her voice was barely a whisper.

"Turn out your headlights. They're blinding me."

"Oh, sorry!"

The area immediately went dark, but my night vision had been washed. I squeezed my eyes shut and opened them a few times, trying to get my night vision back as fast as I could. "What time is it?" I asked.

"Three minutes 'til," Bethany's voice called in my ear. "Should I get out now?"

As my eyes readjusted to the night and the objects around Bethany's car slowly came back into clear view, I called out, "Ten-four."

Bethany cautiously opened her door and walked to the gazebo. She cast a nervous glance over each shoulder as she walked. She positioned herself at the eastern end of the gazebo—directly across from me—and stood with her back to one of the wooden columns. "I'm in place," she whispered.

"I've got you. Can you hear or see anything at all from where you are?"

"Not a peep."

I swept the area again with my scope. The park was empty and so was the adjacent boat launch. As I scanned the park again, I saw a dark figure near a swing set—it hadn't been there a second ago—and it moved. I pulled my scope to a stop and focused on the figure. It was about four hundred yards out. It darted across a small clearing and disappeared behind a tree…it didn't come out the other end. I watched and waited.

"Beth, I've got movement at your three o'clock position. He's directly in front of that oak tree south of the swing sets."

"My side of the tree or your side?"

"Your side."

"I think I see it. Do you want me to go out to him?"

"Negative. Stay put." I quickly tracked to the left. He had come from that direction. There was a patch of grass, the swing set, a sidewalk and then the bayou. I was about to check the edge of the bayou to see if I could find a boat, when I saw it in the upper portion of my scope. There, several yards west of the swing set and slumped on the white sidewalk was a dark humanlike figure. Although it was in the shadows of the surrounding trees, there was no mistaking the pool of dark liquid that surrounded the figure on the cement—

"He's moving again," Bethany called. "Should I get his attention?"

"Negative! There's a subject down!" I whipped my scope back toward where I'd last seen the subject. He was now disappearing behind a large fountain. I watched, but he didn't come out the other side. "Bethany, do you see him?" I tried to keep my voice calm.

"Ten-four," she whispered into her phone. "He's heading straight for me. He's about twenty feet away. Hey! Sheriff's office! Show me your hands!"

A bright beam of light shot out from Bethany's location—her flashlight—and stabbed the darkness in front of her and right into my scope, blinding me.

"Oh shit!" Bethany cried loudly into my ear. Her voice was cut off by two explosive gunshots. Her flashlight fell to the ground, and I caught a fleeting glimpse of a dark figure disappearing behind her car. Before I could place my crosshairs on his back, he was beyond the car and disappeared around the corner of the street. I jerked my scope back to Bethany's location.

CHAPTER 27

"Bethany!" I screamed into the phone. "Are you okay?"

Silence.

"Bethany, come in. Are you okay?"

"Ten-four, I'm okay," she screamed, scrambling to her feet. She snatched up her flashlight and darted toward her car. "That asshole shot at me!"

"Stay put, Bethany! Standby!"

It was no use. She sprinted down River Road and turned right along Main, disappearing behind some buildings. My heart beat in my chest. I searched with my rifle, but I couldn't see over the buildings and trees. She had vanished. "Bethany, where are you? I've lost you! Give me your location!"

I removed the bolt from my rifle, shoved it in my pocket and stormed down the three flights of stairs. I hit the metal grating at a dead run and ran as fast as my legs could carry me, heading east on Magnolia Street. I could hear Bethany's labored breathing and her occasional grunt in my ear mike.

"Bethany! Give me your location!"

"We're heading south…on Main…approaching Sunshine Avenue. Shit!"

Distant gunshots sounded in my ear mike and then there was a volley of much more pronounced shots—four of them—that immediately followed. As the shots were being fired, I'd reached Seventh Street, turned right and ran past Allard toward Sunshine. I turned down Sunshine as the last shot was fired.

"Talk to me, Bethany!" My voice jumped in rhythm with the pounding of my feet against the pavement.

"I'm good," came Bethany's panting voice. "We're moving again...still heading south on Main!"

Three blocks ahead of me, I saw a dark figure whiz by heading south on Main Court, and a few seconds later, I saw Bethany in hot pursuit. "I'm two blocks away," I called, trying to push my legs harder. I was just reaching the end of Sunshine when Bethany's voice came over the mike again.

"He just turned west...on Smith."

I pivoted abruptly to the right and ran between two houses—thinking I might be able to cut them off—and approached a six-foot wooden fence at a full speed. I jumped high into the air, grabbed the top of the fence, and swung my right leg over it. The momentum carried me clean over the fence, and I landed in a stumbling run on the other side. I straightened into a hard sprint, burst out onto Smith Street, took a right. Bethany was twenty yards ahead of me and gaining on the shooter. Her breathing was more labored as she huffed into the mouthpiece on the mike.

The shooter turned left onto Ninth Street, and Bethany followed. No sooner had she cut the corner than more gunshots exploded ahead of me. I heard a sharp yelp, a sickening grunt and a crashing sound in the phone mike, and then it went dead in my ear. More gunshots sounded. I rushed around the corner and raced up Ninth Street holding my pistol out in front of me. I skipped a step and my heart skipped a beat when I saw Bethany lying in the street, clutching her stomach. The shooter was about to disappear around the corner onto Robin Street.

I skidded to a stop on my knees in front of Bethany—shielding her body with my own—and steadied my pistol with my left hand. I closed my left eye, put my front sight on the center of the shooter's back and snapped off five quick shots. The shooter stumbled and fell forward, landing with a thud. Through the dim light from a nearby light pole, I saw him turn onto his side and lift a handgun in my direction. Without hesitation, I blasted off with four more shots...and the shooter lay still.

I dropped my pistol and turned to Bethany, who was writhing in pain. I pulled her hands away from the front of her body and jerked her shirt open. I breathed a sigh of relief when I saw she was wearing my ballistic vest. I rubbed my hand across the rough cloth and felt the backs of four hot projectiles protruding from the vest. "You're okay. It'll hurt like a bitch, but it—"

Bethany groaned, unable to talk, and shook her head. She lifted her hand to my face. My mouth went instantly dry when I saw the blood leaking from her palm and down her wrist. I leaned back to allow some light in and saw the wound…it was above the vest, into the left side of her neck. I ripped a strip of my shirt off and pushed it against the hole. I guided one of Bethany's hands to the cloth. "Hold this here."

I reached behind her neck and ran my fingers down toward her shoulder. I felt another hole. The bullet had gone clean through, but there was no way of knowing what kind of damage it had done. I ripped off another piece of cloth and shoved it against that hole with my left hand.

It was only then that I heard the faint sound of sirens wailing in the distance. I grabbed my phone with my right hand and thumbed nine, one, one. When the operator answered, I rattled off our location. "Corner of Smith and Ninth…shots fired…officer down. Get an ambulance here ASAP!"

"How bad is the officer hurt?" the operator asked.

"Gunshot wound to the neck, four slugs to the vest. She's alert, but in extreme pain."

"Who are you?" There was some frantic talking in the background, telling her to get more information. "Who did the shooting?"

"This is Sergeant London Carter. The suspect is down." Sirens drew rapidly nearer. "I repeat…suspect is down."

The operator relayed that information to the responding officers. The first to arrive was Detective Melvin Ford. He bolted out of his car with a pistol in his hand. He ran toward Bethany and me. "What happened?"

I pointed toward the corner of Ninth and Robin Street, where the suspect was lying motionless. "Check that piece of shit and make sure he can't get his gun back up. If he moves, finish him off!"

"God, it burns!" Bethany groaned beneath me.

"You'll be fine. It looks like it went clean through and it doesn't feel like it hit anything important."

"Are you…saying that I'm not…important?"

I bent and—in the darkness that surrounded us—I planted a kiss firmly on her lips. "At the moment, you're the most important thing in the world to me. Of course," I joked, "that could change."

A strained chuckle ripped from Bethany's throat. "Don't make me laugh. It hurts."

More cars arrived and pulled in from all sides, throwing light around the entire area. An ambulance finally arrived and they backed up very near to where I sat cradling Bethany's head in my lap.

As the medics unpacked their gear and dragged a stretcher from the back of the ambulance, I watched Melvin and a patrol officer cautiously approach the downed suspect, who was lying on his face, his body twisted at an odd angle. Melvin kicked a gun from the suspect's grasp and then he bent to check for a pulse. He turned to look over his shoulder at me, shook his head. "He's ten-seven."

Great, I thought, now we'll never know what he wanted.

The two medics approached me and dropped their bags beside Bethany. "We've got her, Detective," one of them said.

I reluctantly stood and backed away to give them room to do their job. They removed Bethany's vest and tossed it to the side. "None of the bullets went through the vest," one of them announced.

I picked up the vest and watched with concern as they went to work on the bullet hole near her neck.

"Carter," Melvin called from the body. "Come check this out."

I hesitated. Bethany looked up into my eyes, smiled. "I'll be fine," she whispered. "Thanks to you."

I forced myself to walk across the street. "What is it?"

Melvin and the patrol officer were standing wide-eyed, staring down at the shooter. His face was pressed against the rough surface of the road and his right arm was extended at an odd angle. His right leg was pulled up and I could see part of his torso. "What the…"

I leaned closer to verify what my disbelieving eyes were seeing—a badge was clipped to the right side of his belt and a paddle holster was strapped to his waistband. We all traded befuddled looks in the flashing brilliance of the blue and red strobe lights. I swallowed hard. Had I just killed a cop?

With a hand that shook slightly, I grabbed the shooter's shoulder and pulled him over onto his back. He wore a blue ski mask. I reached for it and tugged. It slowly stretched off the shooter's face, and I jerked back when his face came into view.

"Oh my God!" Detective Ford screamed.

A group of patrol deputies and detectives rushed over to see what all the fuss was about. They skidded to a stop and sounded a collective, "Holy shit!" when they saw Captain Michael Theriot's lifeless eyes staring up at them from the dark pavement.

CHAPTER 28

After the initial shock wore off, I shook my head slowly. "This ain't good. This ain't good at all."

"What was he even doing here?" Melvin asked. "We were all told to stay away. What even happened? Why were y'all chasing him? And why'd you shoot him?"

"I don't know what the hell happened. He just approached Bethany from out of the darkness and opened fire. There was no warning." I nodded to his body. "Stand guard over him."

"London!" a voice yelled through the crowd of deputies. "London!"

It was Gina. She burst through the wall of officers and threw herself into my arms, squeezing tight. She pulled back. "Are you okay? I heard the call on the radio. They said an officer had been shot out by the park, but they didn't say who." Her eyes suddenly widened. "Oh, no…Bethany! Is she okay?"

I nodded and walked across the street to where the medics were still working on Bethany. Gina followed. She dropped beside one of the medics when we reached Bethany. "Are you okay?" There was genuine concern in her voice. I even thought I saw a little streak glistening down the side of her face.

Bethany smiled through the pain. "I'll be fine."

"She's ready for transport," one of the medics said.

I waved them off. "Give us a minute."

They walked away, and I squatted beside Gina, feeling for Bethany's hand. "The person who shot you…"

Bethany's eyebrows rose. "Yeah?"

I looked at Gina, then back to Bethany. "It was Captain Theriot."

Bethany gasped. "What? Wait…are you sure? It can't be! There's no way."

I pointed to the group of officers huddled around Theriot's body. "There he is—big as hell and deader than shit. It's him. He tried to kill you. I just need you to try and think of any reason why he would do this."

"How the hell would I know?" she asked. "You know as much as me. We came here to meet that caller… Hey, didn't you say there was a subject down in the park?"

I suddenly remembered the humanlike figure I'd seen on the sidewalk—and my sniper rifle up on the bridge. I bent and kissed Bethany on the forehead, staring directly in her eyes. "I don't know why this is happening or who's behind it, but every last one of those bastards will pay for the pain you felt and the blood you lost."

"You *are* a sweetheart, no matter how hard you try not to be." Bethany lifted a hand and rubbed my face. "Thanks for being here for me. It means a lot."

"Now, get your pretty ass up in that ambulance so you can get better." I stood and waved the medics over. "She's ready."

They lifted the spine board onto a gurney and wheeled her toward the ambulance.

"Melvin," I called to the detective, "can you run up to the bridge and grab my rifle? It's up on the catwalk."

"Can I shoot it?" he asked eagerly.

I pulled the bolt from my pocket and held it up. "Be kind of hard to shoot it without this."

Melvin smiled sheepishly. "It was worth a try."

I then turned to Gina. "Can you drive me to the park? We have to check something out."

"The *downed* subject Bethany mentioned?"

I nodded. "I can't be sure, but I thought I saw a body lying on the sidewalk. It looked like there was a pool of blood around it."

We hurried through the maze of officers and cars and jumped into Gina's car. I pulled off my earpiece and dialed the sheriff's number. As it rang, I moved it away and leaned toward Gina. "Captain Theriot was coming from the area of the body, so he might have had something to do with—"

"Hello? London? What the hell is going on?" Sheriff Burke barked. "I've been calling and calling, but I can't get anyone to respond. Is it true that we have an officer down?"

"Two…we have two officers down."

"Jesus Christ…will the shit ever end?" He let off a long sigh. "Okay, who are they and what happened?"

"Lieutenant Riggs and Captain Theriot. We were—"

"Theriot?" Sheriff Burke echoed loudly. "What are you talking about? Michael's here at the main office."

"No, he's not."

There was a long pause from the other end. Finally, the sheriff said, more to himself, "What the hell was he doing out there? He was supposed to be here."

"I'm not sure what he was doing here, but I think I'm about to find out."

Gina had just pulled into the park and I pointed her toward the area of the park where I thought I'd seen the body. She angled her unmarked car so the headlights shone across the park.

"Was this a trap?" Burke asked. "Did that bastard call just to set y'all up?"

"Yeah, it was a trap, but Captain Theriot's the one who set it. He opened fire on Lieutenant Riggs. She confronted him in the park, and he just opened up on her."

"What did you say?" Burke asked incredulously. "Did you say he tried to kill Riggs?"

"Yep, but he didn't. She took some shots to the vest and one to the side of her neck, but it looks like she'll be fine." I pointed to where the figure was, and said to Gina, "Turn a little that way."

"What? Turn where?" Burke demanded.

"Nothing, Sheriff. I was talking to Detective Pellegrin. We've got another body in the park—probably our contact. We need to go check on it."

"But what about Michael? Did he say why he did that? And how bad is he hurt?"

"He's dead," I said. "I had to kill him."

"*You* killed him? Why? What the hell's going on here? I've lost four captains in a week and we're no closer to finding the killer than we were on day one. This shit is spinning out of control. If we don't wrap this case up soon, the Feds are going to come in here and take over. We've got to get a handle on this shit. Damn!" There was another long pause. "What the hell is going on, London?"

"I'm not sure what's going on, Sheriff, but it's bad. I think Captain Theriot came out here to kill our contact, but we interrupted him. He's mixed up in this case, but I'm not exactly sure how."

"Do you think he was behind the sniper attacks?" the sheriff asked.

"He didn't have the opportunity to take the shots on Abbott and Landry, but it doesn't mean he's not involved."

"How'd it go down? What exactly happened out there?"

I hurriedly explained. "Bethany got into a running gun battle with him across town. She got shot before I could catch up to them. When I got there he was fleeing and I took him out."

Gina's headlights settled on the humanlike figure sprawled on the sidewalk and I gave her a thumb's up. She threw the car in Park.

"Sheriff, we should know more in a minute." I stepped out of Gina's car. "I'll call you when I find out who this guy is." I flipped my phone shut and stuffed it in my pocket, turned to Gina. "You ready?"

She nodded, and we created some distance between each other and made our way toward the body, scanning the area as we went. There were no sounds except for the bayou water lapping against the fishing wharf. Step by step we moved, closer and closer. When I finally stood directly over the body, I nudged it with my foot. Nothing. I crouched beside it and felt for a pulse. Nothing. I holstered my pistol and pulled a flashlight from my back pocket. I shined it around the body. The man had been shot several times in the back from a distance and then twice in the back of the head from close range, while he lay on the ground.

"Captain Theriot did this? *Our* Captain Theriot?" Gina asked. "This is some cold-blooded shit."

I reached into the man's back pocket and removed his wallet. The driver's license told me he was Wesley Guidry—white male, fifty-seven years old. I held it for Gina to see. "Know him?"

She shook her head. "Never seen him before. He's definitely not my type."

"What *is* your type?" I asked as I scanned the area immediately surrounding the body.

"Do you really want to know?"

"Absolutely."

Gina smiled. "You'll just have to keep wanting."

I looked over my shoulder, but couldn't see her facial expression in the night. "Are you toying with me?"

"Maybe."

Something golden sparkled on the ground against the light from my flashlight. I leaned closer. "I've got some spent shell casings."

Gina moved beside me. "They're tiny."

"Yeah, they look like thirty-two caliber casings." I rubbed my chin, my face twisted in confusion. "Captain Theriot pulled a forty caliber pistol on Bethany—this guy was shot with a thirty-two."

"That's not unusual," Gina said. "He probably killed this guy with a drop gun and had plans on ditching it somewhere…or planting it on someone. Y'all surprised him, so he probably just instinctively pulled his duty pistol from his holster. Also, he knows enough about guns to know you don't get in a shootout with a thirty-two pistol. They're okay for close-range surprise assassinations, but they're not worth a shit in a gun battle."

That made sense. I bent back toward Guidry's body and searched him thoroughly, trying to locate the documents he had mentioned on the phone. Nothing. Other than his wallet, he had a set of keys and a pack of gum. "The documents aren't here. I knew that bastard was lying."

"What about Captain Theriot?" Gina asked. "What if he took the documents after he shot him? Didn't you say you saw him coming from this direction?"

"Yeah, he was coming from here. He could have the documents, I guess."

Gina jerked her portable radio from her belt and called Lieutenant Corey Chiasson, who had arrived at the scene of Captain Theriot's shooting and taken charge of the investigation. "LT, can you search Theriot's body to see if he's got any documents on him?"

"Ten-four," Corey called back. After a few minutes, he came back on the radio. "He's got nothing on his person but his wallet, a pack of cigarettes, a lighter and a cheap pistol—a thirty-two caliber."

"That's the murder weapon," I said.

Gina nodded and keyed up her portable. "LT, we've got a murder victim here—shot with a thirty-two pistol."

"Roger that," Corey called. "We'll recover the pistol, and I'll send someone over to process that scene for y'all."

"Ten-four…thanks." Gina fastened her portable radio to her belt and began performing a grid search east of the body. She'd made her way to a dried-out pedestal birdbath that was made of cement. "Hey, I found something here!"

CHAPTER 29

I rushed to where Gina stood. There—at the center of the birdbath—was a small stack of charred paper. The secret document our mystery caller had promised! "Shit!" I blurted. "Can you salvage any of it?"

Gina pulled an ink pen from her pocket and carefully sifted through the pile of ash, training her flashlight on the edges of the paper that hadn't been touched by the flame. "Most of it's burned to shit," she said idly, "but I can read some of the corners."

"What's it say?" I leaned over her shoulder, nearly brushing against her back, straining to see for myself. "Can you make it out?"

"In this corner"—she touched the upper right corner of the top page—"there's what appears to be some kind of letter and number combination, maybe a license plate number?"

"What's the number?"

"It looks like I, dash, zero, nine, zero, two, three, dash, ninety-one—whatever that means."

I pursed my lips, thinking. "When I first started with the sheriff's office, we used to write our case numbers like that. If I remember right, the letter represents the month, the five-digit number represents the total number of complaints up to that point, and the two-digit number represents the year."

Gina studied the number. "So, this case would have happened in September of nineteen ninety-one?"

"Yeah…twenty plus years ago. Can you make out anything else?"

"No, that's it."

"What about the other pages?"

"It looks like there're five pages total and they all have the same number at the top, right. Everything else has been reduced to ash."

I punched the sheriff's number into my cell phone. When he answered, his voice was tired. "Please tell me you've got good news this time," he said wearily.

"Sorry, but the supposed secret documents have been destroyed. It looks like Captain Theriot got to them and burned them."

"Are you sure?"

"I'm looking at them as we speak."

"Are they completely destroyed?"

"Everything but an old case number—I, dash, zero, nine, zero, two, three, dash, ninety-one," I said. "Does that sound familiar to you?"

"Please, London, I can't remember what I ate for breakfast this morning. Do you really expect me to recognize a case number from twenty years ago?"

"Yeah, you've got a point." I looked back at the body of Wesley Guidry. "Oh, by the way, do you recognize the name Wesley Guidry?"

There was a long moment of silence. Finally, Sheriff Burke cleared his throat. "What does Wesley have to do with this?"

"He's the dead guy. Apparently, he's the one who made the anonymous call. Do you know him?"

"Wesley Guidry was a detective when I was a narcotics agent. He quit the department about twenty years ago." After another moment of silence, the sheriff asked, more to himself than to me, "What the hell was he trying to do?"

"Did he have a beef with Captain Landry and all?"

"Not that I ever heard about."

"You know, Captain Theriot thought he recognized the caller's voice on the phone this morning. Did you?"

"Did I what?"

"Did you also recognize his voice?"

"No. Why?"

"Just wondering." I watched Gina try to get all the ashes into a plastic evidence bag. "Sheriff, what about Captain Theriot and Guidry? Did they ever have problems?"

"I don't know."

"What kind of marksmen were they?"

"Average at best," Sheriff Burke scoffed. "They would both struggle each year just to shoot a minimum score on their firearms recertification."

"Thank God for that," I said. "If Theriot would've been a better shot, Bethany might not have been so lucky."

When Sheriff Burke didn't respond, I asked him if he was still there. There was a long sigh on the other end of the phone. "I don't know what to do anymore. It seems like my entire world is caving in. I've got cops turning in their badges nearly every day; my captains can't show their faces in public for fear that they'll get them shot off; the governor's calling to find out what the hell is going on; the media is crawling all over this parish making crazy accusations. I don't know, London. I'm thinking about throwing in the towel and letting the Feds come in and take over this whole mess."

"Don't even think of it," I said heatedly. "Give me more time—"

"For what? So more of us can die?"

"Sheriff, first of all, inviting the Feds in here won't keep anyone safe. Second, I think this Wesley Guidry knew something and—"

"Wesley ain't talking. He's dead!"

"Yeah, he's dead, but he already provided a major break in the case. We have a complaint number that'll more than likely let us know why this shit is happening. Once we know *why* it's happening, we'll know *who* is doing it." I paused. When he didn't say anything, I continued. "My guess is that we'll find even more information at his house. At least give me a chance to toss his house and do some research on that complaint number. If I don't turn up anything solid within a few days, then I'll step aside and let you call in whoever you want to call in."

"Wait, did you just say you'll *let* me call in the Feds? Are you forgetting I'm the sheriff and you're the deputy?"

"Not at all, but you did say you owed me for saving your life, so I figured this was me cashing in on that debt."

There was another long sigh from the other end of the phone. "Okay…two days. If you don't find anything definitive, we're pulling out and letting the Feds get involved. Maybe they'll burn the whole place down like they did in Waco and we'll be able to come back in here and start all over, clean slate and all."

When I hung up with the sheriff, I called the radio room. A dispatcher answered in a strained voice.

"Hey, this is London. Can you check an item number for me?"

"Sure. What is it?"

"I, dash, zero, nine, zero, two, three, dash, ninety-one."

The phone went silent except for the tapping of computer keys. "Nothing," she finally said. "No record at all. I'm kind of new here, so let me check with my supervisor to see if I'm missing something."

A second later, Mallory, a dispatcher with almost thirty years, got on the line. "London, we won't have anything from that far back. We would've destroyed it."

"What? Why on earth would y'all have done that?"

"Sheriff's orders. A few years back he ordered us to destroy everything prior to him taking office in 2000. We were running out of storage space, so he ordered the mass destruction. We went out to the hospital and used their incinerator—"

"Shit, Mal...we need that information."

"Sorry, there's nothing I can do about that."

My mind raced. "Hey, you've worked here forever. What do you make of the shit that's going on? You have any theories about why this is happening?"

"Hold on...I've got another call." The phone went quiet, clicked and then Mallory was back. "We were on a recorded line, and I don't want anyone hearing what I'm about to say. Look, I don't know if I should be saying anything, but I think I need to tell you something. It means nothing to me, but it might mean something to you." There was a pause and then she continued. "I'm not sure what's going on, but I'm good friends with Carmella and she's been acting a little strange lately, ever since the killings started."

"What do you mean by *strange?*"

"She won't go into any details, but she says this is some sort of revenge killing spree and she thinks her turn's coming."

"By *her turn,* she means..."

"She's going to be killed. I told her it was nonsense, but she insists that this is the past coming back to haunt them."

"Did she ever say who's included in *them?*"

"No, and I don't think she ever will. Whoever they are, she seemed to be afraid of them."

I pondered this information. Captain Carmella Vizier had spoken up in the meeting, but she had been shot down by Captain Theriot. Why? What did they both know? "Did she and Captain Theriot get along?"

"She hated him. In fact, I think he's the person she was most afraid of."

"Will she talk to me?"

"God, no...and please don't tell her I told you. She spoke to me in confidence."

Confused, I asked, "But why are you telling me all of this?"

"You killed Captain Theriot, so you can't be a part of *them.*"

I flipped my phone shut and filled Gina in on what I'd learned. She listened while sealing the evidence bag that contained the remnants of the burned document. "Let's talk to her when we get back," she suggested.

"Mallory doesn't want her to know that she told me."

"She doesn't have to know. We can bring all of the commanders in one at a time and interview them. When we get to her, we can just work her until we get the information. With Theriot dead, she might be willing to spill it."

"I don't know…"

With a gloved hand, Gina held up the set of keys I'd recovered from Wesley Guidry's pocket. "Hey"—her face twisted into a scowl—"where's his car?"

I glanced around, trying to penetrate the surrounding darkness with my eyes. The keys jingled in Gina's hands. A second later, headlights flashed in the distance and the faint sound of a horn blowing twice disrupted the tranquility of the night. I pointed toward the Payneville Bridge. "There it is—under the bridge! Good thinking."

"It's just habit," Gina said, slipping the keys in an evidence bag. "I have to use the keyless remote to find my car every time I go shopping."

Just then, Detective Melvin Ford drove up and parked near Gina's car. We met him as he was stepping out of his unmarked cruiser, and he handed me my rifle. "Thanks a bunch," I said and shoved my thumb in the direction of the body. "Can you keep an eye on our victim—make sure he doesn't go anywhere?"

Melvin stifled a chuckle. "Yeah, no problem."

"Lieutenant Chiasson's sending a team up to work the scene," Gina offered. "We're heading up there"—she pointed along River Road—"to check out the dead guy's car. After that, we're heading to his house."

"Cool," Melvin said. "Want me to meet y'all at the house when the crime scene team gets here?"

I nodded, as I shoved my rifle in the back seat of Gina's car. "The address is two zero six Dustin Street."

We jumped in Gina's car and she shot up River Road, then stopped under the bridge beside the truck. It was new, but dirty. Gina pressed the UNLOCK button on the keyless remote through the evidence bag and the locks popped up. I pulled on a pair of latex gloves and carefully opened the driver's door. Gina entered through the passenger's door, and we sifted through the clutter in Wesley

Guidry's truck for over an hour, but found nothing that brought us any closer to finding out why our captains were being targeted.

"Ready to check out his house?" Gina asked, tossing a stack of old receipts back into the ashtray.

"Yeah," I said.

A wrecker driver was waiting across the street with orders to tow the truck to our motor pool. A patrol deputy was waiting with the driver and it was his job to escort the wrecker. Fifteen minutes earlier, Captain Theriot's unmarked detective car had been located two blocks away and had already been secured in the evidence garage at our motor pool.

I waved the wrecker driver and the deputy over and slapped the hood of the truck. "She's all ready to go."

As they made preparations to tow Guidry's truck, Gina and I slipped into her car. She turned off River onto Sixth and sped to Dustin Street. When we found his house, I had to look twice at the faded number on the mailbox. "At least," I said, staring at the knee-high grass that surrounded a wooden house in desperate need of a facelift, "the house is messy like his truck."

Gina picked her way across the dew-drenched grass, swatting at the army of mosquitoes that rose up to greet her, and cursed under her breath. "Would it have killed him to cut his grass?"

"Nope, but not cutting it did." I followed Gina to a set of shaky steps. She donned a pair of gloves and removed the keys from the evidence bag and inserted one in the doorknob. After wiggling it in the keyhole, she was finally able to get the door open. An unfamiliar stench emanated from the doorway. Gina grimaced and covered her nose as we entered. She flipped the light switch and gasped. There were dirty dishes piled high in the sink, on the countertops and on the table. There were two garbage bags filled with trash on the floor and a third bag was still in the can, but it was overflowing. A few aluminum beer cans, a milk jug and a frozen pizza box were on the floor around the garbage can. The living room was littered with dirty clothes, newspapers, old frozen food cartons and more beer cans.

"Do we have to search this place?" Gina wailed. "I mean seriously…this is a health hazard."

"Who lives like this?" I kicked an old bottle of orange juice out of the way as I walked across the kitchen. I pulled open the freezer. A few ice trays had been shoved in randomly and the inner walls of the freezer were covered with yellow ice from an exploding can of beer. A few frozen dinners occupied the rest of the space in the small compartment. The refrigerator was no better. A few packs of sandwich meat—two of them expired—and a jug of milk were among a horde of plastic containers that held leftover food. "Wesley's housecleaner must've died twenty years ago and he never got around to hiring another one."

"From the smell of this place," Gina agreed, "her body's still in here somewhere."

We slogged through the house, searching one room and then the other, making sure to touch and examine every object in the place. We had finished his bedroom and were about to walk out the hallway when Gina pointed to a door at the end of the hallway. "Did you check that closet?"

I shook my head, idly pushed a pile of dirty clothes aside with my foot and turned the knob. When I opened the door, I was surprised to find a spacious—but neat—room on the other side. This closet had been converted into an office and it seemed to be the only clean space in the entire house. A wooden desk and a row of filing cabinets lined the far wall. A computer monitor, a laser printer and a yellowed stack of newspapers were positioned neatly on the desktop. On a shelf above the desk was a row of books propped in place by a large three-ring binder.

Gina whistled as she entered behind me. "It looks like we're walking through a portal into an alternate universe."

I sifted through the newspaper articles. "These are all from 1991, with the—"

"Holy Smokies!"

I turned. Gina had shut the door we'd just entered and was gawking at a faded newspaper cutout taped to the back side of the door. It was a full-page article and there were a dozen photographs on it. I moved beside her and read the newspaper heading:

DEPUTIES TO TESTIFY IN FEDERAL COURT TODAY

There was a caption beneath the photographs: *Top Row: Anthony Landry, Trevor Abbott, Matt Garcia, Michael Theriot, Martin Thomas and Tyrone Gibbs; Bottom Row: Carmella Vizier, Lawrence Doucet, Ronald Day, Calvin Burke, Justin Wainwright and Wesley Guidry.*

The only commander not listed was Captain Carl Boutin—the commander of the detention center. I scanned the pictures. They were all younger, slimmer, had more hair and—

I suddenly froze. Abbott, Landry and Wainwright's pictures were crossed out. This was the hit list!

CHAPTER 30

"The date on the clipping is February third, 1992," Gina said. "The complaint number on the burnt document was from 1991. That can't be a coincidence."

I nodded and walked back to the desk, sifting through the pile of newspapers until I found the earliest date—September 7, 1991. There on the front page, above the fold, was what we'd all been looking for...a motive for the sniper killings. I read the story with mouth agape, heart pounding. When I reached the end of page one, I hurried and flipped to page five, where it continued. When I finished the article, I slowly shook my head, then handed the paper to Gina. "This is it."

As Gina read, I heard boots pounding along the hallway outside the door, drawing nearer. I palmed my pistol and pulled the door open—

"Whoa there, tiger!" It was Detective Sally Piatkowski. "It's just your friendly neighborhood detectives coming to offer a hand with this mess."

Detective Melvin Ford walked up behind her.

"What's going on back at the scene?" I asked.

"Lieutenant Chiasson's been on the phone with Sheriff Burke," Sally explained, "and Sheriff Burke put him in charge of the detective division. He's the new captain."

"The way they've been dropping," Melvin blurted, "I think I would've turned the promotion down. Being a captain around here is more dangerous than tongue kissing a cobra."

We all snickered, and Sally continued, "*Captain* Chiasson has crime scene teams at each of the locations and they're both almost done processing them. There were no real surprises at the scenes. We"—Sally shoved her thumb in Melvin's direction—"went to the motor pool and searched that ex-cop's car, but we didn't find anything worth noting."

I stepped back so they could enter the office. When they were inside, I closed the door behind them and pointed to the article. "Check this shit out."

Their mouths dropped open in unison as they realized what they were looking at. "That guy in the park—Wesley what's-his-name—is he the killer?" Melvin asked.

I shook my head. "He was a target."

"So was Captain Theriot." Sally looked at me and then turned back toward the clipping. "You and Captain Theriot helped the killer move one step closer to accomplishing his goals." She traced a crisscross pattern over Theriot's picture with her index finger and then did the same over Guidry's picture. "That's five down and only seven left to go."

"I bet he's saving Sheriff Burke for last," Melvin mused.

"Yeah, well, he'll never make it to him because"—I nodded toward Gina, who was reading the articles—"we now know his motive and we'll be able to identify him soon."

"What is the—" Sally began, but was cut off by Gina's outburst.

"They killed a *baby?*" Her face was red with rage. "It's no wonder they're being gunned down."

That got Melvin and Sally's immediate attention and they scrambled to read over Gina's shoulder. Gina surrendered the paper when she was done and turned to me. "How in the hell was this not the very first thing that came to their minds when this shit started happening?"

"I have no clue," I said. "But it explains why they're barricaded in the main office, scared to death to show their faces."

Sally's mouth dropped open as she read. "I never heard about this!"

"I was in high school when this happened," Melvin said. "I remember my mom and dad talking about it."

None of the earlier stories mentioned the names of the family or the officers involved, but when I got to the newspaper articles that covered the preliminary court proceedings, I caught a break that sent chills down my back. I read it quickly at first and then went back over it more carefully. When I'd reached the end of the article, I sighed. "You were wrong, Gina."

"About what?" Gina had moved to the filing cabinets where she and Sally were digging through one of the drawers. Neither of them even looked up at me.

"James five-sixteen is not a Bible verse." I now had the attention of the whole room. I paused, allowing that revelation to sink in.

Gina had stopped what she was doing and she now waved her hand impatiently. "Well, what the hell is it? You know I hate to wait for shit, so hurry and tell me."

"The house they hit was located at five-sixteen Cottonwood Street. The family that lived in the house…guess what their last name was?"

Gina stared blankly. "What? What is it?"

"James?" Sarah blurted, her eyes widening as realization set in.

"Bingo," I replied.

Gina's mouth dropped almost to the floor. "No kidding?"

"James five-sixteen—big as shit." I turned the article so they could read for themselves. "The dad's name is Lenny James and the mom's name is Michelle. Wait a minute—Lenny James…" I scratched my head, scanning the recesses of my memory. "For some reason, that name's familiar to me. Shit, I can't figure out why I know it."

"You'll remember tonight when you're sitting on the toilet and not even thinking about it anymore," Melvin said.

I shook my head to clear it. "Anyway, this is the reason the captains are being killed, and there's no way in hell they didn't know what this shit was about. They've been holding out on us. The night we found Wainwright's body and that message in the field… From that very moment they knew what this was about."

"But why would they keep that from us?" Gina wanted to know. "I find it hard to believe they would've intentionally kept this quiet if it meant more of them being killed. This case is their best chance of stopping the killings, so why not tell us about it? I just don't think they realized what it stood for. After all, it was twenty years ago, and they've done a lot of shit since then."

I considered her point, as I began reading over the news articles that detailed Sheriff Burke's testimony in federal court. "What if they lied in court? What if the lady's the one telling the truth? What if there's a lot more to the story than what the sheriff and all testified about?"

Gina scowled. "You think they'd commit perjury and risk going to prison? That's a hell of a risk."

"Unless telling the truth would land them a longer prison sentence," I said. "After all, Wesley Guidry did say he had some original documents that would prove what really happened that night." I hefted the newspaper from September 7, 1991. "There's no doubt this is the night he was talking about, and I'm betting those documents would've burned the sheriff's ass—or at least Captain Theriot's ass."

The room went silent. I thought I heard a few gulps as I spelled out my suspicions. Finally, Melvin spoke up, but it was barely over a whisper. "Are you accusing the sheriff and his entire command staff of being involved in a cover-up? Those are serious allegations against the man who signs your paycheck."

"It's a stamp," I said.

Melvin's face twisted in confusion. "What's a stamp?"

"His signature on the check—it's not his signature. It's a stamp. He doesn't even see the checks. His secretary stamps his signature on all the checks." I waved my hand to dismiss the issue. "But that's irrelevant. What is relevant—and quite telling—is the fact Captain Theriot *murdered* a man who claimed to have a document revealing the truth behind these sniper killings. If that truth is worth killing for, it's got to be bad...*really* bad."

No one spoke for a while. We all stood there staring at each other. Gina finally broke the silence. "Let's say you're right. What do we do? How do we take down the chief law enforcement officer of the parish, with absolutely no evidence?"

"Good question," I admitted.

"Couldn't we be fired just for talking like this?" Sally asked. "I heard the sheriff fired a couple of deputies a few years ago because they were complaining about something stupid—like the stripes on the squad cars—and they said the sheriff didn't know what he was doing."

"That's true," Melvin said. "I worked with one of the guys. He was a good cop, but the sheriff didn't care. One of the brass overheard them complaining and told the sheriff. He fired their asses on the spot."

The room went quiet. Sally and Melvin stared at each other, their faces slightly paler. Gina's jaw was set. She stared directly at me, her eyes unwavering. "I was looking for a job when I got this one," she said. "If he's dirty, I don't want anything to do with him."

I grinned. "I love the way you think." I turned to Sally and Melvin. "What about y'all? Are y'all in or out? If we find out the sheriff and his command staff committed a crime, are y'all going to stand up for what's right? Will y'all move against them with us?"

Sally swallowed hard. "We're *his* deputies and we get our powers from him, so what exactly can we do? Who would believe us over him and his captains and majors? They've got more clout than we'll ever have."

"Could be what the killer was thinking," I said. "He probably figured his only real chance at justice was to start assassinating them. But we need to show him there's another way. If we uncover evidence proving the sheriff is involved in some sort of crime and cover up, we'll take him into custody and contact the district attorney."

"What if they resist?" Sally wanted to know. "What if Sheriff Burke tells some of his more than three hundred deputies to take *us* into custody? What then?"

"We'll have to keep this quiet and take him by surprise." I studied their faces one at a time, the severity of the situation casting worry lines on all of them. "We can count on Lieutenant Riggs and the entire sniper team to help us out, and I have a few buddies on the SWAT team who'll stand with us if I ask."

"Lieutenant—I mean *Captain*—Chiasson's above board," Gina offered. "He'll assist us."

Melvin rubbed his face. "I can't believe we're even having this conversation. This is crazy! Do you realize what you're saying, London?"

"I know full well what I'm saying." I looked into his eyes. "If we develop evidence that proves Sheriff Burke has been involved in the commission of a felony, I'm going to arrest him...and everyone who stands in my way. You'd better think long and hard about what you do next. When the earth opens up, you don't want to be standing on the wrong side of the crack."

Melvin took in a deep breath, held it for a moment, and then exhaled. "Okay, if you find evidence—*convincing* evidence—that proves Sheriff Burke is dirty, I'm in. *But*...I won't risk my job over suppositions or theories, only hard evidence."

I nodded. "Fair enough."

"I'm in, too," Sally said.

I tossed the newspaper to the desktop. "Great. Can y'all finish up here? I want to head to the hospital and check on Bethany. And I want to run this by her. I'm sure she'll have some thoughts on what to do...how to approach the sheriff and all."

"I'll come with you," Gina said hurriedly.

I shook my head. "I need you to stay here and spearhead the search. You and I were first in and made the discovery, so it's best if one of us hangs around. You've also been involved early on in the case, so you know what to look for."

"Why don't you stay here and I go to the hospital?" she suggested.

I held out my hand, ignoring her comment. "I'll need your car."

"How am I going to get back to the office?"

"Melvin or Sally can bring you to the park to pick up Bethany's car."

"This is bullshit."

"Your keys, please," I insisted.

Gina bristled, as she dug her keys out of her tight jeans. She flung them at me and turned back to the stack of newspapers, muttering under her breath. I couldn't be sure, but I thought she said something about me going screw myself.

CHAPTER 31

Bethany's eyes were closed, face relaxed, hair spilled across her pillow. The bed sheet had been pulled up to her shoulders and a thick bandage bulged from under her hospital gown, enclosing the wound on her neck. I walked into the dimly lit room, where medical equipment hummed quietly, and sidled up to the side of her bed. I leaned over and brushed my fingers across her forehead. Her eyes opened and she recoiled in brief horror.

"Oh, God," she breathed the words. "It's you."

"Who else would it be?"

She touched her chest and sighed. "I don't know, but you scared the shit out of me."

"Sorry about that." I pulled a chair close to the side of her bed, dropped in it and leaned my forearms on the bedrail. "There's been a major break in the case that we need to discuss."

Bethany pulled herself more upright. "What is it? Hurry...tell me."

"Twenty years ago, on September seventh, 1991, the sheriff and all the current commanders—except for Captain Boutin—were involved in a drug raid where a baby was killed. They had—"

"How do you know that? Where'd this information come from?"

"Wesley Guidry's house. We found a stack of newspaper articles dealing with the incident, along with a hit list taped on the door to his office. He'd crossed out the pictures of Wainwright, Landry and Abbott."

"Who in the hell is Wesley Guidry?"

"He's the dead guy in the park...the guy Captain Theriot killed."

"Do you think he's the sniper?"

"Definitely not. I think he was trying to blow the lid on a cover up."

"Cover up? What kind of cover up?"

"I'm not sure, but"—I raised my eyebrows—"I was hoping you could figure it out for me. After all, you're the brains of the operation."

"I'll try. Tell me about the raid."

"Sheriff Burke—a narcotics agent at the time—was heading up a drug case and had sent an undercover officer into a house to purchase drugs. Later that day, he prepared a search warrant and a judge signed it. Burke requested the SWAT team's assistance in executing the search warrant because it was a no-knock warrant. They approached the house in the early morning hours on the next day— the paper said it was two o'clock AM—and they crept through the front yard and made it to the front door with no incident. One of the officers crashed the door down with the battering ram and the other officers filed into the house.

"According to court testimony, one of the officers tossed a flash bang into the back bedroom, where the suspect was known to hang out with his semi-automatic rifle and several handguns, and, at that point, all hell broke loose."

I took a deep breath, continued. "According to the wife's statement to the media later that morning, the flash bang landed in a baby crib, where her three-month-old baby was sleeping, and it went off, killing the baby. She said her husband jumped up out of bed and tried to rush to the baby crib, but one of the officers cracked him across the skull with the butt of his rifle. When the husband tried to defend himself against what he believed to be a home invasion, one of the officers fired at him with what she described as machine gun fire. He died at the scene along with the baby."

"How'd he try to defend himself?" Bethany asked.

"According to the wife, he was unarmed and he simply tried to push what he thought was an intruder out the door...and they killed him for it."

"What about the wife?" Bethany asked. "What happened to her?"

"She was arrested and charged with possession with intent to distribute cocaine, resisting an officer and attempted murder of a police officer."

"Attempted murder? What did she do to warrant *that?*"

"According to the officers at the scene, the husband brandished a gun and they had to shoot him in self-defense. When the husband went down, the wife picked up the gun and took a shot at them, so that's where the attempted murder came from."

"Why didn't they shoot her, too, if she took a shot at them?"

"That question was actually posed to them at a hearing and they—actually, it was Sheriff Burke who answered it—testified that other officers were in the crossfire, so they were forced to tackle her to the ground."

Bethany leaned back and bit her lower lip. "So, the cops are saying the husband had a gun and the wife is saying he didn't?"

"Right, but that's not all. The wife claimed she never did drugs in her life and neither did her husband. She said she'd never even seen cocaine and she offered to take a drug test. The newspaper reporter described her statement as a 'tearful and heart-wrenching plea for justice.'"

"This statement was made before her arrest?"

"No." I shook my head. "She made it to the media during the suspect walk. I think they probably regretted walking her out in front of the media because she began running off at the mouth and they were unable to shut her up."

"So, she denied selling drugs to the undercover agent?"

"Not only does she deny the allegation, but she says they royally screwed up by hitting the wrong house. She claims the house they were supposed to hit was the one across the street."

"Was there any validity to that claim?"

"The reporter did some digging and found that the police had been called out to the house across the street a dozen or so times for various complaints—including suspicion of drug activity. So, it looks like the wife might've been telling the truth." I took a deep breath. "Of course, that didn't do her much good. A grand jury indicted her on all counts and she was held in jail on a one million dollar bond."

"Where is she now? What happened with the trial?"

"As of the latest article we found, the lady hadn't been tried. It seems she had a mental breakdown in jail and had to be hospitalized after a failed attempt at suicide. She was deemed incapable of assisting in her own defense and was unable to stand trial. For all we know, she could still be in a mental institution today."

Bethany was silent for a few moments. "This could all be a coincidence and one might have nothing to do with the other."

I smiled smugly. "But you haven't heard the real kicker yet."

"What is it?"

"The house the cops hit that night—it was located at five-sixteen Cottonwood Street and the family's last name was James."

Bethany's eyes widened. "James five-sixteen!"

"Our killer was pointing us directly to that night—to that incident. And you know what's even worse?"

"What?"

"I think the sheriff knew all along what it meant. I think they've been holding out on us."

Bethany scowled. "Why would they do that? It would be suicide."

I glanced over my shoulder to be sure no one had entered the hospital room. "Look, Captain Theriot wouldn't take a shit without Sheriff Burke approving it. I think Theriot's been riding the coattails of this investigation waiting for us to make a break in the case. I think they were waiting for us to uncover who's doing this so they can take him out...kill him to shut him up. I think that woman might have been telling the truth about them hitting the wrong house."

"I don't know, London. Those are serious allegations."

"I know, but it's the only thing making sense right now. Think about it—Captain Theriot beat us to Wesley Guidry and killed him. If they all told the truth back then, if they didn't do anything wrong, why kill Wesley? I'll tell you why—because he was about to expose them. He said he had the only proof about what *really* happened that night. That means the rest of them are lying."

"What if this Wesley guy was a nut?"

"Well, this incident definitely happened—we have an ass-load of newspaper articles to prove it—and I can say with confidence there's a correlation between the incident and the sniper killings. I also believe the sheriff knows more than he's saying and I plan to confront him when I get back to the office."

"Do you really think he'll just come out and admit that twenty years ago they covered up the murder of a baby? During an election year?" She shook her head. "No way. Besides, you'd have to believe every cop out there was dirty and they all lied about that night. Look, you said Captain Landry was like a father to you. Do you really think he'd be involved with something like this?"

I tried to look at the situation from every angle, searching for a hole in my theory, but I couldn't find one. "Do you know how driven and committed a person has to be to wage war on the police? This sniper has signed his own death warrant and he knows it, but he doesn't care. He feels his actions are totally justified. To my way of thinking, it can only mean one thing...the cops hit the wrong house and then lied about it. It's the type of emotionally charged injustice that can lead even a good person to believe he has the right to carry out his revenge.

"If the James family were truly drug dealers, I don't believe these killings would have started. The sniper would've understood the James family was to blame for the death of their own child—they were the ones who brought the police to their home—and it would've been the end of it. Sure, whoever he is, he would've been distraught, probably for a long time, but he wouldn't have lived for twenty years just to randomly wage a war against the officers involved with the incident…not unless the allegations the mother raised were true."

"What if it's not true, but the killer perceived it to be true and is killing cops for nothing? For something they didn't do?"

"Ah, that's certainly a possibility. A perceived injustice can be just as powerful a motivator as an actual injustice." I smiled. "That's why I wanted to come here and talk to you. You have a way of bringing order to the chaos that is my brain."

Bethany held up a hand. "Now, don't go acquitting them just yet. I'm only saying it's *possible* the sheriff and all were telling the truth and we should investigate further before coming to any conclusions. Of course, if they were telling the truth, why would they be so afraid of Wesley Guidry? To the point of having to kill him?"

"You're right," I said, nodding in agreement. "Wesley Guidry was definitely killed because he knew too much and he was about to expose them. There's always the possibility Captain Theriot acted alone, but I seriously doubt it."

"I agree."

I sat thoughtful for a moment and then asked, "What would you suggest if we found evidence implicating the sheriff in the commission of a crime?"

"I'd suggest taking him down. It doesn't matter who you are—if you break the law, you need to pay the price. No one is above the law."

"I was hoping you'd say that."

"But I don't think we'll ever find any evidence and I know he'll never confess to anything," Bethany said. She started to speak again, but broke out into a fit of coughing. She winced in extreme pain. I jumped to my feet, leaned over her and placed my hand on her shoulder. "Are you okay?"

She nodded weakly. "They took X-rays, but I haven't heard from the doctors yet. They think a few ribs are cracked from the impact of the bullets."

"What about your neck?"

"The bullet went clean through. Like you said, it didn't hit anything important." She started to chuckle, but winced again. When the pain had subsided, her eyes turned warm and she reached for my hand. "You saved my life out there—first by giving me the ballistic vest and then when you shot Captain Theriot. After all of this shit is done, I'll look forward to spending the rest of my life trying to repay you."

While the prospect of a long-term relationship with Bethany Riggs sounded extremely appealing, it was overshadowed by the guilt I felt. I frowned, staring at my hands. "No, I let you down. I'm the one who placed you in danger. I told you I'd protect you, but I didn't. If it wouldn't be for luck, you'd be..." I shook my head. "You'd be dead."

Bethany squeezed my hand and pulled me close to her. I stared into her moist eyes. "I'm a cop, even though you don't think I'm a real one," she chided playfully, "and I'm fully aware of the risks associated with my job. I went into that situation with my eyes wide open and it wasn't luck that saved my ass—it was *you*."

I cracked half a smile. "And what a nice ass it is."

Bethany feigned shock and lifted her arm to smack my stomach, but suddenly clutched her torso. "Damn, I've got to remember this rib."

"Yeah, I don't like seeing you—"

A knock at the hospital door behind me interrupted my comment. I turned to see a nurse in pink scrubs. "Hey, can I borrow my favorite patient? We need to redo the X-rays."

"Sure." I turned back to Bethany. "Do they know how long you'll be here?"

Bethany looked at the nurse. "What did the doctor say—a couple of days?"

"Yes, ma'am," the nurse said. "Once we're sure there's no internal damage from the gunshots to the bulletproof vest and we figure out the extent of your rib injury, you should be able to go home."

I squeezed Bethany's hand. "I have to go meet with the sheriff. I'm going to tell him what we found and see what he says and how he reacts."

CHAPTER 32

When I arrived at the main office in Chateau I had to park two blocks away from the building. Other than the cop cars littering the streets and parking lots in close proximity to the sheriff's office, there were a dozen vans and cars bearing the logos of our local papers, television stations and radio broadcasters. In addition, satellite trucks from each of the major news organizations in the country were taking up parking space around the office. It was the busiest this street had ever been at five in the morning.

I pushed my way through the mob of reporters gathered on the sidewalks surrounding the building and pulled on the front door. It was locked. As I dug for my keys, cameramen and women shoved their video cameras in my face and reporters rattled off questions.

"Is it true that Captain Assassin is dead?" asked one female reporter. "And that he was one of your own?"

I chuckled, shook my head. As corny as it sounded, the name they'd given the killer was catchy. "How long have y'all been here?" I asked her.

Sensing she might establish a dialogue with me, she leaned in eagerly. "We received the call at eleven and got here twenty minutes later," she said. Then, quickly, "Is it true? Is the killer dead?"

There was something about this woman I liked. I couldn't quite put a finger on it, but I was instantly drawn to her. Maybe it was the way her words tripped off her tongue—suggesting she was new— that made me feel sorry for her. Or maybe I just admired the look of sincerity in her eyes—also suggesting she was new—that was absent from the eyes of the other sharks surrounding me. Whatever it was, I broke standard protocol and spoke to the press. "No, ma'am"—I scanned the surrounding night air—"the killer is not dead. He's still out there somewhere…waiting for his chance to strike again. And he *will* strike again."

"Is it true the entire command staff of the Magnolia Parish Sheriff's Office will remain hidden in this building until Captain Assassin is captured or killed?"

I checked out her nametag. Kelsey Cavanaugh. "Sorry, Ms. Cavanaugh, I've already said too much."

I shoved the key in the door and pushed it open, leaving a chorus of rapid-fire questions in my wake as I entered the building. I glanced over my shoulder. Kelsey Cavanaugh was still standing there, microphone dangling from her hand, staring at me. I smiled and nodded in her direction before the door shut behind me. I thought I saw her smile back.

"London! Is that you?" Sheriff Burke's voice hollered from down the hall.

I followed his voice and found him in the conference room. His face was gaunt and cluttered with stubble. His commanders—what was left of them—were seated around the conference table, worry lines cutting deep gouges in their faces. No one spoke when I walked in.

"Close the door," Sheriff Burke ordered.

I did.

"Tell me you've got something. Tell me you know who did this…that you at least have an idea who's out there hunting us like animals. Tell me anything at all to keep that"—Sheriff Burke pointed toward the front of the building—"mob at bay."

I surveyed the group, measuring my words. "I don't know exactly who's doing this, but I know why it's happening."

There were nervous glances around the room; someone coughed softly. Sheriff Burke raised his eyebrows impatiently. "Well? Why's it happening?"

"Does the name Lenny James mean anything to y'all?" I asked. The gasps that sounded around the room provided the answer I needed. I continued. "It seems every officer who was involved in that case is being targeted. Particularly, every officer who testified in federal court." I let the information sink in.

Sheriff Burke had walked to one end of the room and stood with his back to the rest of us, staring at the blank television screen. "How sure are you?"

"Positive. We found a hit list taped to the door of Wesley Guidry's office." I pointed around the room. "All of your faces were on the list except for you, Captain Boutin." I paused with my finger pointed in his direction. He sighed audibly, relief pushing the color back into his cheeks. The room stood quiet for what seemed like too long. I finally broke the silence. "Sheriff, what happened out there that night? Really?"

The sheriff waved his hand to the rest of the officers. "Leave us alone."

The commanders stood and hurried out the door. When we were alone and the door closed, Sheriff Burke took a seat at the end of the conference table and nodded for me to sit. I did.

"That night is a night many of us have tried to forget. It was definitely not our brightest moment. Anytime a baby is hurt..." Sheriff Burke shook his head somberly.

"Hurt?" I scowled. "Sheriff, I thought that baby was killed."

"Yeah, regrettably, the baby died. We tried to save him, but there was nothing we could do. The flash bang landed in the crib and the coroner said the explosion killed the baby almost immediately." Sheriff Burke shook his head. "There's nothing worse than drug dealers who put their own children in the line of fire."

"Who shot the husband?"

"Michael opened fire first and then Anthony and Matt. They almost had to shoot the wife. She just went crazy. Freaking out. She picked up her husband's gun. Of course, it was understandable under the circumstances."

No shit, I thought. "Do you think she still wants to kill some cops?"

"What do you mean?"

"Well, if she tried once, I'm sure she's capable of trying again."

The sheriff scoffed. "That woman was a clumsy housewife. She's definitely no skilled assassin."

"Maybe she hired someone, or there's another member of the family out for blood."

"We tried to locate some family members after the incident, but we couldn't. They weren't from here originally, and if they even had family, it seemed they didn't really care about what happened."

"What happened to the wife, Michelle James?"

Sheriff Burke shrugged. "For all I know she's still in the mental hospital up in Davenport. She never was deemed competent to stand trial."

"She was sent to an insane asylum?"

"Yeah. She went berserk in jail. Some kind of traumatic something or other that she suffered from."

I made a mental note to visit the hospital in Davenport. "You were the case officer, right?"

Burke nodded.

"Would you still have a copy of your investigative report—the search warrant and stuff like that?"

"That was twenty years ago. I doubt we still have a copy in records even."

"We don't. I checked." I pulled out a notebook, where I'd scribbled some information from Wesley Guidry's house. "Michelle James made some statements to the media on the night of the incident and said y'all hit the wrong house."

"That was bullshit."

"She also said her husband was not a drug dealer, that she'd never seen cocaine before in her life and that they didn't own a gun."

"What would you expect her to say?" Sheriff Burke sneered. "That bitch and her husband sold drugs to Martin—"

"Captain Thomas?"

Sheriff Burke nodded.

"I thought he worked patrol back then?"

"He did. He worked the north area, so we used him a few times to go undercover in the southern part of the parish where nobody knew him. We'd also use patrol officers from the south side to buy drugs from the north. They loved that shit. It got them out of the squad car and the polyester for a few hours." Burke cleared his throat. "Anyway, Lenny James sold drugs to Martin the day before the raid and he did it in the presence of their baby. I just wish it had been the mother who died instead of the baby."

"But, according to the newspapers, neither one of them were ever charged with a drug crime—or any crime, for that matter—before that night."

"It doesn't mean they didn't do it. How many people have you arrested for murder who didn't have a criminal record? How many drunk drivers have you arrested for vehicular homicide whose first arrest was the one that resulted in the death of another person?" Sheriff Burke nodded. "The same thing here. They'd been selling drugs for some time, but that was the first time they ever got caught."

"But the papers said they interviewed all the neighbors and no one ever saw any suspicious activities or a high volume of traffic coming and going from the house. In fact, the neighbors told the reporters the people who lived across the street from the James were known drug dealers who had multiple arrests for distribution."

Sheriff Burke waved it off. "People never talk bad about the dead. Take Justin Wainwright. When he was alive he busted a lot of cops, and they all hated him. Did you hear them at his funeral? Some of those same cops who used to openly profess their hatred for him were crying their eyes out and saying what a great man he was." Burke shook his head. "Lenny James was a hardcore drug dealer, but you'll never get his neighbors to say it now that he's dead."

It suddenly dawned on me that Sheriff Burke was explaining himself...trying to convince me that he was telling the truth. An innocent man—an innocent sheriff speaking to his underling— should have become indignant at my implications. "Sheriff, who did what out there?"

"What do you mean? And why is that important?"

"Who threw the flash bang? Who found the drugs? Who worked the shooting? Stuff like that. I think it'll help us figure out who the biggest targets might be."

The sheriff sighed and rubbed his tired head. "Wesley...Wesley Guidry threw the flash bang. He was never the same after that night. He only stayed on the job another year or two and resigned right after the hearings. We were all cleared of any wrongdoing, but he still felt responsible for killing the baby. Of course, he was just a kid at the time—we all were—and he didn't know how to cope with the pressures of the job."

"Why do you think he came forward after all these years? And what did he mean by having a document that proved what really happened that night?"

He shrugged. "I have no clue. I guess he just finally lost his mind. Had a nervous breakdown. He probably realized he was getting up in age and was getting closer to dying, so he figured he'd try and do something to help get his sorry ass to heaven."

"If that's the case, he certainly had something worth seeing...and Captain Theriot thought it was worth killing for. Maybe Theriot did something behind your back?" I was baiting him, studying his expression as I posed the theory. "Something you had no way of knowing about?"

Sheriff Burke's face lit up, as he suddenly realized a way out of his predicament. "You might be right. Maybe Michael did something inappropriate the rest of us didn't know about. It could be why the killings are happening." He was beaming now. "We could put an end to all of this! All we need to do is make a public statement saying Michael Theriot had acted inappropriately in the investigation and he acted alone. Maybe it'll stop any further killings."

This was not the reaction I was anticipating. I pursed my lips.

Bethany would've known how to play this out. "Sheriff, I think we have to keep digging—"

"Get Kimberly in here and she can draft a statement. We'll send it out to all the major news organizations, and I can have a press conference in here later in the day...say, about noon."

"But we don't know for sure what really happened."

"It doesn't matter what we know or think. It only matters what the killer thinks. We need to make him think this is over, the people responsible are dead. If they're all dead, he has no reason left to kill, which will buy us some time so you can track the sonofabitch down. Your number one priority is to identify him." He clenched his fist and shook it in the air. "Once you do, I'm issuing a shoot on sight order for the bastard and we'll staple wanted posters on every light pole in the parish!"

I opened my mouth, but Sheriff Burke's jaw was set. There was no arguing. I started to walk out the room, but his voice stopped me. "London, when this is over, there'll be a nice promotion and a raise for you and Lieutenant Riggs."

"Not necessary," I said slowly. "I just want to do my job, and right now it's learning everything I can about what happened that night so I can figure out who's doing this."

"Well, go home and get some rest tonight so you can get back to doing your job tomorrow. You've had a long day and made a serious break in the case. I have a good feeling about this. Everything's going to be over soon and we can get back to preparing for the election."

CHAPTER 33

Monday, August 22, 2011

It was almost ten o'clock AM when I returned to CID. I'd spent the early morning hours at the hospital with Bethany and had managed to get three hours of sleep in a small chair next to her bed. Although she insisted on being discharged so she could come to work with me, her doctors refused to let her leave. They said it would be another day or two before she could go home.

I marched straight to the evidence section and approached the doorway marking the entrance to the immense warehouse-type storage area. The top half of the split door was open. I looked in and saw the evidence custodian sitting at her computer.

"Cindy, do you have a minute?"

Cindy Folse spun around in her chair, stood and met me at the door. "For you, I always have time."

"You might regret saying that when you see what I need."

Cindy opened the door and let me in. I tore a page from my notebook and handed it to her. Written at the top of the page was the case number we'd found in the birdbath out at the Payneville Park.

"What's this?" she asked.

"I need to know if you have any evidence at all from that case number."

"I was two years old in ninety-one," Cindy said when she realized the year on the case number. She sat at her computer and started stabbing at the keyboard with slender fingers. "So, what kind of evidence am I looking for?"

I walked close and looked over her shoulder as she typed the case number into the search field. "Well, I know they recovered a gun and some cocaine. They should've also logged a spent flash bang into evidence."

"Is this connected to all the murders that have been happening?"

"I think so."

"I can't believe that about Captain Theriot. It feels kind of weird around here today. A bunch of news people were in the parking lot most of the morning." Cindy turned from her computer. "Everybody's being hush-hush about what happened, but from what I heard, Captain Theriot deserved what he got."

"He tried to kill Bethany Riggs, so yeah, he got what he deserved."

"Gina came in this morning with Bethany's shirt and Captain Theriot's gun and his uniform." Cindy shuddered. "It was kind of eerie seeing clothes somebody I knew was wearing just a few hours earlier."

I nodded toward her computer, where the search screen showed one result for the case number. "Is that it?"

Cindy spun back around and stroked a few more keys. A long list of evidence appeared on the screen. I leaned close to scan the list in search of a gun...there were four of them. Three nine-millimeter pistols and a three-fifty-seven caliber revolver. "Please tell me you still have the evidence here."

Cindy switched to a different screen that tracked the status and location of each piece of evidence. "The semi-automatic pistols belonged to the officers involved in the shooting and were returned to them three months later. As for the revolver..." She searched for a few more seconds. "Hey, you're in luck. The revolver's still here." She wrote down the bin storage number and stood. "Come on. It's in here." She led the way deeper into the office and through a solid steel door at the entrance to an enormous vault. It was where all guns and drugs were stored, and it contained thousands of guns.

Although everything was organized, it was no easy task locating the box containing the revolver Sheriff Burke and his crew recovered from the home of Lenny James. Cindy gave a triumphant shout when she located an aged box on a top shelf in the far corner of the room. "This is it!"

I reached out for the box and then held her hand while she stepped down from her rolling ladder. We moved to her desk and she sliced the evidence tape with a letter opener. I donned a pair of latex gloves and removed the revolver to examine it. The serial number had been scratched off. "Do you have a screwdriver?" I asked.

"I think so. Why?"

"Some guns have hidden serial numbers under the grip."

Cindy reached in a filing cabinet drawer and pulled out a flathead screwdriver. I used it to remove the single screw holding the handgrip in place. When I popped the wooden side-plates off the grip, I sighed. "I guess this isn't one of the gun manufacturers that hide serial numbers on their guns."

"What's that?" Cindy was pointing to one of the wooden side-plates. Something was burned into the underside of the wood.

"It looks like a social security number," I said, making a note of the number. Cindy pulled up a computer program and typed the social security number into a search field. After she clicked on the search button, almost instantly a full page of results appeared, each line containing the same name, Zeke Hadley.

"Can you print that out for me?" I asked.

Cindy nodded and her printer fired to life. I grabbed the printout and studied it. There were six different addresses and three different phone numbers listed for Zeke Hadley. The date range was from 1988 to 2011. I pointed to the 2011 listing. "Is that his current address and number?"

"Yeah," Cindy said.

I whistled. "This is some cool shit. What is it?"

"It's a new law enforcement data base. I can find anyone with it."

"How'd you get it?"

"You should have access to it now that you're in detectives."

I reached for Cindy's phone to test her program's accuracy. A woman picked up on the second ring. After telling her who I was, I explained my problem. "I need to find your husband to verify if this is his gun."

"He's on the road, but I can give you his cell number."

I copied the number and dialed it next. A smooth-spoken voice answered the phone. "This is Zeke."

"Hi, I'm London Carter, a detective with the sheriff's office, and I'm calling to see if you ever owned a silver, three-fifty-seven revolver."

"I sure did," Hadley said without hesitation. "It was stolen twenty years ago from my truck. They caught the punks, but they never recovered the gun. Why? Did you recover it?"

"I might have." I glanced down at the social security number I'd copied from the wooden plate. "The serial number's been scratched off—"

"Not a problem," Hadley said. "If it's mine, all you have to do is remove the grip and you'll find my social security number scratched into the metal or burned into the wood on the grip. I do that with all my firearms."

"No shit," I said, impressed. "Well, this is it. This is definitely your gun."

"Where'd you find it? I figured it was lost forever and I'd never get it back."

"I, well, I found it in our evidence locker. It's been here for twenty years."

"Evidence locker? What was it doing there?"

"It appears it was used in a shooting."

Hadley didn't immediately respond. When he finally spoke, his voice was cautious. "Was anyone hurt?"

"It's a complicated case and two people were killed, but no one was hurt with your gun."

"Is that the case they're talking about on the news? They said the sniper who's been killing cops has been linked to a case from twenty years ago. I saw it on the news earlier today. Is it involving my gun?"

"Do you know anyone by the name of Lenny James?"

"No, never heard of him. Why?"

"He was in possession of your gun on the night he was killed. He allegedly pointed it at some officers, and they returned fire, killing him. His baby had been killed when the SWAT team accidentally threw a flash bang into the baby's—"

"I remember that case!"

"Yeah, it was pretty big news back at the time."

"No, I remember it because I had to wait to get my other gun back. The detective who worked the burglary of my truck was also involved with that shooting. Shit, I think he's the one who capped the man." Hadley sighed. "Of course, I don't blame the man for picking up a gun. No offense to you, but if a bunch of cops kicked my door down in the middle of the night... Let's just say I don't think it would end well."

I nodded absently, not hearing the last part of what he'd said. I was still stuck on his *other* gun. "You said you had to wait to get your other gun back?"

"Yeah, I had a snub-nose thirty-eight that was stolen, too, but I got that one back with no problems. It took a little while, but I got it back nonetheless."

"Was the serial number scratched off that one?"

"No, it was in perfect condition. Just like it was when I left it in my truck."

"You wouldn't remember what detective worked your case, would you?"

"Yeah," Hadley said, "it was Detective Ronald Day."

"And the kid who stole your guns?"

"Oh, now you've got me." The line went quiet, with the only sound from the other end being Hadley tapping on his steering wheel. "Look, I might be able to find his name in some old court papers. I keep everything pertaining to my guns and I know I kept those documents somewhere."

I left my number with him and thanked him. Just as I hung up the phone, a knock sounded on the door behind Cindy and me. We both turned to see Sally Piatkowski standing there.

"Hey, Sally, how are you?" Cindy asked.

Sally pointed at me. "I'm looking for him."

"What's up?" I asked.

"I need to run some things by you. It's about the case," Sally said with a sense of urgency.

I thanked Cindy and followed Sally out of the evidence section and down the hall to the conference room. It was empty. Sally waited for me to enter and then pushed the door shut. "I was reading through the newspaper clippings and I might've found something."

"Where's everyone else?" I asked.

"A bunch of them went to the autopsies this morning—Gina, Melvin, Captain Chiasson and Rachael."

As she talked, I walked to the conference table where dozens of yellowed newspapers were scattered along the lengthy tabletop. They were organized by date. I recognized some of the articles from earlier in the morning. "What did you find?"

"Now we've pretty much nailed down the motive for these killings, I figured the killer has to be a family member or a very close friend. So, I went through all of these articles, searching for a name, an interview, anything that might offer a clue as to their next of kin. I'd almost given up when I found this." Sally folded one of the newspapers vertically and pointed to an article on the right half.

My brows puckered when I saw the tall, slender man in the picture. "This guy looks oddly familiar," I said slowly. I glanced down at the caption and almost choked on my heart when I read his name beneath the picture—Kenny James. "Screw me!"

Sally's eyes widened. "Seriously? Like, really?"

I waved her off and stabbed the picture with my finger. "I know this guy."

"How? The article says he's from Tennessee and last I checked, your ass hadn't left Magnolia Parish in a *long* time."

"I don't *know* him, like for real. I mean, I've never met him, but I certainly know *of* him." My mouth dropped in disbelief. "This is crazy. I don't know why I didn't think of it before."

"Think of what?" Sally asked impatiently. "How do you know him?"

"I have two of his books."

"Books?" Sally's face twisted in confusion. "You read?"

"What's that supposed to mean?"

"I don't know. You just don't look like the reading type."

"Really? So what does the reading type look like?"

Sally blushed, looked away from my piercing stare. "I don't know. Less...physical, I guess."

I scowled. "Is that a compliment, or should I be insulted?"

Refusing to answer me, she pointed back to the article. "Come on; spill it. How do you know this guy? And what is it you should've thought of?"

"A few years ago, I received an ad in the mail to join this exclusive book club. You could get five or six books at like a dollar each, but you had to agree to buy five or six more over the course of a year or eighteen months. Anyway, I picked my five or six books and I decided to order the others right then because I knew I'd forget about them over the next twelve or eighteen months. Since I'd already picked all the books I could find by a few authors I'd already known about and there were no other books I just had to have, I decided to order the two-book set by Kenny James."

I shook my head, still stunned from this revelation. "This is huge, Sally. You just blew this case wide open."

Sally threw her hands up. "What are you talking about? What did I blow wide open? What do your books have to do with this case? Why is—"

"They were *sniper* books."

Sally choked on her words. "What did you say?"

"He wrote two instructional books on sniping. He's a former military sniper and he now works as a sniper leader for a rural county out in Tennessee. And better than that, his preferred aiming point is the left eye."

CHAPTER 34

"Sheriff, I think we've identified the shooter!" I thought I could hear his jaw hit the floor through the phone.

"Wait…what…how?" Sheriff Burke stammered. "Who…who is it? Is he in custody?"

"Sally found a picture of Lenny James' brother—Kenny James. He was there during the hearings in federal court. He watched y'all testify. He knows who y'all are!"

"Wait a minute…is that it? Is that all you've got?"

"Oh no, there's more," I said triumphantly. "He wrote two books on sniper training—I have them both—and he leads a sniper team in Tennessee. Furthermore, and this is the real kicker, he trains snipers to aim for the left eyeball!"

There was an audible gasp from the other end. "Where is he? Have y'all been able to track him down?"

"Sally and Rachael are on the phone right now calling every hotel, motel and bed-n-breakfast in the state to see if he checked in within the last few months."

"Good! Keep at it. I just got off the phone with Corey. He's just leaving the autopsies and he's heading back to CID with Gina and Melvin. Get him up to speed and have them help y'all track down that piece of shit. I want him in custody before nightfall!"

"Sheriff, there's a chance he's back in Tennessee—"

"Contact the sheriff's department up there and have them take him into custody immediately. I don't want that asshole putting his head on a pillow tonight unless that pillow's on a prison cot!"

"This guy is a hero in the sniper community. His books are required reading, and his word is often the *last* word on issues relating to sniping. He's been certified as an expert on sniper techniques in nearly every state in the US, so I'm sure he'll have—"

"That doesn't give him the right to gun down my men!"

"No, it doesn't, but he'll undoubtedly have an ass-load of sympathizers and supporters in Tennessee." I paused, letting it sink in. "I feel good he's our guy, but we don't have any hard evidence at this point. Maybe I should head up there and see what I can dig up. If I find something that absolutely ties him into the murders here, it'll be harder for the Tennessee cops to ignore our requests. Sally located an address for him on Bear Mountain Road in Gatlinburg. We can be up there in ten hours."

"Okay, I like that. If y'all don't turn up anything with the hotels and motels, get up to Tennessee and see what you can find out. Keep me informed on all developments."

I started to tell him about Zeke Hadley's gun, but my phone began beeping. "Okay, Sheriff, I have to go. I have another call coming in and it might be about the case." I checked the number. It was Zeke Hadley. I pressed the green button to pick up the call. "Mr. Hadley, how's it going?"

"Good...I found that information for you. The guy who stole my guns was Jarvis Griffin. His address was on Tunnel Lane off of Highway Fifty-One."

I jotted the information down and thanked him. After flipping my phone shut and turning to my computer, I tried to find that database program, but couldn't. A shadow fell over me and I looked up to see Gina Pellegrin.

"What's going on?" Gina asked. "Corey said there's been some major development in the case."

I stood and nodded to my seat and handed her the note I'd jotted. "Can you look up this name in that database I'm supposed to have access to but don't? I'll fill you in on what's going on while you do it."

She plopped into my chair and her fingers danced across the keyboard. "Go ahead...fill me in."

I told her about Zeke Hadley's stolen gun and my suspicions that Major Ronald Day had recovered the gun back when he was a detective and had scratched off the serial number and planted it on Lenny James' body. "If I can talk to Jarvis Griffin, I bet he'll verify he never scratched the serial number off that stolen revolver and that *Detective* Ronald Day recovered it at the same time he recovered the snub-nose."

"Um," Gina said, leaning back in the chair, "you won't be able to do that. Jarvis Griffin's deceased." She pointed at the screen. There was a large red "D" beside Griffin's name.

"Are you sure?" I asked.

"Positive. Look at the address. He would've been about thirty when he died."

I leaned back against the wall of my cubicle, feeling deflated. "Shit, I needed him. Can you see how he died?"

Gina continued hacking away at my keyboard. After several quiet moments, she pointed to the screen. "He died in a car wreck. He was driving drunk and hit a cement flood wall in 2002. There were two other people with him and they both died as well."

I shook my head, and we joined the others in the conference room. Captain Chiasson had just hung up one of the many phones they'd set up in there and shook his head. "That was the last one on my list. What about y'all?"

Sally, Rachael and Melvin all shook their heads.

"He didn't check into any motels in the state," Rachael said.

"I checked over a hundred apartment complexes and none of them have even heard of this Kenny James," Melvin said. "Shit, I never even heard of him."

I looked at Sally. "Anything?"

She frowned and shook her head.

"Well, it looks like we'll be making a road trip," I said.

Melvin threw up his hand, waving it in the air. "I want to go on a road trip!"

"If I have to be in the car with someone for ten hours," I joked, "I'd rather it be Sally than you."

"Oh, *now* you want to hang out with me?" Sally chided. "I remember that not too long ago you weren't into cops and—"

"Hey, can we just forget about the past and go get packed?" I asked. "We have a long trip ahead of us."

Gina sneered. "Why does she get to go with you?"

"If it hadn't been for her, we wouldn't even know about Mr. James." I stood to leave, but Captain Chiasson lifted a hand.

"Can you hold up a minute, so I can have a word with you?" he asked.

I nodded, and he waited until we were alone to close the conference room door. "Look, Gina told me about your conspiracy theory, where you think our superiors, including the sheriff himself, know more than what they're saying about what happened that night twenty years ago."

"At this point, I think it's a little stronger than a conspiracy theory."

Captain Chiasson shook his head. "I'm betting you're right, but if you have anything less than a videotape catching them in the act, you'd better be careful who you say that to. If the sheriff finds out you're going around saying that, he'll have you fired and he'll find a way to have you arrested."

I studied Chiasson's face, my jaw set. He threw his hands up and hurriedly said, "I won't say anything, but, if asked, I'll deny knowing anything about your theory. I have a wife and kids to think about and only seven years left before retirement."

"Well, if I get concrete evidence proving the sheriff and his henchmen hit the wrong house and wrongfully killed Lenny James and his baby, you can bet I'll be going to war with him...and you won't want to be on his side."

Captain Chiasson pursed his lips. "If you get that concrete evidence, I'll stand by your side."

I nodded, before I hurried out the door.

Sally was waiting in the parking lot and asked, "Where do you want to meet?"

"I'll meet you here in an hour and you can drive. I just want to run to the hospital and see Bethany before we set out."

CHAPTER 35

"Tennessee?" Bethany bolted up in bed, then gasped in pain. Face twisted in agony, she gingerly slid back down. "Why are you going to Tennessee?" she asked through clenched teeth.

When I explained what was going on and who Kenny James was, she frowned. "That doesn't make sense. Why would this guy wait twenty years to exact revenge? He'd be slower, weaker, have poorer eyesight. It doesn't make sense."

"I'm just as fast and strong today as I was twenty years ago," I contended.

"Maybe so, but will you be able to say that in twenty more years? This hero of yours, wouldn't he have to be in his late fifties, early sixties? While he might be able to still get around good *for his age,* there's no way some old grandpa shot Captain Abbott in the cemetery and then disappeared before we hit that abandoned schoolhouse."

"He's not my hero," I muttered. "I just own two of his books." I sank into a nearby chair and brooded over this commonsense revelation. "Why do you always have to piss on my parade?"

Bethany reached out a hand and stroked my arm. "I'm sorry. I guess it's just the investigator in me. This case is like a giant puzzle and my mind's constantly working...trying to stick pieces here and there...evaluating what fits and what doesn't. The first thing I do when I get a new piece is try to explain why it *doesn't* fit. If I can't do that, then I start looking at why it *does* fit. I've found that by approaching my cases this way, I tend to put fewer pieces in the wrong place."

"I knew there was a reason I liked you," I said with a smile.

"Wow, a guy who appreciates me for my mind."

"And a lot of other things." I stood and squeezed her hand. "I have to meet Sally Piatkowski at CID."

"Why?"

"Like I said, we're going to Tennessee to find Kenny James."

"But why? Like I said, old as he is, there's no way he committed these crimes."

"Yeah, but I still want to check it out to be sure. Maybe he'll lead us to someone who *is* capable of doing it."

"Why don't you just call the police up there and ask them to check him out? It'd save you a lot of wasted time."

"We think the police up there might not be as open-minded as we are about his possible involvement. While he might not be my hero, I'm sure a lot of those Tennessee cops hold him in high regard."

Bethany was silent for a moment, thoughtful. "Tell me again why Sally's going with you?"

"Well, she's the one who broke this wide open, so it's only right that she gets to go."

Bethany faked a pout. "I don't know if I like that."

"If you hadn't gone and got yourself shot, you'd be coming with me."

"But do you even need to go? There's no way Kenny James did this, so why not let Melvin go instead of you? That way you can stay here in case another attack takes place."

"I think Kenny might be able to shed some light on what really happened during that raid, and I don't want anyone screwing that up. Kenny should know if his brother was ever involved with drugs and he should be able to tell us if Lenny James ever owned any guns. By the way, listen to this…" I told her about Zeke Hadley's gun and Jarvis Griffin.

"I knew they were dirty!" Bethany shook her head. "There's got to be someone out there who knows something…someone willing to talk."

"Until we find that person, we'll have to try and backdoor this case." I turned to leave, but stopped by the door. "One last thing…be careful who you talk to about our suspicions. Captain Chiasson said the sheriff doesn't take kindly to being questioned."

CHAPTER 36

Tuesday, August 23, 2011

It was something after midnight when Sally and I walked into the lobby of the Smokey Inn in Pigeon Forge. It was our last hope—all the other hotels and motels in the area were booked solid.

"What can I get you for?" the clerk, an elderly lady with thinning hair and a salt-and-pepper mustache, asked from behind the cluttered counter.

"We were hoping to get a couple of rooms." I pulled out my wallet.

The clerk shook her head before she started punching into her computer. "We only have one room available…a king on the second floor. The party just cancelled."

I looked at Sally. She shrugged, the makings of a smile tugging at the corners of her mouth. "I'm cool with it if you are."

I hesitated. "Um, do y'all have any cots?"

The clerk raised an eyebrow. "Excuse me?"

"You know," I explained, "a roll-away cot."

"No, we don't have any cots left." The clerk looked from me to Sally and then back again. "Even if we did, why would you want one? You afraid of her?"

Sally giggled. I blushed.

Suddenly, the front door burst open and a lady walked briskly to the counter. "Are there *any* rooms available in this Godforsaken town?"

Before the clerk could open her mouth, I shoved my credit card across the counter. "We'll take it."

The clerk broke into a toothless smile. "Sorry, ma'am, the last room in this Godforsaken town has just been rented."

The woman stormed out of the lobby, leaving behind a tirade of choice words, and the clerk took my information and gave us the swipe card to our room. "Enjoy your stay," she said pleasantly.

We carried our bags up the two flights of cement stairs and stopped outside our door. Leaning against the metal railing, we stared out at the busy strip of highway that passed in front of the motel. A cool breeze blew in from the not-so-distant mountains, and I heard Sally sigh. "This place is so beautiful."

I nodded and, after spending a few more minutes admiring the nightlife along the highway, we turned and entered the room. It was modest, with a king-size bed, a television table holding a twenty-five-inch television, a round table with a squared-back chair and a small nightstand. Across from the entrance was a lavatory, complete with coffee pot and hairdryer, and to the right was the doorway to the bathroom. I dropped my bag near the round table and stared at the bed. "Um, what'll we—"

"I call it. I get this side," Sally said, and plopped to the left side of the bed, nearest the bathroom. She rolled onto her back, smiling up at me. "I want to be the first one in the bathroom in the morning. I can't let you see my morning face."

I wondered how Bethany would feel about me sharing a bed with another woman and, for a fleeting moment, I thought about crashing on the floor. Sally must've seen me eyeball the floor because she shook her head. "Don't even think about it. We're both adults...professionals...and we're both single. There's no reason we can't crash in this giant bed for a few hours to recharge our batteries, me on one side and you on the other. We're on the job. It's not like we took a vacation together to the Bahamas."

"I guess you're right." I dropped my shoulders in resignation. "There's no reason to get all worked up over this situation. We close our eyes for a few hours and then we get back to work...and we never speak of this to anyone. You know how our coworkers are—if you look at someone too long it means you're sleeping with them, and neither of us needs that grief."

"Grief?" Sally frowned.

"You know what I mean. We don't need to hear their jaw-jacking over something that never happened."

"I guess so." Sally grabbed her bag and went into the bathroom to get ready for bed.

I took the opportunity to call Sheriff Burke to let him know we'd made it and where we were staying. After twenty minutes of back and forth, I was finally able to end the conversation and call Bethany. She was fit to be tied.

"They released me a few hours ago," she complained. "I could've gone with you if you would've waited!"

"I didn't think they were releasing you today."

"Neither did I, but all the tests came back good, so they said I could go. If I didn't know better, I'd think they did that just to screw me out of going up there with you."

"Yeah, no shit."

"Think about it…we could've saved the department money by renting only one room and we could've spent another night together…away from here, in a romantic location, with no early-morning interruption, no time schedule, nothing to interfere with our time together."

I smiled. "Yeah, that does sound nice. Maybe we can find another excuse to come up here."

Sally opened the bathroom door right at that moment, dressed in a thin T-shirt and very short shorts, and I quickly threw my finger to my lips. She nodded her understanding and tiptoed across the floor. She shoved a tuft of wet blonde hair over an ear and eased onto the bed. Leaning her back against the headboard, she pulled her sleek and tanned knees to her chest and squirted a handful of body lotion into the palms of her hands. She began applying the lotion to her right leg first, rubbing from the ankle to the knee—using long, deliberate strokes—and then she moved to her left leg.

"Hey, are you there?" I heard Bethany ask over the phone.

"Yeah, I'm here."

"Well? Did you?"

"I'm sorry. I didn't hear the question—did I what?"

"Did you all find Kenny James?"

"Not yet. We're going out to Bear Mountain Road in the morning. The sheriff wanted us to visit the house tonight—catch him by surprise—but I think a more diplomatic approach will get us more information. If he *is* Captain Assassin, like the media dubbed him, I'm not just interested in catching him, I'm also interested in finding out why he's doing this. Sure, he'll have to pay for his actions and nothing justifies murder, but if the sheriff and his cronies hit the wrong house and killed an innocent baby that night, they're going down."

"How're you going to make that happen?"

"I'm not real sure." I glanced at Sally again. She had straightened her legs and was now applying the lotion to her upper thighs, using the same slow and deliberate motion. When she caught me looking, she smiled coyly. I quickly adjusted my eyes, cleared my throat. "Well, Beth, I think I'd better get some rest. It was a long drive up here."

"Oh…okay," Bethany said, sounding disappointed. It was clear to me that she wanted to keep talking. "You sound distracted, distant. Is everything okay?"

"Yeah, everything's great. I'm just fried. I didn't exactly get a lot of sleep this morning."

"I don't know how you even fell asleep in that tiny chair," Bethany agreed.

"Yeah, it certainly wasn't my granddaddy's recliner."

"It was nice of you to be there. Having you with me helped to make my situation more bearable. Plus, it was so romantic of you to sleep by my bedside."

"I was glad to be there." The fingers of guilt began to tug at my conscience like a nagging child pulling at his mother's dress, begging for a candy in line at the grocery store. "Well, I guess I'd better get to bed."

"Hey, London…"

"Yeah?"

"You're not feeling any weirdness over what happened last night, are you?"

"None at all."

"You'd tell me if you did?"

"Yeah, absolutely."

"Okay." She sighed. "Will you call me in the morning?"

"Absolutely. I'll call you as soon as I wake up." I flipped my phone shut and carried my bag into the bathroom. When I was done showering, I stepped out the bathroom to find the room cloaked in darkness. I grounded my bag outside the bathroom door and shut off the light. I felt my way to the bed, using the sound of Sally's soft breathing as a guide. When I reached the bed, I eased under the sheets—trying not to shake the bed too much—and lay there motionless. I remained on my back for several minutes. My muscles began to relax. My eyes closed. My mind gradually faded to black.

Just as I began to doze off I felt Sally move beside me. The bed shifted as she turned onto her side. Her hand brushed against my leg and it inched upward to my chest. My heart began to race. She slowly moved her bare leg over mine, the touch of her cool skin sending shivers reverberating up and down my body, and her hand began to explore my chest.

CHAPTER 37

I peeled my eyes open, but shut them as sunlight bled through the curtains and blinded me. I turned away from the window and eased them open again.

I gasped and jerked to a seated position when I saw Sally Piatkowski lying naked beside me. The events of the previous night came flooding back, and I groaned and sank back to the soft mattress, cursing myself silently. Sally stirred beside me and stretched like a lazy kitten that had just eaten a hearty meal.

Her blue eyes sparkled when she opened them and saw me staring at her. "Good morning."

Although guilt tugged at my heart as I thought about Bethany lying alone seven hundred miles away, I couldn't help but smile. "I…I thought last night was a dream."

"It sure felt like a dream," Sally agreed. "Even better than I'd anticipated."

"Oh, you were anticipating what happened last night?"

"Ever since I first met you."

My face flushed a little. I rolled out of the bed and padded to the bathroom to run water for a shower. I was surprised, but didn't object, when Sally joined me a few minutes later. After we showered and dressed, we hurried through eggs and bacon at Momma Black Bear's Breakfast, then drove out onto the strip and headed toward Gatlinburg, with Sally driving and me reading the map. It took about twenty minutes to reach Gatlinburg, and Sally cruised along the crowded street, passing tattoo parlors, gift shops and a fudge store. Even at that early hour, the sidewalks and shops were crowded with tourists.

"Stay on this strip until you get to Traffic Light Ten. It's at the other end of Gatlinburg...should be coming up." I traced my finger along the map. "And then you'll take a right at that light and go up Bear Mountain—"

My phone screamed from my pocket. I pulled it out and checked the number. It was Bethany. *Shit!* I'd forgotten to call her first thing in the morning. I threw the phone to my ear, trying to sound pleasant. "Hey, Bethany, how's it going?"

"I thought you were going to call me when you woke up?"

"Yeah, I'm sorry about that. We were in a hurry to leave and I just got busy packing up, finding a map, checking out...stuff like that." I heard Bethany huff, but she didn't reply. I waited for several long moments, but nothing. "Hey, are you still there?"

"Yeah, I'm here," Bethany said in a low voice. "I just feel played."

Sally touched my arm, pointed to the last traffic light and the sign that read Bear Mountain Road. I nodded, she took a right and we left the jostling street behind.

"London, did you hear me?" Bethany asked.

"Yeah, I'm sorry. We're turning onto Bear Mountain Road right now and we should be getting to the house pretty soon."

"Okay, I'll let you go."

Before I could answer there was a sharp click and the line went dead. "Bethany?"

Nothing.

Sally frowned, touched my hand. "I'm very sorry."

"About what?"

"About you and Bethany...about what happened last night. I don't know what came over me. I guess it's just been a while and—"

"Wait...what do you mean that you're sorry about me and Bethany? She has no idea anything happened, and she's not going to."

"I'll certainly never tell, but I do have to warn you that women know when these things happen. They can sense it."

I pursed my lips, cursing myself for not being stronger. *What the hell is wrong with me?* I continued to beat myself up internally as Sally wove her way along what turned out to be a sharp, narrow and winding mountain road. There were no shoulders, just steep drop-offs and dangerous switchbacks.

"If you make a wrong turn, you're dead," Sally commented, gripping the steering wheel with both hands.

I stared idly out the window, wondering how on earth I would even begin to patch things up with Bethany. I hadn't been in a legitimate relationship in years and I'd finally found someone I felt I could connect with—someone who seemed to have so many things in common with me—and I'd thrown it all away for one night of...of what? What was that exactly?

We had rounded a bend and were traveling along the outer edge of Bear Mountain, where the right side of the roadway was clear of trees. About a quarter mile away was a neighboring mountain that was thick with trees and void of any signs of civilization. As I tried to penetrate the shadows of that mountain's underbrush, searching for traces of Gatlinburg's infamous black bears, I spotted a familiar flash of light. I squinted, curious. It appeared again and a third time. I suddenly realized it was out of place in the remote wilderness—

"Get down!" I grabbed Sally's neck and jerked her toward me just as the windshield exploded and shards of glass peppered our faces. My eyes blinked shut and my cheeks burned. The car careened out of control and shot off a narrow embankment to the left side of the road and slammed into a tree. A second shot blew through the back window and smashed into the radio, sending plastic debris flying into the air.

Kenny James!

CHAPTER 38

I checked the hole in the back windshield against the hole in the radio and calculated the angle of the trajectory. The shooter was at our seven o'clock position. I did a quick-peek over the dashboard and planned an escape route through the forest.

Sally moved under me, cursing, and it was only then I realized she was okay. "What's going on?"

"We're being shot at…it's Kenny James!" I fumbled for the driver's door and pushed it open just as a third shot blew out the back passenger's door window. I shoved Sally ahead of me and out the door, falling on top of her. She grunted as all of my weight smashed into her, and I scrambled to my hands and knees, dragging her with me down a shallow gully and behind a large outcrop of rock. Several more bullets whizzed overhead and one smashed into the rock opposite our position.

Sally's breath was coming in labored gasps, her chest rising and falling rapidly. "What's going on?"

I dropped to the ground behind the outcrop and carefully craned my neck to see around it, searching for another glint of sunlight against the sniper's objective lens. Another bullet smashed into the rock, kicking dust into my eyes. "Call nine, one, one," I said to Sally, rubbing my face, "and stay behind these rocks!"

While Sally dug out her phone and began dialing, I scurried up the mountainside, keeping the giant trees and thick foliage between my location and the sniper's position, and made my way to a spot where I could safely try and get an eyeball on the shooter. Cursing myself for not having brought my rifle on the trip, I strained to penetrate the shadows of the distant mountain. One thing I'd learned from studying Kenny James' books was that he put a lot of emphasis on marksmanship, but not much on camouflage and concealment.

I thought I caught a glimpse of movement in the area where I'd first seen the sun reflecting off the rifle scope, but I couldn't be positive it was the shooter. I was about to move to a position where I could get a better visual on the sniper's location, when a large twig snapped behind me and it was followed by a rustling sound. I spun around and found myself staring right into the eyes of a large black bear. It was about twenty feet from me, its bottom jaw dangling, exposing a row of menacing teeth.

"Whoa there, buddy," I said, placing my right hand on my pistol. I stood my ground and watched as the bear ambled toward me. He stopped, turned his head and looked through the forest toward Bear Mountain Road, which snaked below us. He lifted his nose, tested the air, and then turned and bounded off in the opposite direction. I breathed a sigh of relief, as I wiped the sweat from my brow. A moment later, I heard the faint sound of sirens echoing through the mountains. *Damn, that was quick.*

After watching the sniper's last known position for several minutes and not seeing any movement, I made my way, slipping and sliding, back down the mountain to where Sally still crouched behind the rocks. Just as I reached her, the sirens became louder and a fire truck appeared around the bend, but it raced by us without slowing. Moments later, a second fire truck passed by and it was followed by a Gatlinburg police car. A second squad car rounded the curve and skidded to a stop several feet away from our unmarked car. A short, stocky patrol officer stepped out and approached us.

I pointed toward the shooter's last known location. "There was a sniper up there…be careful."

The patrol officer glanced over his shoulder, scowled. "A sniper?"

"Yeah, someone took some shots at us," Sally said. "Didn't the dispatcher tell you?"

The officer shook his head. "We're en route to a house fire. Jimmy radioed me to say he passed you all wrecked into the side of the mountain." He walked to our car and surveyed the damage. "Are you all cops?"

I handed him my identification. "We're here on official police business. We're looking for a suspect we believe killed three of our commanding officers—"

"Magnolia," he said, reading my identification card and

butchering the name of our parish. "No shit! I heard about this on the news." The officer stared off toward the neighboring mountain. "You think the killer's from here? That's he's out there?"

"We suspected it at first, but we're sure of it now," I said. "Somehow, he found out we were coming and set out to ambush us."

The officer moved beside us behind the rock outcrop and spoke into his police radio. The dispatcher let him know she had a team of investigators and SWAT officers en route to our location. When he was done, he turned back toward us. "Do you have any idea who the shooter is? A name? Description? Anything I can relay to the responding officers?"

I glanced at Sally. She nodded. I turned back to the officer. "We do have a name. It's Kenny…Kenny James."

The officer immediately shook his head. "That's not possible."

"Why's that?" I asked, although I'd already expected strong resistance from the members of the well-respected sniper's home agency. No law enforcement officer would ever want to believe someone they thought they knew so well—especially someone of Kenny James' stature—could do something as despicable as slaughter some of their own in cold, calculated fashion.

"Lieutenant James is dead."

"Dead?" Sally and I echoed in unison.

"Yeah, dead…like he ain't alive no more."

"When? What happened?" I asked.

"He died about two weeks ago. His neighbor found him in his living room. It looked like he died of a heart attack. He was up in age, you know."

I glanced at the bullet holes in Sally's unmarked car. "If Kenny James is dead, then who did that?"

"Your guess is probably better than mine, but I'm sure we're about to find out." He pointed toward the neighboring mountain, where a team of heavily armed SWAT operators were scurrying like ants through the dense forests, converging on the spot Sally had described to the dispatcher and where the shooter had been concealed twenty minutes earlier.

An eerie thought entered my mind and I hurried away from Sally and the patrol officer, digging my phone from my pocket as I did. I punched in Bethany's number. She answered on the second ring. "London? Hey, did you find Kenny James?"

"No," I said. "He's dead. But somebody just ambushed us. They fired a half dozen shots at us, almost killed Sally in the process. Lucky for us, the bastard didn't know how to conceal scope glare. I need you to somehow find out if any calls were made from our sheriff's office phones to the Gatlinburg area code—or any Tennessee area code, for that matter."

"Wait—*what?* First off, are you okay?"

"Yeah, there's nothing like getting shot at to make you appreciate the time you have here on earth. I feel great."

"Who shot at you all? What the hell is going on? You're not a captain, so why in the hell were you shot at?"

"I don't know…maybe we're getting too close to the truth."

"You think the sheriff sent someone out there to ambush you?"

"It could be him or anyone on that hit list—or any other person in the world, for that matter. At this point everyone's a suspect." An idea occurred to me. "I need you to get your hands on all of the commanders' cell phones and see if any of them made a call to a Tennessee area code."

"How am I supposed to do that? I haven't been cleared for duty yet."

"Call Gina or Melvin. They're onboard with us. You can trust them. Get one of them to get it done."

"How are we supposed to get our hands on their phones? Do we just walk up and demand to see their call history? Even if they had nothing to do with the attack they'll tell us to get lost."

I thought about that for a few seconds. "I've got it! Get with Debra in accounting. She has real-time, online access to all cell phones through the sheriff's office. Play your IA card and make her show you the records."

"Okay, I'll get right on it. Oh, and London…"

"Yeah?"

"Please be careful."

I flipped my phone shut, then rejoined Sally and the officer. A detective had arrived and was questioning Sally about our reasons for being there, when we got into town, where we stayed.

"If I didn't know better," I interjected, "I'd think we were suspects."

The detective, a plump fellow with silver hair, turned to me. "And you must be London Carter."

"That I am." I stuck out my hand, but Detective Plump ignored it.

"What time did you all roll into town?" he asked in an almost accusing tone.

"We arrived at the Smokey Inn in Pigeon Forge at midnight. We stayed there until this morning when we checked out. We ate at Momma Black Bear's Breakfast—you can verify that with our waitress, a brunette named Natalie—and we drove straight here, where we were almost killed. Why are you asking all these questions? Is there something we need to know?"

Before walking to his unmarked four-wheel drive, Detective Plump turned to the patrol officer. "Keep an eye on these two lovebirds for a few."

My blood started to boil. I opened my mouth, but Sally caught my eye and shook her head. I took a deep breath and paced back and forth until the detective returned. He nodded, extended his hand. "Sorry about that, but I had to be sure."

I shook his hand, confused. "Sure about what?"

"That it wasn't you all who started the fire. I had my boys check Momma Black Bear's and they pulled the video. You all were sitting there in Pigeon Forge when old man Redmond called about the fire here in Gatlinburg, so there's no way you all started it."

"Of course we didn't start a fire," I said. "Why would you even think that?"

"Lieutenant Kenny James was one of our own. He died a couple of weeks back. Anyway, his place burned to the ground a few miles up the mountain. Deputy Conner here"—the detective indicated the deputy with a nod—"got suspicious when you all mentioned Lieutenant James' name, in light of his house was burning down just up the mountain. Burnt right to the ground."

Sally and I traded shocked looks. "His house burned to the ground?" I asked. "How? Was it arson?"

The detective nodded. "You can smell the gasoline from a quarter mile away. Do any of you know anyone who might want to burn his house down?"

I walked to Sally's car and reached into the backseat for my case file. I dug out a copy of the newspaper article with the picture of Kenny James and handed it to the detective. "Your Lieutenant Kenny James was related to the family in this news story. We believe this incident is connected to the recent sniper attacks in our parish. Somebody must've found out we were coming up here and they're obviously trying to hide something. Whatever it is, it has to be inside Kenny James' house."

Sally frowned. "I guess now we'll never know."

I pursed my lips, trying to figure out our next move. I turned to Detective Plump. "Does Kenny James have any family around here?"

He shook his head. "The only family he had in these parts was a daughter, but she moved away a bunch of years back."

"What was her name?" I asked.

"I'm not real sure. I never met her. But I bet Larry Durham could tell you. He's an old friend of Kenny's. He's even mentioned in some of Kenny's books. If you wouldn't know better, you'd think they were brothers—that's how close they were. Inseparable. If anyone would know anything, it'd be Larry."

"How can we find him?"

CHAPTER 39

After acquiring a loaner car from the Gatlinburg Police Department, we followed Detective Plump's directions and found Larry Durham sitting on the front porch of an ancient log cabin that jutted off the side of a steep mountain. He was bent over a rough table chopping on some type of wild game. He didn't look up when we approached, but a lop-eared pit bull that had seen better days stood slowly to his feet beside the old mountain man and bared a row of rotting teeth.

"Don't even think about biting them, Cletus. I wouldn't want you to lose another tooth. Lord knows, you only got two or three left." After squirting a stream of brownish tobacco liquid from his mouth, he wiped his lips with a dirty shirtsleeve and turned to us. "I hear you want to know some things about Ken. Why should I tell you anything? Way I heard it, you all killed his brother and his brother's baby and then lied about it in a court of law."

"Did Kenny tell you that?" I asked. "Did he tell you anything else? Anything that would help me nail the bastards who did that to his family?"

Larry Durham squinted suspiciously. "You'd turn against one of your own for a complete stranger?"

"It's quite possible one of our own just tried to murder us." I stepped forward. "Look, I know you don't know us, and I certainly don't expect you to trust us, but if you'd just give us a chance and help us figure out what Kenny knew about what happened twenty years ago, I guarantee you we'll do everything in our power to make it right. We didn't take an oath to protect the interests of the sheriff's office, we took an oath to uphold the laws of our state and country, and we intend to do that regardless of who committed the crime. Besides, I'm a fan of his work. I've studied both of his sniper books."

"All Ken ever wanted was justice," the old mountain man said, a deep frown tugging at the corners of his mouth. "He died without finding his justice."

"If you give us a chance, we'll do what we can to honor his memory. We certainly know that someone out there"—I pointed my thumb toward the surrounding forest—"didn't want us seeing what was inside Kenny James' house, and we know there's a reason behind it. Was there something in there that might help us uncover what happened back in Magnolia?"

Larry shrugged. "Just a house full of history...that being *his story*. That house was a shrine of his life. He had pictures all over the walls, copies of his own books and every other sniper book he could get his hands on, an old magazine collection and, of course, lots of guns." Larry spat another stream of juice to the ground and shook his head sadly. "He must be turning over in his grave knowing all them guns got destroyed. They were his pride and joy. He loved them almost as much as he loved Liz."

"Liz? Was that his daughter?" I asked.

Larry shook his head. "Ken didn't have no kids. Never even got married. Nope, Liz was his niece."

My eyebrows furrowed. I hadn't realized Lenny had two brothers. I glanced at Sally, who shrugged, and then turned back to Larry. "A niece? Who was her father?"

"Lenny James." When he saw the look of shock on my face, he grinned. "Didn't know that, did you?"

"There's no record of her in any of the newspaper articles," I said.

"There won't be...Ken made sure of it. The night this all happened, Ken received a call from his sister-in-law, Michelle, and she told him what had happened. He rushed down there, but by the time he showed up Michelle had been arrested. The law wouldn't let him see her and they wouldn't tell him anything about his brother or his brother's baby—that is until he told them who he was and threatened to bring the FBI down. They got all scared-like and told him some bullshit story about his brother selling drugs. Told him Lenny dragged iron on them when they raided his house.

"At his demanding, they finally let him see Michelle in a private room for five minutes. He tried to find out what all happened, but all Michelle could do was cry. He said she kept saying over and over that they were set up, and she kept crying for her little baby that was killed. He asked her about Liz, and she finally got herself together enough to tell him that Liz was sleeping at a girlfriend's house. It was like she had forgotten all about Liz until Ken mentioned her. Ken was able to get a phone number from Michelle before the guards came in and took Michelle away. That was the last time he was able to talk to her before she was shipped off to a mental hospital. He called the lady who was keeping Liz, picked her up and took her back to Tennessee with him."

"She stayed here with him?" I asked.

Larry nodded. "He raised her like his own. Taught her everything he knew about everything. He had that girl—"

"Holy shit!" I said, my blood turning to icicles. "Did he teach her how to shoot?"

"That's the first thing he taught her to do—and she was good...*damn* good! She was out-shooting grown snipers on the sheriff's department team by the time she was twelve." Larry shook his head. "That little Liz was something to see. I been on a number of hunts with Kenny and her. I seen that girl drop an elk with one shot from eight hundred meters, seen her drop a four-hundred-pound black bear that was charging directly at her, seen her blow the eye out of a coyote at four hundred meters." Larry nodded fondly, as though he were seeing it through his mind's eye. "You name it, that girl could do it with a gun. Kenny was some proud of his little sniper. It nearly killed him when she moved away."

"Moved? Where'd she move to?" I asked.

"I'm not real sure. She got married for five minutes to some guy she met up around Sevierville. They didn't stay married long. She divorced him and moved away. She'd come back to visit every now and again, but things just weren't the same for Ken with her gone. It was like she took his soul with her when she left."

"Who'd she marry?" Sally asked. "What's the guy's name?"

Larry shook his head. "I never did hear his name called."

"Any idea where she moved?" she asked.

"Nope. I just know she moved away and it killed old Ken."

We all stood silent for a few minutes—me trying to think of what to ask next, Larry going back to work on supper and Sally scratching Cletus' head. Finally, I thought to ask if Liz ever talked about the night her father and baby brother were killed.

"Not to me," Larry said, "but she did say something to Ken about it. Ken wouldn't bring it up much because it made him sour and he didn't want to dig up old wounds for Liz. But when he'd get to drinking, he'd sometimes talk about it if we were alone. One night when he was hitting the moonshine extra hard—it was after Liz had moved on—he told me that he knew his brother was set up. Said he could prove it."

"Did he say how he could prove it?" I asked.

"The law down there said they bought drugs from Lenny and Michelle the day before the raid, but"—Larry shook his head—"Liz was home and she said they didn't get no visitors...none. She also said her dad didn't own no guns. In fact, when Ken tried to give him one at Christmas a few years before he was killed, Lenny went off about how a man with a family shouldn't keep guns around the house. Too dangerous, he said. Ken believed every man should own a gun and teach his family how to use it—you never know when they might need it—but Lenny, he was a different breed. Thought every situation could be talked out. He sure didn't have a chance to do any talking that night."

"Did he ever tell anyone what Liz told him? Did he report it to the authorities in Magnolia or to the FBI?" I asked.

"Ken knew how the law worked. Liz was a little girl and her word wouldn't stand up against a bunch of cops. Nope, after all his attempts to get justice failed, he just settled into teaching her to let go of the bitterness and get on with her life. Taught her that those that do wrong get theirs in the end—that the Man upstairs settles all scores sooner or later. It was a lesson that took a long time to take root."

Larry shook his head. "That little girl was some bitter. Ken would've had an easier time breaking a wild mustang with that attention disorder all them youngsters claim to have nowadays. I always said she would grow up and become FBI and go after them bastards, but I don't really know what became of her."

I jotted some notes from Larry's statement and then turned to Sally. "Can you think of anything else?"

"Yeah—two things," she said. "First, what's Liz's real name and—second—whatever happened to Michelle James?"

"Liz's name was Elizabeth...Elizabeth James. As for Michelle"—Larry shook his head—"she committed suicide in the mental hospital. It was a bunch of years ago, when Liz was still a little girl. That really hit Liz hard—set her back a bit—but Ken stuck at it and got her head back on straight. He always had a way of making things better for her and helping her through things. Of course, now that he's gone..."

"Have you seen her since Kenny died?" Sally asked.

"She was at his funeral, and I meant to talk to her, but didn't get the chance. Ken was kind of popular and the funeral was a big deal—newspapers, TV crews, cops from all over the country—and with all that crowd, I lost track of her. One minute she was there and I started making my way through the crowd. By the time I got through, she was gone."

"Would you have a picture of her?" I asked.

"Never did own no camera—never had a need for it. Now Ken, he had pictures of her all over his house. He'd buy some of those throw-away cameras and would stand in line at the pharmacy for hours waiting for them pictures." Larry grinned, a stream of tobacco juice leaking from his lower lip. "Liz would fuss when they had company over because Ken had hung those pictures everywhere. He had pictures of her at the shooting range, swimming in the river, hunting and just kicking around the mountain. Liz would bitch something awful about them pictures. She wasn't one for attention, that girl."

"What was Liz wearing on the day of the funeral?" Sally wanted to know.

I stared sideways at her, wondering what was on her mind.

Larry shrugged. "What everybody wears at funerals—black."

"What did she look like when you last saw her—color and length of her hair, height, eye color—as best you can remember?"

Larry struggled through a description and as Sally wrote down the particulars, I reached down to check my phone that was vibrating. It was Bethany.

"Hey, did you all leave yet?" she asked.

I walked toward the loaner car. "Not yet. We're talking to an old friend of Kenny James."

"Who?"

"Some mountain man named Larry Durham."

"Larry Durham? Did he tell you anything?"

"Did he ever! I think we're looking for a female sniper—Lenny James' daughter."

"I think your Larry Durham has been drinking too much moonshine," Bethany said. "Lenny James didn't have a daughter. He only had a baby boy and his baby was killed in the raid. Gina and all have already combed every newspaper they could find on the case and they even found his obituary, but there's no mention of a daughter."

"Yeah, this little girl has been a well-kept secret. She's the key to everything. When we find her, we'll find the killer."

There was a long pause from the other end. "Are you saying the killer—the sniper—is Lenny James' daughter? That she's killing everyone involved in the raid?"

"At this point, she's our best bet."

"Does this girl have a name?"

"Elizabeth James."

"Elizabeth?" Bethany echoed.

"Yep."

"Hold up a second..." Moments later, the sound of fingers pattering against a keyboard came through the phone. Bethany finally spoke again. "I'm running her name and there seems to be a few of them, but none from Tennessee. There's one from Anchorage, Alaska, one from Chicago, Illinois and one from Denver, Colorado. I doubt if any of these are our girl. Maybe this Durham fellow is shooting you a line of shit."

"Where are you?" I asked.

"Home...why?"

"How're you checking the database from home?"

"It's a web-based program. I can check it from anywhere that has an Internet connection."

"A what?"

"Never mind that. Do you have any more information that'll help get us closer to this girl?"

"Larry did say she moved away and got married, so she could be going by a different last name, but I still think we need to check these women out. Get officers from each of their hometowns to visit them and see what they're up to. If any of them are out of town, we need to find out where she's supposed to be and what she's supposed to be doing and try to verify that information. The real Elizabeth James is here somewhere...creeping around in these mountains."

"I'll call Gina or Melvin and have one of them get right on it," Bethany said. "By the way, when are you coming back?"

"We're about done here, so we should be leaving soon."

"Good...I miss you."

Sally walked up and motioned to the car, and I followed. "I miss you, too," I murmured, hoping Sally hadn't heard. I flipped my phone shut and slipped into the driver's seat. "Ready to head home?"

"We have one stop to make first," Sally said.

"Where's that?"

"The local newspaper. Larry remembered that Elizabeth James got the flag from the funeral and he said a number of photographers were shooting during the presentation."

"No shit! Great idea."

Sally had made a phone call and got the directions from Detective Plump. Within the hour we were going into the office of the *Gatlinburg Gazette* and we were shown to the desk of the reporter who'd covered the funeral.

"That was a couple of weeks ago," Courtney Hackenburg said, sliding her chair back and turning to rummage through a stack of articles. She finally found the one she was looking for and handed it over. "Here it is."

I unfolded the paper and scanned the front page, with Sally leaning close. There was a picture of the flag-covered casket with rows upon rows of uniformed officers in the background. A few other photographs depicted the color guard, officers crying and the sheriff giving his speech. The story ended at the bottom of the page and directed me to page five. I flipped through the pages and found more pictures from the highly publicized funeral.

"This guy was popular," I commented.

Courtney nodded. "He was very well-respected around here. Cops from everywhere attended the funeral. The governor even—"

"Holy shit!" My stomach suddenly went sour and I felt an intense urge to vomit.

"What is it?" Sally asked, craning her neck to see over my shoulder.

I dropped the paper to the desk. My head swam, knees felt unsteady. The room began to swirl. "Jesus…Christ," I muttered through numb lips.

Sally stared down at the picture that had stopped my clock in its tracks and she gasped violently. There in the picture, receiving the United States flag from the casket of Kenny James, was Elizabeth James…known to us as *Bethany Riggs!*

CHAPTER 40

I rushed out onto the sidewalk and vomited against a nearby lamppost. Several tourists swore out loud and made wide circles around me as I stood slumped over, gasping for breath.

"Amateur," one of them scolded.

"Learn how to handle your sauce," another chided.

I jerked my shirt up and wiped my face. My mind raced. *How had I been so blind? What in the hell had I been thinking? What was I going to do?* Bethany's voice…her smile…her soft lips…her naked body in bed beside me…all of those images strobed through my mind, making me dizzy. I felt a hand on my shoulder.

"Are you okay?"

I looked up. It was Sally. I straightened, fought to keep from swaying, and nodded. "I'll be okay. It just…it just surprised me is all."

"I know she meant a lot to you," Sally said in a soft voice. "I'm really sorry."

I took a deep, cleansing breath and exhaled. My shock started to fade and I began to seethe. I'd told my deepest, darkest secret to Bethany Riggs—Elizabeth James. She had lied to me…used me. She'd cold-bloodedly murdered three police officers. Kenneth Lewis had taken his own life, Wesley Guidry had been killed and I had been forced to kill Captain Theriot. A lot of lives had been lost and others ruined—all as a result of her actions. And all this time I had been sweet on her.

"She means nothing to me," I said.

"Just like that?" Sally asked doubtfully.

"Just like that." I spat on the ground for emphasis. "After all, if she'd meant so much to me, last night would've never happened." I walked away and left Sally standing there trying to digest what I'd said. Before I made it to the parking lot where our car was parked, my phone rang. I glanced down, then hurriedly waved Sally over. "It's Bethany's cell!"

Sally's eyes shifted to the rooftops across the road from us and then up and down the crowded streets. "You think she's watching us? You think she knows that we know?"

I glanced at my watch. "We were shot at nine hours ago. She could be almost back in Magnolia by now."

Sally pursed her lips as my phone continued to ring. "Aren't you going to answer it? If you don't, she might get suspicious."

I flipped it open, trying to sound casual. "Hey, Bethany, what's up?"

"Nothing much. I was able to track down all three women named Elizabeth James. Officers from all three jurisdictions went right out to the houses when I told them what was going on here. All of the women were home, they all have families and none of them have any criminal record of any type. It looks like that name is a dead end."

"Yeah, here, too," I said. "We haven't found anything worth pursuing. In fact, we're on our way back. This whole trip was a huge waste of time."

"What about the ambush? Do they have any leads?"

"Nothing. They scoured the mountainside, but they didn't even find a trace of the shooter. He must've been long gone before we even made the call."

"Oh, by the way, I called Debra from accounting and asked her to pull up the online call logs for all sheriff's office phones within the last twenty-four hours. I told her it was a confidential IA matter, like you said, and it worked like a charm. She e-mailed them to me, and I was able to check the call logs from my home computer. I went through—"

"You can do all that from home?"

"I can do it from my laptop in my car if I wanted to."

"Your car?" I blurted, then silently cursed myself.

"Yeah, why's that so hard to believe?"

"No reason," I said quickly. "Anyway, what did you find out?"

"There were no calls to or from anyone living in Tennessee."

"Nothing at all?"

"Nothing at all."

Of course there weren't, I thought, because you're the shooter!

There was a long pause and I finally said, "Well, let me go so we can get out of here."

"London..."

"Yeah?"

"Will I get to see you when you get back?"

"It'll be early in the morning when I roll back into Magnolia. Probably around two o'clock. Maybe we can get together tomorrow afternoon?"

"Hell, no!" Bethany said. "That'll be too long. Why don't I just meet you at your place at around twoish?"

My mind raced, trying to think of the right course of action. Yesterday I would've jumped at the chance of having Bethany spend the night—or morning—with me. Yesterday I couldn't wait to see her again. But today... Well, today things had changed. Sensing I was taking entirely too long to respond, I blurted, "Why don't I call you as I'm rolling into Magnolia? And then you can meet me at my house. It should be no later than two, two-thirty."

"That sounds great, but I have to warn you...you won't be getting much sleep until around four or five. I've been lying in that hospital for two days dreaming about our next time together."

"What about your neck? Won't that be a problem? I mean, doesn't it have to heal up first?" I tried to sound concerned.

"London Carter, are you trying to make excuses? Is there something I need to know?"

"No...no...not at all," I stammered. "I just don't want to hurt you. I don't want to hurt your neck."

Bethany laughed. "I'm kidding. No, the doctors said that was nothing. They were more concerned with whether or not I had any internal injuries from the bullets impacting the vest, but I got the all clear from them."

"Very funny," I said, relieved she hadn't suspected I was on to her. "I'll see you in the morning then." I flipped the phone shut, then turned to Sally. "What the hell am I going to do?"

"I think you need to call Sheriff Burke right away and tell him what we know."

"No way," I said, shaking my head. "He'll have her killed. I might be mad at her, but I don't want her to die. I mean, part of me understands why she's doing this—if it *is* her who's doing it."

Sally studied my face. "I think we've moved beyond the what-if-it's-her phase. I think we should be concentrating on what to do next, and that shouldn't include doing nothing."

"I'm not saying we do nothing. I'm just saying we handle it

ourselves—take her in alive—see if she confesses. She's the missing puzzle to what happened twenty years ago. Like Larry said, she can tell us if there ever was a drug deal in the first place. If she talks, we'll have what we need to put Sheriff Burke away and—"

"Whoa, cowboy, let's not get ahead of ourselves," Sally cautioned. "Even if she does admit to being Elizabeth James and she says what we think she'll say, do you really think a jury would believe her? She's a cop who killed three other cops in cold blood. She's not exactly the best witness in a police corruption case."

"She's the perfect witness," I countered. "No one would go through all that trouble and risk the death penalty for a lie, or for something that didn't happen."

"What if she kills again before we get to her? Are you willing to live with another cop's blood on your hands?"

I leaned against the car and crossed my arms in front of my chest, considering the prospect. After thinking about it for about three seconds, I nodded. "Yep, I can. If you ask me, everyone involved deserves to die anyway. Sure, not the way she's doing it, but by lethal injection. If she gets to one or two of them before we get to her, it'll save the state a few dollars. Besides, the sheriff and his cronies are hiding under their cots at the main office. They won't stick their heads outside until the killer is locked down solid."

Sally shook her head slowly. "I can't believe I'm considering going along with this. But, more than anything, I really hate dirty cops, especially those who would kill a baby and then lie about it. Okay, what's the plan?"

CHAPTER 41

I didn't call Bethany until I was pulling into my driveway. I'd wanted to make sure she didn't beat us to my house. Her voice was groggy when she answered. "Hey, I'm sorry I fell asleep. I tried to stay awake. What time is it anyway?"

"Three forty-five. We got stuck in traffic."

"Is Sally still with you?"

"No, I dropped her off." I pressed my finger to my lips, cautioning Sally not to make a sound. "You know, we can wait until tomorrow, if you want. You sound tired—"

"Oh, no! I'm coming over right now. I want to see you. I *need* to see you."

I shut off the engine to the loaner we'd gotten from the Gatlinburg Police Department and Sally and I rushed into my house. Once we were inside, Sally looked around. "What's the plan?"

I unlocked my gun closet. "Why don't you hide in here until she gets inside? As sure as we're standing here, she'll give me a hug. Once she does, I'll latch onto her and not let go. At that point, you can rush out and handcuff her."

Sally nodded and slipped into the dark closet. "Sounds like a plan."

I closed the door behind Sally and sat on my sofa, trying to act casual. We spoke in low whispers as we waited, but we didn't have to wait long. A car hummed into my driveway and came to a stop.

"Okay, get ready, Sally."

I remained seated as I heard the car door slam. It wasn't until I heard heels echoing right outside the door that I stood to my feet. My heart beat a steady drum in my chest. There was a knock at the door.

I took a deep breath, moved to the door and opened it. There Bethany stood, dressed in jeans and a tank top. She appeared cautious. I noticed her pistol was strapped to her waistband and her hand was dangling close to it. I smiled and moved in to hug her. "God, I've missed you so much!"

Bethany seemed to relax in my arms; she hugged me back. I held her for several seconds, then turned and stepped into my house. I pushed the door closed and opened my arms to her. She fell into them and squeezed me tight. I sighed, realizing she was no longer suspicious and—

"What is it?" Bethany asked, pushing back to stare up into my eyes.

"Nothing. Why?"

"I felt you take a breath, like you were relieved or something."

I smiled. "I am relieved…relieved to see you again."

There was a creak behind her, and she jerked her head around, yelping when she saw Sally coming toward us. I jumped forward and wrapped her in my embrace, then pulled her toward the ground on top of me. Her right hand reached for her pistol as she screamed, "What the hell?"

Bethany and I crashed to the ground, and I wrapped my legs around hers, pinning them to me. Her right hand was on her pistol and she was trying to drag it from its holster. Sally jumped onto Bethany's back and jerked her right hand behind her back. After a brief struggle, Sally secured Bethany's left hand behind her back and slipped cuffs on her. Bethany struggled to free herself, but it was no use. Sally pulled her off me and we stood.

Bethany kicked at me, smashing the heel of her shoe against my left shin. I winced, but brushed it off. "Settle down, Bethany," I said. "It's over."

"Get these cuffs off of me now!" she screamed. "I'll have you both arrested for false imprisonment!"

"Sorry, Bethany, it's over. We know everything." I pulled her to her feet and guided her to the sofa and let her sit. She stared up at me, face red with anger. As I began reciting Bethany her Miranda rights, her eyes grew wider as I spoke.

"London, this is not funny," Bethany said, panic starting to tighten its grip on her throat, making her voice shake. "I'm serious. Take these cuffs off me. I don't know what you're talking about, but you're wrong. If you just stop this right now, I'll forget this ever happened and I won't file any charges."

I sat on the coffee table across from her, and Sally sat beside me.

I shook my head. "It's over, Liz. We know everything...*every*thing."

"Why did you call me that?" Bethany asked. "I don't know what you're talking about. Please, London, you have to believe me. I don't know anything." Tears streamed down her face. She stared desperately from Sally's cold eyes to mine. "London, you need to listen to me. I don't know what you're talking about."

I turned to Sally, nodded. She quickly got up and exited the house. When she was gone, Bethany slipped off the sofa and knelt in front of me. "Please, London, I'm begging you to let me go. I know you have feelings for me and I have feelings for you. You and I can be together, just like we both want. This is all a big mistake. Just let me go so I can prove it to you. Please, London...I love you. Let me show you how much I love you and give me a chance to prove to you that I'm not who you think I am. I'm the girl you fell for—nothing more, nothing less. Just give me a chance."

The door slammed shut and Sally reentered the living room. She handed me the newspaper article we'd acquired from Courtney Hackenburg. I flipped through it until I found the picture of Elizabeth James and turned it so Bethany could see. "Are you denying this is you?"

What was left of Bethany's color drained completely from her face, leaving a deathly shade of pale on her cheeks. "How... Why... Where'd you get that?"

"As you already know, this picture was taken at your uncle's funeral. Now, you can continue to lie to us about who you are or you can keep your mouth shut. It makes no difference to us. We'll lock you up and we'll toss your place and retrace every step you've made in the last ten years. We'll get the evidence we need to convict you of first degree murder and the district attorney will seek the death penalty—and he'll get it. You'll go to prison and remain there until you're put to death. You'll be known as some crazed female sniper who began killing cops because she was bitter and blamed everyone else for life's problems."

I took a breath and exhaled. "Or you can tell us the truth about what happened. You can help us prove the sheriff and his thugs hit the wrong house twenty years ago and they killed innocent people and then lied about it. If we can prove they're nothing but rogue cops with blood on their hands, a jury will have a very difficult time sentencing you to death because no one has any sympathy for dirty cops. Hell, they might even find you guilty of something less than murder...maybe even find you temporarily insane. Who knows? They might even let you walk. What is certain, though, is if you keep your mouth shut, you'll be sentenced to death or you'll be killed by Sheriff Burke and his men."

Bethany hung her head and cried. Sally placed a gentle hand on her shoulder. "Look, if you talk to us, we can protect you. We'll get you shipped out of here and we'll see to it that the sheriff and his men are taken down. You have our word."

After a long moment of silent weeping, Bethany looked up into my eyes. "Promise me they'll pay for what they did."

"I promise," I said.

"No, I want to hear you say that the sheriff and his men will pay for killing my little brother and my dad and for framing my mom. They can't get away with it or everything will—" Bethany broke down in uncontrollable sobs. When she'd calmed down a bit, she continued. "If they get away with it, then everything I've done will have been for nothing and my family will never get justice. I'm the last chance they have."

I cradled Bethany's face in my hands. "I promise you this; the sheriff and every single one of those bastards responsible will be brought to justice. They'll be arrested, tried and convicted for murder. I give you my word."

Bethany appeared to relax a little and took a deep breath. "Okay, I'll talk under one condition…you get me out of Magnolia Parish as soon as we're done here. Put me in another jail—any jail—just as long as it's not Magnolia. If you lock me up here, I'll never live to see justice served for my family. You already know that."

"Arrangements have already been made," I said, "but we need to hurry. Tell us what you did and why you did it."

"That's me in the picture," Bethany began softly. "I'm Elizabeth James."

Although I already knew that to be the case, I was still shocked to hear her say it out loud. "Go on," I coaxed.

"I was sleeping at a friend's house the night Sheriff Burke—he wasn't the sheriff back then; he was a narcotics agent—and his team killed my dad and baby brother and framed my mom. Afterward, I went to live with my uncle, Kenny James. He raised me like I was his own daughter. He taught me how to take care of myself. He taught me how to fight, how to shoot, how to cook, how to clean my own kill, how to do everything. He was like a dad to me."

"What about the court hearings?" I asked. "Did you attend any of them?"

Bethany shook her head. "Uncle Kenny wouldn't let me. After I told him what I knew, he insisted I stay away. He didn't want anyone knowing I existed. He was afraid if the sheriff and his men found out about me, they'd try to get at me."

"What did you tell him?" Sally asked. "What is it that you knew?"

"I told him I was home the day before the raid and I knew the cops were lying about the drugs because no one came to visit that day. Not a narcotics agent, not a cop, no one. I remember that day like it was yesterday, every little detail. It's funny how a traumatic event can burn even the most mundane parts of a day into your mind." Bethany sighed, then shifted uncomfortably on the sofa. The chains from the handcuffs rattled as she moved. "After the last court hearing, Uncle Kenny told me they declared my mom legally insane and placed her in a mental hospital. He and I would go visit her as often as possible, sometimes as much as two or three times each week.

"And then one day"—Bethany bent her head and cried softly—"we went to the hospital and they wouldn't let us see my mom. They took Uncle Kenny into another room while a nurse stayed with me and then he came back and told me…he told me that my mom was dead. The hospital called it a suicide, but I know it was the medicine. They did it. They gave her too much medicine. My mom would never commit suicide. She loved life too much. She loved me too much. She would never leave me alone…ever."

"What happened after that?" I asked. "After your mom died?"

"The case just went away. The district attorney considered it closed, and even after my uncle pulled enormous strings, the FBI refused to launch a full investigation. They claimed to have looked over the case and didn't find any evidence of misconduct. They said everything checked out and that it was all my dad's fault, but I knew better. The sheriff and his gang of outlaws stole everyone I loved away from me. They destroyed my childhood…my entire life."

Sally moved over to sit beside Bethany and dabbed at Bethany's eyes with a napkin. After a few moments, I asked Bethany to continue.

"After that night, there wasn't a day I didn't think about getting revenge. Like you"—Bethany nodded toward me—"I fantasized about killing each and every one of them bastards."

Sally turned a curious eye my way and mouthed the words, What the hell?

I shrugged like I didn't know what Bethany was talking about.

"Each time I'd shoot a target with Uncle Kenny, I'd imagine I was shooting one of them right in the eyeball. Little did he know I was preparing myself for the day I'd return to Magnolia Parish...the day I would claim the souls of those who wrecked my life."

I stared at the beautiful woman in front of me, my heart going out to her. I knew all too well how she felt. She and I were so much alike, with the only difference being she acted out her fantasy and mine had remained in my head. "So, you admit to being the one who killed Captain Landry, Captain Abbott and retired Captain Wainwright?"

Bethany nodded slowly.

"Why'd you wait so long?" I asked. "You worked here for years, so why'd you start when you did? Why not kill them sooner?"

"I couldn't do it as long as Uncle Kenny was alive. He would've known it was me and it would've destroyed him. From the first day he took me to live with him, he began working hard to teach me to let go...to forgive them for what they did. He said God would punish them in the end and that I should move on with my life. He said my family would've wanted it that way." Bethany slowly shook her head. "I wasn't like him. I couldn't forgive them, no matter how hard I tried, and I couldn't wait for God to punish them."

"So, your uncle was the only thing holding you back?" I asked.

Bethany nodded.

"And when he died—"

"When he died, I was lost. I had nothing to live for. Nothing holding me back anymore. I was free to carry out my plan, to make those bastards pay."

"How'd you get hired on without the sheriff or anyone else knowing who you were?" Sally asked incredulously. "And how'd you get rid of your real name?"

"I didn't. My real name is Bethany Elizabeth James. Everyone always called me Elizabeth or Liz. After I got married, my name legally turned to Bethany Riggs."

"Your uncle's friend said you didn't stay married long," I began. "What happened?"

"I tried to follow my uncle's advice, tried to move on with my life. I got married to a guy who seemed nice enough, but he turned out to be a real prick. I ended up divorcing him six months later. After that, I decided to move back home."

"Here in Magnolia?" I asked.

"Yeah. I got the job with the sheriff's office and began trying to gather as much information as I could about that night."

"You killed Wainwright first," Sally said. "Why?"

"I couldn't find the reports from that night in any of his files at work, so I figured he might've hidden them at his house."

"Did you find anything?" I asked.

"I found the doctored police report. Most of it was a lie, but it did name every officer who was involved with the incident and it gave me exactly what I needed."

"Your hit list?" I asked.

Bethany nodded.

"How can you sit here so calmly and talk about how you killed fellow cops?" Sally wanted to know. "Cops you worked with day in and day out? How can you do it?"

"They're not cops," Bethany explained. "You and London are cops. Them...they're parasites. They're no better than the criminals you all put away every day. Being dead just means they won't be able to hurt anyone again...ever."

After several moments of silence, I asked, "What was the deal with Captain Landry? Why'd you take him out in the middle of a hostage standoff?"

"Why *not* do it then?" Bethany looked confused. "It was the perfect time. I was passing on the bridge just as everything was going down and realized I could see the scene from up there. We had the roads blocked off, so there was no danger of anyone passing by and seeing me. It was the perfect setup."

"But why Captain Landry? Were you going in any particular order?" I pressed.

"He was the only one I could get my crosshairs on...the only one who showed his eyeball," Bethany said flatly. "If the sheriff had been standing there, it would've been his ass going down. In fact, you saved his life at the funeral."

I cocked my head sideways. "What do you mean?"

"I planned to take out the sheriff right after I took out Abbott, but you tackled him to the ground before I could get a clean shot on him, and I wasn't about to risk hitting an innocent person. I was going to try to get another shot at him, but when I saw you lift your phone over the stage, I knew you had my location pegged. I slipped out, put my rifle in my car and melded into the officers who were running around the cemetery."

I mused over what I'd just heard, feeling a little stunned that I'd actually closed my eyes and slept right next to this cold-blooded killer—without having a clue what she was up to. My mind then drifted to Kenneth Lewis. "Did you know about the affair between Kenneth and Captain Landry's wife?"

Bethany's head drooped. "That's my only regret in this whole situation. Captain Landry had come to me with his suspicions, and I began doing surveillance on Lewis. I caught him with Landry's wife and I started to tell Landry about it, but then I decided Lewis would make an excellent scapegoat at some point. So, I told Landry I hadn't found out anything. I knew Lewis was a sniper and when I heard about that hostage call, I was going to try and shadow his position to make it look like he took out the sheriff—or whoever I could take out at that time. When he didn't show up, it made my job much easier. I just didn't bank on him killing himself."

"That's what happens when you decide to take the law into your own hands," Sally scolded. "Innocent people die or get hurt. You should've known that from your own experiences."

Bethany only nodded, tears beginning to stream down her face again.

I stood to get more napkins, but the front door to my house crashed open. The doorframe splintered; glass shattered. A brilliant flash and a violent explosion erupted within the room, blinding everyone inside and rendering us helpless.

CHAPTER 42

Dark shadows darted through the smoke and gunpowder. Loud voices bellowed amidst the chaos, but were muffled by the ringing in my ears. They barked orders of some sort while rough hands—a dozen of them—grabbed at me and stretched my limbs in different directions. I fought to free myself, managed to get one arm loose, and I punched out at one of the dark shadows. A blunt object struck the back of my skull. The chaos seemed to fade for a brief second. I shook my head and continued to struggle. Two sharp barbs stabbed into my back and a surge of electricity reverberated through my muscles. My arms locked up. My jaw tightened. I groaned and tried to resist the shock. It was no use. Several sets of hands pulled my weak arms to my back. The vice of electricity suddenly released me and I went lax. Before I could jerk my arms forward again, I felt steel fingers ratchet around my wrists.

Realization suddenly hit me…I had been shot with a stun gun and handcuffed!

I was jerked to my feet and shoved onto my own sofa. As the smoke began to dissipate, Bethany and Sally came into view. Sally had been cuffed, and she was seated on the loveseat beside Bethany. A dozen SWAT officers—clad in black ninja garb, complete with masks and goggles—stomped around my living room.

"What the hell is going on?" I demanded.

One of the SWAT officers peeled his mask off. It was Dave, one of the assault team leaders. "Sheriff's orders," he said. "We were told you were harboring the killer sniper."

"Who told you that?" I glanced at Bethany. Her eyes were wide.

She knew the end was possibly near.

"I did," said Captain Corey Chiasson from the doorway. "Bethany Riggs is the killer, but I guess you already knew that, didn't you?"

I jerked my head around. Corey was flanked by Detectives Melvin Ford and Rachael Bowler. They all stared accusingly at me.

"What... How'd y'all know?" I asked.

"This is from an ATM machine camera." Melvin pulled a grainy black-and-white photo from a file folder. He held it so I could see. It was a surveillance photo that showed a woman in the driver's seat of a car taking a picture with a high-powered camera. There was no mistaking Bethany's beautiful face. "The pictures y'all found in Justin Wainwright's house, the ones of Kenneth Lewis and Starla Landry having an affair"—Melvin pointed his thumb toward Bethany—"she took them. She knew about the affair and set Kenneth up for killing Captain Landry and Captain Wainwright. She planted the photos in Wainwright's house the day she killed him and she ransacked his place to make it look like Kenneth was looking for them."

I looked over at Bethany. She mouthed the words, Please help me.

My mind raced. I had to get her out of here or they would kill her for sure—especially if they found out her real identity. "All you have is a picture of Bethany with a camera. We don't know when the other pictures were taken, so there's no way to tell if this surveillance shot has anything to do with those pictures."

"Actually," Melvin said, "a judge agreed with us that there was enough probable cause to search her house. We found this..." He held up a memory card. "On it are copies of all the pictures y'all recovered from Justin Wainwright's house. Better than that, the date and time stamp on two of the pictures coincide with the date and time from this surveillance video."

Knowing how foolish it would sound, I said it anyway. "So she took a few pictures—big deal. That doesn't make her a killer."

"No," Lieutenant Chiasson said, "it doesn't. What makes her the killer is the sniper rifle we found hidden in the floorboards of her house, along with a case of three-o-eight bullets—minus three—and a report from 1991 that was written by Justin Wainwright. It details a certain incident involving Lenny James. It lists the names of the dead captains, most of the living captains, our majors, the chief and the sheriff. The names of Wainwright, Abbott, Theriot, Guidry and Landry were struck through. She was going to take them all out one by one, all the way down to the sheriff. The only thing I can't figure out is what's in it for her." Corey approached Bethany and squatted beside her, leaned his face close to hers. "What's your connection to this case, Bethany? Why are you doing this?"

"I-I don't know what you're talking about," Bethany said quietly. "I'm not a killer. I'm a cop. I'm an internal affairs officer. You all are making a huge—"

"Bullshit!" Corey spat in Bethany's face. He stood abruptly to his feet. "You're going to die for what you did, you little bitch!"

"Corey, we need to talk," I said, motioning toward the kitchen with my head, "in private."

"There's nothing to talk about," Corey said. "The sheriff's on his way. When he gets here, you can plead your case to him. Last he mentioned, you and Sally were facing principal to first degree murder, which also carries the death penalty."

As if on cue, tires screeched outside and several vehicles pulled into my driveway. The front door, which was hanging precariously by its hinges, burst open and the early morning light flooded in. Sheriff Burke pushed through the splintered mess on the floor. He was followed by his entire command staff. They all looked disheveled and desperately in need of sleep, but they no longer walked in fear. The swagger had returned to all of their steps—that cockiness that consumes many commanders who forget from whence they had come—except for Captain Carmella Vizier. On a face that once sported an obvious look of fear, there was now a look of shame and regret.

"Where's that bitch?" Sheriff Burke bellowed as he approached the SWAT officers in my living room. They quickly separated and left an opening straight to the loveseat and sofa where we sat cuffed. Sheriff Burke's eyes locked onto Bethany and he raced across the living room. He punched her full in the face. "You bitch!"

I jumped to my feet. "Cut that shit out, you—"

Electricity flooded through me once again—I'd forgotten about the stun gun probes in my back—and I stiffened up. After five seconds, it suddenly and unexpectedly released me and I collapsed violently to the floor. After I took a few deep breaths to clear my head, I looked up to see Sheriff Burke standing over me.

He shook his head. "And you... You're the worst of them all. I trusted you. I gave you everything you asked for. And this is how you repay me? This is how you thank me? All for a piece of ass?"

"What're you talking about?" I asked. "We just got back from Gatlinburg. I already called and told you everything. Bethany just got out the hospital and she met us here to hang out, see if we needed anything. We were going to get something to eat and then get to bed and—"

"Cut the bullshit, London. The first major clue you're full of shit is that you had the bitch cuffed." His face broke into a wicked and triumphant grin. "Your second mistake was calling Sheriff Tyler and asking him to send his deputies into *my* parish to transport Bethany back to *his* jail. What, did you think he would just take the word of some random detective—well, ex-detective now—and send his deputies down here to arrest a cop killer without verifying your information first? You think he would make a move against a sitting and neighboring sheriff just based upon a phone call he received from some bullshit detective? A detective who was admittedly getting his information from a killer—a *cop* killer at that! What world do you think you live in, boy?"

I sighed heavily, hung my head. The plan had sounded good at the time and Sally had even agreed. The radio operator had patched me right in to Sheriff Tyler's cell phone—woke him up, actually—and he seemed like a standup guy. Gave me his word he would keep things under wrap and provide all the assistance I needed...said he hated dirty cops just as much as the next one...said whatever he thought he needed to say to convince me everything was cool.

"God, I'm such a fool," I murmured.

"What'd you say?" Burke asked, shoving my shoulder with his boot. "Whatever it is, it'd better be a prayer to the Good Lord, because you're going to need it where you're going." He walked to Sally and grunted. "You know, Piatkowski, it's a shame you got caught up in London and Bethany's scheme—you were a good detective. Unfortunately for you, principal to first degree murder carries the death penalty. Maybe if you turn state's evidence they'll spare your life."

"I ain't turning shit," Sally said defiantly.

Sheriff Burke smiled and turned to the group of SWAT operators who had gathered by the doorway. "Get these maggots out of here. We have a press conference to attend."

The sheriff and his entourage moved out into the sunlight, then gathered just outside my doorway on the cemented driveway. One of the masked operators moved toward me and jerked me to my feet. He grabbed my hand with his and slipped something into my palm. It was a handcuff key. "Just be cool and go along," he said. "We've got this under control."

It was Jerry Allemand!

While other SWAT operators pulled Bethany and Sally to their feet and began escorting them outside, I leaned toward Jerry and whispered, "What's going on?"

"Gina contacted the FBI," he mumbled back, "but we're not waiting on them to get here. Gina should be waiting for us at the main office by now with Dean, Ray and Alvin. Once we get there, we'll bust y'all out and head to New Orleans, where a team of FBI agents should be waiting for—"

"Let's go!" Sheriff Burke called from outside. "The media's starting to arrive. Who called them anyway?"

Jerry and I reached the doorway first and we were met by Chief Garcia and Major Ronald Day. "We've got him," Garcia told Jerry, and they each grabbed one of my arms and turned toward the group of reporters that had gathered at the end of my long driveway. They walked with chests poking out, slightly behind me, pushing me toward the nearest squad car.

We were still a dozen yards from the squad car when I felt a whisper of air fly by my right ear. My right arm suddenly dropped and I heard a dull thump behind me. A second whisper whizzed over my left ear and met with the same results—the grip on my left arm was relaxed.

CHAPTER 43

Screams sounded behind me, and I turned just in time to see Captain Tyrone Gibbs collapse to the ground, just a few feet behind Garcia and Day, who were sprawled on my driveway, a small hole between their eyes and a mess of blood and brain matter staining the cement behind their bodies. A fourth bullet whispered by and Major Lawrence Doucet joined his counterparts on the cement, thrust into the afterlife.

Without thought, I dropped to the ground and rolled behind a nearby squad car. Captain Martin Thomas had just stepped out of my house. He was escorting Bethany and was holding onto one of her arms. Captain Carmella Vizier and Jerry Allemand were right behind them. A look of shock fell over Thomas' face when he saw the bodies of his comrades lying in pools of blood and brain matter on the ground, but his reaction time was no match for the sniper's bullet. It entered Thomas' head through the tip of his nose, destroying his medulla oblongata so instantly that his facial expression didn't even change when his body collapsed into a lifeless heap on my doorsteps.

Jerry grabbed Bethany and jerked her into my house. Carmella screamed and followed Jerry, disappearing into the shadows of the room. There was a slight pause in the shooting and I realized the sniper was reloading. I bolted for my front door and dove through it, kicking it shut behind me. It slammed against the splintered frame and dangled there, a beam of sunlight spilling through the large crack from the damage.

I scrambled to a corner of the room and rolled to my shoulder, struggling with the handcuff key Jerry had given me. I found the hole in one of the cuffs and freed my left hand. I brought my right hand around and stripped that cuff off as well, before I tossed them aside. I scanned the room and found Bethany lying on the ground behind the loveseat. Jerry was leaning against her, shielding her body with his own. Carmella was across the room cowering against the wall.

"What the hell's going on?" I asked Jerry. "Is this what you meant by busting us out?"

He shook his head, eyes wide with excitement. "That's not us, London. I…I don't know who that is."

"Where's Sally?" I asked.

"Back here," she called from the kitchen.

"Jerry, take Bethany to the kitchen and get those damn cuffs off Sally—she did nothing wrong—and then y'all hunker down in the hallway bathroom. There're no windows in there and the walls are reinforced for tornadoes, so you'll be safe from sniper fire."

Semi-automatic gunfire erupted outside. Without looking, I knew the SWAT operators were spraying the area they thought the sniper to be, but they were wrong. From my house, there was only one place those shots could've originated from—the water tower located three hundred yards to the west. Another burst of gunfire sounded and bullets pattered off the steel exterior of my front door.

"To hell with the sniper," I called. "Y'all need to worry about friendly fire from those overzealous idiots out there." I crawled to my closet and pushed the door open. I threw my semi-automatic rifle over my shoulder and grabbed my sniper rifle. Next, I crawled to where Carmella sat. Her knees were pulled to her chin and she was shaking uncontrollably. "Come on," I coaxed. "Go down the hall and into the bathroom. Stay there and don't move until—"

"They're coming for me!" Carmella wailed. She clutched my arm, her nails ripping at my flesh. "They're going to get me! I'm next! Oh, God, I'm next! You need to help me! You need to protect me! I didn't want to do it! I didn't want any part of it, but Sheriff Burke said I'd go to prison if I didn't do what he told me to do! I didn't have a choice!"

"Do what?" I asked, raising my voice above the thunderous gunfire still erupting outside. "What are you talking about?"

Tears streamed down Carmella's face and her chin bounced as she spoke. "I-I wrote the search warrant that night. It wasn't for Bethany's family's house—it was for the one across the street."

"What?" That got my attention.

"We hit the wrong house."

"What about the court hearings? Y'all testified Thomas bought drugs from Lenny James the day before the raid."

"We…we lied. They made me lie. They made me change the warrant and then they told me if I said anything I'd be arrested. I-I didn't have a choice. I was afraid. They threatened me! The sheriff threatened me! It was all his idea. He promised to take care of everyone who went along with him and threatened to destroy anyone who went against him. I had no choice! It was all of them against me. You've got to believe me—if there'd been a way for me to do the right thing I would have. I-I had no choice!"

"Do you still have a copy of the warrant?"

Carmella nodded her head, as she rubbed tears from her face. "I have the original. It's in a fireproof safe at my mom and dad's house, in my old room. I'll give it to you—I don't care—just protect me!"

I grabbed her by the arm and dragged her to her feet. I ushered her across the living room and toward the hallway. As we passed the doorway, it flung open and Sheriff Burke—his face pale—and several SWAT operators rushed inside and took cover behind the furniture. I shoved Carmella. "Keep going! Get into the bathroom with Jerry and Sally and lock the door!"

I hurried to my spare bedroom that faced west and jerked the curtains open a few inches, letting the sunlight flow through. I backed out into the hallway, dropped to the ground and set up my rifle. I flipped open my scope caps and aimed through the crack in the curtain, searching for the water tower. When I found it, I cranked the power on my scope to ten and scanned the catwalk. Nothing. Not even a whisper of movement. The sniper was gone.

CHAPTER 44

I left my sniper rifle on the floor and swung my semi-automatic rifle off my shoulder, then walked to the living room to face Sheriff Burke. He was hiding beside my entertainment center. The SWAT operators were scattered around the room.

"The sniper's gone," I announced.

There was a collective sigh around the room and everyone stood slowly to their feet. The sheriff eyed me coldly. "How'd you get out of your cuffs? Nothing's changed. You're still under arrest."

With a subtle shift of my hands, I swung the muzzle of my rifle in his direction. "Sheriff, it's over. We know about the search warrant, the false testimony, everything. You're going down for murder."

The SWAT operators began to fan out, so I quickly shouldered my rifle, settling the front sight on Sheriff Burke's head. "Don't move—none of you! The FBI's en route to take Calvin Burke into custody. If any of y'all try to help him, y'all are going to prison, too."

The operators hesitated, exchanging glances through their goggles.

"London, he's the sheriff," one of them said. "The *sheriff!* You'd better have proof before you start making those kinds of accusations."

"I have all the proof I need." I scanned the group while keeping my front sight trained on Burke. "Keep your hands where I can see them and move slowly toward the left."

They hesitated for several moments. Finally, one of them nodded his resignation, moved toward the left, stripped off his mask. It was Jake Reynolds—he'd graduated from the police academy with me.

"I've always known you to be a standup guy, London, and I'll give you the benefit of the doubt. I don't need to tell you what'll happen to you if you're wrong."

"I'm not. We have all the proof we need to put his ass behind bars forever."

"Bullshit," Burke bellowed. "I'm ordering y'all to take London Carter into custody this very moment!"

The other operators hesitated, but Jake waved them toward his side of the room. "Do what London says. I have a feeling he's on the right side of this fight."

I relaxed, but kept my rifle pointed at Sheriff Burke. At that moment, tires screeched outside, doors slammed and there was a knock at the front door.

"It's us," called a familiar voice. "We're the good guys—don't shoot."

It was Ray Sevin, my number four sniper. He cautiously opened the damaged door and walked in when he saw me standing there. Alvin Reed and Dean Pierce followed him. Ray handed me his phone. "It's Gina. She needs to talk to you."

"Hey, stranger." I held the phone in one hand while holding my rifle steady with the other. "What's going on?"

"Are y'all code four?" she asked, wanting to know if everything was cool and we were safe.

"Yeah, we're good now, but there's a second shooter out there."

"Jerry called me and told me y'all were under attack," she said, "but I haven't been able to get back in touch with him. I was worried sick."

"We're good right now."

"Good?" Gina's voice was incredulous. "Jerry said there're a number of officers down. How's that *good?*"

"I said we're good *now.* The sniper's gone."

"What about Sheriff Burke?" she asked.

"He's right here. I'm about to put him in handcuffs." I didn't have to say another word. Ray moved forward, spun Sheriff Burke around and slapped a set of cuffs on him. I lowered my gun.

"Let Jerry know I'm just getting into New Orleans," Gina said. "The director of the FBI wants me to meet with the federal prosecutor and tell him what we're dealing with. He's assembling a team from across the country to come in and conduct a thorough investigation into everything that's happened…from twenty years ago to now."

"How long will it take y'all to get back to Magnolia?" I asked.

"He said most of the team members have already flown into New Orleans. I think he's waiting on one or two more to get there. I'm guessing a couple of hours at most."

"Okay. I'll have a few officers stay here and secure the scene and the rest of us will get back to CID."

"Please be careful," Gina warned.

"Yeah, I'll have Jerry and the rest of the snipers secure a route to the office. We'll be fine. Get back here with the FBI as soon as you can." I handed the phone back to Ray. "You've got things under control here?"

Ray nodded, so I made my way toward the bathroom. I knocked on the door. "It's me—London."

Jerry pulled the door open, and I stepped in. Bethany and Carmella were on the floor, leaning against the edge of the bathtub, and Sally was seated across from them on the countertop. "Jerry, can you take Carmella to the living room? Sally and I need to talk to Bethany."

Jerry nodded, led Carmella out of the room and closed the door behind them.

I set my rifle on the counter and squatted in front of Bethany Riggs, staring intently into her eyes. "Who are you working with?"

Bethany's mouth dropped open. "I'm not working with anyone!"

"Don't give me that shit, Beth. Someone's out there finishing what you started, and you know exactly who it is."

"I don't know anything. I admit I shot Wainwright, Landry and Abbott, but I don't know who's out there doing this."

I looked up at Sally. She shrugged. I turned back to Bethany. "Look, I don't want to hurt you, but I will if I have to."

Bethany's mouth dropped open. "What are you talking about?"

"You know damn good and well what I'm talking about. Start talking or else—"

"That's a threat! Even if you do make me talk, you won't be able to use anything I've said against me in court because any statements I make will be made under duress and the threat of violence. You can't do that!"

I smiled. "Bethany, I don't plan on using your next statement in court. I'm only going to use it to save lives."

"You'd never hit a woman," Bethany said, shaking her head positively. "I know you too well. You're bluffing!"

I stood and stepped back. Sally moved in my place and leaned close to Bethany. "I'll knock the piss out of you with a good heart."

Bethany's eyes widened. "This is ridiculous! I don't know

anything. You all can't—"

Sally swiftly leaned her head back and smashed her forehead into Bethany's face. Bethany yelped as blood appeared in an open gash above her right eye and also spilled from her nose. "You bitch!" she screamed.

Sally followed that with an uppercut punch to Bethany's solar plexus. Bethany doubled over and groaned, blood dripping from her face and staining my bathroom floor. "Who's working with you?" Sally asked.

Bethany strained to catch her breath. "You can go to hell! I'll never talk."

Sally grabbed a handful of Bethany's hair and jerked her head back. "You just admitted there's someone working with you. Now who is it?"

As Bethany pressed her lips together, she shook her head in defiance. Sally looked up. I frowned. "Forget it. She won't say anything. Let's just turn her over to Sheriff Burke and forget about her family. If she won't do the right thing, why should we? To hell with her dad and her baby brother. If she won't talk, we won't help."

Tears rolled freely down Bethany's face. "You…you promised!"

"You rendered that promise null and void when you got your accomplice to start killing more cops." I jerked her to her feet. "Let's go. I'm turning you over to Sheriff Burke—"

"Wait!" Bethany pleaded. "Just wait. Okay, I'll talk. It…it's my ex-husband, Troy Riggs. He's out there watching over me. We had a plan. If I got captured, he was supposed to finish what I started, and he did. He took out everyone but Sheriff Burke. I told him not to touch Burke. Killing him would be too easy. I want him to live to regret the day he destroyed my family."

"You're full of shit! These are just more of your lies."

"No, it's the truth. Think about it…if he wanted Sheriff Burke dead, he would've been the first one to drop. Troy took out everyone except for Burke because I told him not to touch Burke. I want the sheriff going to jail."

I started to talk, but Bethany interrupted me.

"London, it's over. I'm over. I accept that. All I want now is to see Burke in jail. I know I'm going to jail. I know I'll probably be sentenced to death. I accept that. I just want him to get what's coming to him."

I thought that over, then slowly nodded. "Okay, where do we find Troy?"

"I don't know. He's probably long gone by now. I told him to leave as soon as it was done—as soon as it was finished."

"What's his cell number?" I pressed.

"I don't know."

"Bullshit," I said. "There had to be a way for y'all to communicate, for you to tell him what to do and who to do it to."

"We figured it would be best if we didn't contact each other. That way, if one of us got caught, the other would be able to fulfill the mission."

"Mission?" Sally echoed. "This wasn't a *mission*...this was *murder!*"

"Where'd you see him last?" I asked. "Where were y'all when y'all concocted this plan?"

"I...I ran into him at Uncle Kenny's funeral—in Tennessee. That was the last time I saw him. And then he...he called me about a...a week ago. It was from a payphone. He said he was coming here."

"Did he say where he was staying?" I asked.

"I...I think he was staying at the Payneville Motel. I'm not positive, but I thought I saw his car there one morning when we drove by."

I jerked my phone out and called Detective Rachael Bowler. She answered on the third ring, her voice excited. "London, what's going on? I heard over the radio that—"

"I don't have time to explain right now. I need you to check the Payneville Motel for a guy named Troy Riggs. He might be traveling under a different name, so get the names and information on every occupant who stayed there over the last week. I also need you to run his name and find out everything you can about him—his address, criminal history, driver's license, vehicle registrations, next of kin—everything."

"Got it," Rachael said. "Does this have anything to do with the sniper killings? Is this guy related to Lieutenant Riggs? I heard she was the killer."

"We're getting information this guy is working with Bethany Riggs—he's her ex-husband. We think he's responsible for the killings this morning, so be extra careful."

"Okay, got it."

CHAPTER 45

I shoved my phone in my pocket, walked out into the hallway and grabbed my sniper rifle. Jerry was just getting off his phone. He turned to me. "We're all set to go. We've drawn out a safe route from here to the office, and we have officers stationed at every intersection. There shouldn't be any problems."

"What about the water tower?"

"I sent Dean up there. He's got an excellent view of your house and the surrounding area. Last I checked, all was clear."

"Let's move them." I walked to the living room and Jerry followed. Sheriff Calvin Burke, Captain Carmella Vizier and Lieutenant Bethany Riggs were all handcuffed and being guarded by Alvin Reed, Jake Reynolds and several SWAT operators. I glanced from one to the other. "Y'all ready?"

They all nodded, and Jake took two operators with him and moved to the doorway. They stepped out—guns poised—and did a quick check of the perimeter and returned to the doorway. "All's clear," Jake called.

Holding my sniper rifle at port arms, I led the way out the door and toward the squad cars. The bodies of Gibbs, Day, Doucet and Thomas still lay where they had fallen—bloodstained white sheets covering their lifeless forms—and I had to zigzag my way around them. When I reached the first squad car, I scanned the area. Most of the news crews had moved a mile or so up the road, but two or three of them had remained at the end of my driveway, where they now huddled beside their news vans, cameras still rolling.

I glanced up at the water tower three hundred yards away and shielded my eyes against the bright sky. I could make out a dark figure on the southern side of the catwalk—Dean Pierce. I waved up at him, and he lifted a hand into the air, letting me know all was well. I turned to Jerry, who stood by my door, and nodded.

Jerry stepped back and waved the prisoners through. Alvin and Jake escorted Sheriff Burke to one of the squad cars and secured him in the backseat. His face was pale, but he was defiant. He cursed Alvin and Jake and threatened their jobs. I walked over and slapped the top of the squad car. Burke looked up at me and I said, "Shut up or I'll climb back there and beat your face in!"

Burke swallowed hard and hung his head.

Two SWAT operators came out of the house next with Captain Vizier. They locked her into the squad car behind the first one and then stood beside it while Jake and two other operators walked Bethany to the last squad car. When she was secure, I lifted my hand to signal everyone to take off, but stopped when my phone rang. "Let's get ready to roll out of here." I slung my rifle over my shoulder and pulled my phone out. "Hey, it's London."

"I found your guy," Rachael said.

"You found Troy Riggs? Already?"

"Yep, but he's not in Louisiana."

I glanced through the window of the last squad car. Bethany was sitting there, unmoving, staring directly at me. I thought I saw a smile tug at the corners of her mouth. "Go on," I said to Rachael, trying to interpret Bethany's expression.

"I found an address in Sevierville for a Troy Riggs and there was a home number listed, so I called it, thinking a wife or other relative could tell me where to find him, but he answered."

"No, he's around here somewhere. You must've called a cell phone with a Tennessee area code."

"That's the first thing I verified before I made the call. It's definitely a landline and it's in Sevierville."

I scowled, started to walk toward the squad car that held Bethany. "Did he know Bethany?"

"Yeah," Rachael said, "and she's not who you think she is."

"What do you mean?"

"Troy Riggs divorced her after only a few months. He got the marriage annulled."

"Wait a minute…I thought she left him?"

"Nope, he caught her—"

Glass suddenly exploded from the side window of the first squad car. I turned quickly and was just in time to see blood, bone and glass smash into the opposite window, causing it to shatter and spill onto the cement. Where Sheriff Burke's head once was, there was now an empty mass of broken flesh and bone. Everything above his ears was gone. I dropped my phone, dove to the ground and scrambled on my elbows and knees to the rear of a nearby detective car, pulled my rifle around and flipped open my scope caps.

Behind me, Jerry screamed over the radio. "Dean, where'd that shot come from?"

The radio was silent except for a brief moment of static. Jerry repeated the radio traffic—more silence. Just as I shouldered my rifle and turned it toward the water tower, the second squad car exploded in broken glass and someone screamed that Captain Carmella Vizier was down. Footsteps pounded the cement all around me as officers scrambled for cover, trying to seek out the shooter's position.

Just as I attained proper eye relief, I caught a flash of movement through my scope. A dark figure disappeared around the southern side of the water tower. I moved down to the bottom of the catwalk where Dean was supposed to be...he was gone. On the opposite side of the water tower a length of rope dropped toward the ground. Before my mind could process what was happening, a dark figure raced down the rope as the killer rappelled toward the ground. Without thought, I dropped my crosshair to the sniper's feet and squeezed off a shot. I thought I saw the figure lurch slightly. I aimed at the knees for my second shot and fired twice in rapid succession. The sniper's arms went limp, and he crashed toward the ground at breakneck speed.

"I got him!" I hollered, confusion scrambling my thought process as I wondered what in the hell Dean Pierce had to do with Bethany Riggs, or Elizabeth James.

I pushed myself to my feet and bolted across my property, keeping my rifle poised. My legs were pumping at their full potential by the time I reached the street and raced across it. I jumped my neighbor's fence, landed at a stumbling run and straightened out as I caught my stride and zipped across his property and through a patch of barren fields. I was still fifty yards from the water tower when I saw a dark spot in the thick grass, still attached to the rappelling rope. I slowed to a fast walk and leveled my rifle at the figure on the ground. I took several deep breaths to help slow my heart rate. I stalked quietly toward the downed sniper, every one of my senses on high alert, straining to detect even the slightest hint of life, my right index finger brushing the trigger on my sniper rifle.

"Don't move!" I called out, but when I got a little closer I realized I was speaking to the dead. The body, dressed in typical ninja-like SWAT garb, was twisted like a pretzel and blood oozed from three bullet holes—one in the neck and two in the torso. Unless it was the odd angle of his body, it looked like Dean Pierce had lost a few pounds. A sniper rifle—like the one I'd issued to all the snipers, including Dean Pierce—was positioned on the ground several feet away. I approached the body and used the muzzle of my rifle to strip the ballistic hood and the goggles from the sniper's face.

I recoiled in horror…my knees went weak…I sank to the ground…my rifle fell from my grasp.

CHAPTER 46

"You okay, London?"

I looked up to see Sally Piatkowski walk into the conference room. I nodded my head, took a sip of coffee—something I never drank—and pointed to the chair beside me. "Have a seat. You're a lot easier to look at than that damn FBI agent they sent to debrief me."

Sally smiled, took the seat and slid her hand across the tabletop, squeezed my arm. "How are you holding up?"

"I'm fine."

"Really?"

"Sure."

"They said you were a bit shaken up."

I looked into her sparkly blue eyes and recognized the concern on her face. I smiled to reassure her. "Seriously, I'm fine. I'm more pissed at myself than anything."

"Why are you pissed?"

"Two reasons. First, I failed to properly prepare myself mentally to take that shot. Second, I was such a fool for not realizing I was being played."

"Well, the important thing is you *did* take the shot and you saved a lot of lives today."

"Speaking of that—how's Dean?"

"He got out of surgery an hour ago. They expect a full recovery."

I sighed. "That's a relief. It didn't look good for him."

"The doctor did say his heart stopped beating a couple of times while they were working on him, but they were able to save him.

He's very lucky."

I took another sip of coffee. I found it hard to keep my eyes off Sally. My mind wandered to that night in Gatlinburg and I had to fight to bring it back to the present. "Did Bethany make a statement to the FBI?"

"No. She refused to say anything. I guess it's a good thing she confessed to us."

"Yeah…" I thought back to earlier that day and doubt started to creep back into my head.

Sally cocked her head sideways. "Something's on your mind. What is it?"

"Had I known, I don't think I could've taken the shot," I admitted out loud for the first time. "I would've hesitated."

"I don't believe that."

"I'm very honest with myself, Sally. If it hadn't been for that ballistic mask, I really think I'd've had a hard time squeezing off the shot. Hell, I wanted to kill the person who shot Captain Landry until I found out it was Bethany. I let her get inside my head. I got too close to her."

"That's where we differ. I could shoot Bethany Riggs with a good heart."

"You don't think she was a little justified—morally, at least—for killing the people responsible for killing her family? You don't feel a little sorry for her?"

"That's not why I want to shoot her," Sally admitted, a twinkle in her eye. "I want to shoot her for sleeping with you."

I felt my face flush, but my embarrassment soon turned to anger. "How could I have been such a fool? She was using me from the very beginning. She was never interested in me. Shit, I'm not even her type, but I actually thought we made a connection…that she was something special. Well, until you and I took that trip to Gatlinburg. If she'd really been special, I guess…"

I let my voice trail off.

"I guess you were both lying to each other and to yourselves. Stop beating yourself up about it. We were all fooled…about everything. Let's just put this all behind us and move on. In a few weeks or months, none of this will even matter anymore." Sally touched my face softly. "And maybe we can pick up where we left off in Gatlinburg."

"That would be very nice," I said, smiling. I leaned in and kissed Sally Piatkowski for a long moment. When I pulled back, her eyes were half closed.

She purred. "I could get used to that."

"You'll have to." I stood. "But first, there's one last thing I need to find out."

"What's that?"

"I want to know how Bethany did it."

"You think she'll talk to you?"

"She talked to us before. Why wouldn't she talk now?"

"You're right. She has nothing to lose." Sally stood to follow me out the conference room.

As we walked down the hallway, I asked over my shoulder, "Does she even know?"

"Nope, no one told her. The FBI agents figured if she found out she'd be too distraught to talk—she'd have no incentive."

"Where is she now?"

"They're getting her ready for transport. I think they're going to keep her at the women's prison until the trial."

CHAPTER 47

We found Captain Corey Chiasson in his office. He looked up and jumped to his feet when he saw us. Three FBI agents were seated across the desk from him. "London! How the hell are you?"

"I'm good."

"Is there anything I can get for you? Anything I can do? You've done a hell of a job and there's no way we can ever—"

"I want to talk to Bethany Riggs one last time," I said.

Captain Chiasson started to speak, but one of the FBI agents interjected. "That won't be possible. She's already exercised her right to remain silent. To talk to her now would be a violation of her rights."

I ignored the suit, addressed Captain Chiasson. "Where is she?"

"She's in interview room number two. Tell the guard I said to leave y'all alone with her."

"Captain," said the same FBI agent, "we have already attempted to interview the suspect and she refused to speak with us. We've employed the most advanced interview techniques, yet still she refused. I must inform you that if your detective attempts to speak with her it'll be a violation—"

"I don't give a shit what techniques you *employed* and I'm not interested in your opinions," I retorted, taking a step closer to the agent and staring down at him. "You had your crack at her and you failed. Get over it and stay out of my way!"

Captain Chiasson stifled a grin to wave us out of his office. "Let me know when you're done with her."

The FBI agent started to object again, but Captain Chiasson shut him down. "You forget you're here at my request, and at any moment that request can be rescinded."

Sally ripped the case file from Detective Melvin Ford's hands and met me outside the interview room. "Ready?" I asked.

She nodded, and we pushed through the door. Bethany's head was resting on the table. She lifted it when we walked in and came instantly alert. "London? What're you doing here? I thought the FBI had taken over the case."

"We kicked them out." I smiled. "Wouldn't you rather speak to me than them anyway?"

"Of course I would." She smiled back. "What do you all want to talk about? Like I told those FBI pricks, I already made my statement to you and Sally, so there's really nothing much left to say."

"Ah, but there is." I took the chair nearest Bethany and leaned close to her. "I want to know who was helping you."

"I already told you. It was my ex-husband. His name's—"

"Troy Riggs." I pursed my lips. "The only problem with that is Detective Rachael Bowler—you remember her, don't you?—talked to Troy Riggs. He's in Sevierville, where he lives with his new wife."

Bethany's face paled a bit, but she was quick to recover. "She must've spoken to the wrong Troy Riggs. You see, the Troy Riggs I married was from—"

"Oh, it was the right Troy Riggs... and he certainly remembered you." I leaned back in my chair and folded my arms across my chest. "It seems you lied about the way things ended with y'all."

Bethany tried to remain casual. "What're you talking about? I didn't explain why I divorced him."

"That's just it—you didn't divorce him; he divorced you."

"He told you that? That's bullshit!"

"Is it also bullshit he caught you cheating on him?" Sally asked, her voice cold.

Bethany swallowed hard. "He...he's lying."

"No," I said thoughtfully. "I don't think any man would lie about something like that."

"No way," Sally agreed.

"As it turns out," I continued, "he still remembers the name of the person you cheated on him with. Well, the first name anyway. He said he forgot the last name."

At this point, Bethany Riggs' eyes were watering, and a tear dangled precariously from the corner of her left eye. "Please...I already admitted what I did. There's no need to involve anyone else. I'll take responsibility for everything...even the murder of Sheriff

Burke and the others this morning. Give me the death penalty. I don't care. My life is over anyway. Please, just don't involve anyone else in my mess."

"I'm sorry, Bethany, but we're not involving anyone else—you're the one who did that." I uncrossed my arms and leaned close, touched her knee. "Look, there aren't many women named Gina. It was Gina Pellegrin, wasn't it? He caught you in bed with Gina Pellegrin, didn't he?"

Bethany's face turned to ash. She stared desperately about the room. "Please, I'm begging you…don't involve her in my mess. I admit we were having an affair, but she had nothing to do with the sniper killings. That was all me. She had nothing to do with any of it."

"She had everything to do with it," Sally said. "Not only did she kill the sheriff and all this morning, but she's also the one who shot at London and me in Gatlinburg."

"That's impossible," Bethany pleaded. "She had nothing to do with any of it!"

"You know, it's one thing to kill a bunch of dirty cops," I said, "but she definitely crossed the line when she shot Dean Pierce just so she could take up his position. A jury *might* have been a little sympathetic toward you with regard to the others, but attempted murder of an innocent cop? No way! They'll regard you as nothing less than a common cold-blooded murderer."

Bethany looked from me to Sally, confused. "Me? Just me?"

I nodded. "Just you."

"So you won't go after Gina?"

"Well, you did say Gina didn't have anything to do with any of it, right?" I asked.

"That's right. She didn't know anything about it. In fact, Jerry told me she was in New Orleans meeting with the FBI, so you all could take down Sheriff Burke. If she was in New Orleans, there's no way she's involved."

"Then how do you explain this?" I dug in the file and pulled out the picture of Gina Pellegrin's lifeless body lying beneath the water tower, holding it so she could see.

Bethany's scream was bloodcurdling and ripped at my eardrums. The door burst open and the guard rushed in, his eyes wide, not knowing what he would find inside the room. Once we convinced him everything was okay, he left, and Sally and I turned back toward Bethany. She was bawling like a newborn, mouth wide and tears spilling like blood from an artery. Because her hands were cuffed behind her back, she was unable to wipe her face. Sally quickly left the room and returned with a handful of napkins. I took them from Sally and dabbed at Bethany's face. After nearly ten minutes of dabbing and consoling, we finally calmed her down enough she could speak.

"What...what happened to her?"

"I had no choice," I said.

Bethany's eyes turned to slits. She lunged at me, spat full in my face and tried to kick at me, but the chain from the leg shackles went taut and she fell hard. I wiped my face on my sleeve and then helped her to her seat.

"You bastard," she wailed. "You killed the only person I had left in my life!"

I started to apologize, but Sally stopped me and grabbed Bethany by the face. "Get a grip on yourself and think about it. *You* did this! You killed Gina. Had you not involved her in your insane plan, she'd still be alive today. But it's over. There's nothing you can do about it now—except help us understand why she'd do something like that. Help us explain to the world why she'd turn rogue and kill fellow cops."

I nodded. "We know why you did what you did. Help us understand why she did it."

Sniffling uncontrollably, Bethany sighed. "She did it for me. She loved me more than she loved her own life. She would've died for me—hell, she *did* die for me!"

"I don't understand how you two hooked up," I said. "You were raised in Tennessee, and she was raised here. Your husband caught you in bed with Gina before you moved here. How'd y'all even meet? What was she doing in Sevierville?"

Bethany frowned, her chin trembling. "I've known Gina my whole life."

I scowled, confused. "How's that possible?"

"The night my dad and brother were killed, I was not home. I was sleeping at a friend's house. That friend was Gina Pellegrin. Uncle Kenny picked me up from her house."

My jaw dropped open. "What the—?"

Sally was equally shocked. "Gina Pellegrin—*our* Gina Pellegrin—has known Elizabeth James—*you*—all this time?"

Bethany nodded. "We kept in touch, and her family would come visit every year, sometimes twice a year, and she even came to stay with us over the summer two or three times. She meant everything to me. She was the one person who saw me through everything, who kept me going when I felt like giving up. I-I don't know what I'm going to do without her."

As much as I didn't want to, I couldn't help but feel sorry for Bethany Riggs—and I felt like an idiot for misreading her, and a complete fool for misreading Gina. I stood and placed my hand on her shoulder. "If it makes you feel any better, I would never have been able to pull the trigger had I known it was Gina. She had that mask on, so I thought she was a man."

"You mean that?" Bethany asked.

"Yeah. In all of my years of training, I never prepared myself mentally to kill a woman, especially a woman I knew well—or thought I did—and liked a whole lot. That's one shot that'll haunt me for a long time."

After we were done with Bethany, Sally Piatkowski and I exited the interview room and walked out into the parking lot. The sun had long since gone down on what had been Magnolia Parish's darkest hour. I sighed and leaned against Sally's unmarked car. She hesitated by the door, her keys dangling from her hand. "You want to come over…maybe have a drink or something? Put this day and this case behind us?"

I studied Sally's face, trying to see deep inside her to gauge what type of person she really was.

"What? Why are you looking at me like that?"

"I'm trying to figure out what you want."

"Huh?" Sally's brows puckered.

"Bethany and Gina pretended to be interested in me because they wanted something from me, and like a fool, I really believed they were into me." I squinted, studying her face some more. "I just don't want to make that same mistake again—"

Sally grabbed the back of my head and pulled my mouth to hers, kissing me long and passionately. When she pulled back, her eyes were moist and her chest was heaving. "Any more questions?"

Made in the USA
Monee, IL
02 January 2022